Ric-A-Dam-Doo

The Snow Devils

Ric-A-Dam-Doo

Wayne A D Kerr

Cover by
Tanya James

Canusa llc

CANUSA LLC
871 S Paseo de la Lira
Green Valley, AZ 85614

www.waynekerrnovels.com

Publisher's Note: This is a work of fiction. Names, characters, places, and incidents are a product of the author's imagination. Locales and public names are sometimes used for atmospheric purposes. Any resemblance to actual people, living or dead, or to businesses, companies, events, institutions, or locales is completely coincidental.

Book design © 2013, BookDesignTemplates.com

Ordering Information: Special discounts are available on quantity purchases by corporations, associations, and others. For details, contact the publisher at the address above.

CANUSA LLC – First Edition

ISBN 978-0-9904179-5-8

Printed in the United States of America

Thank you to the men and women of the Canadian armed forces for all of their sacrifices and services.

I wish to thank my friends and siblings

for all of their input and encouragement.

I especially want to thank my wife. Without

her efforts this book wouldn't have been possible.

Tanya James produces one great cover after another.

Prologue:

At the outbreak of World War One, Hamilton Gault raised a private army to assist in the efforts overseas. He had both the blessing and assistance of Canada's Department of Militia and Defense. Britain's Duke of Connaught and Strathearn was the Governor General of Canada at the time. The Governor General proved to be an invaluable resource for Gault in his quest. They named the newly-formed battalion after the Duke's daughter, and the Princess Patricia's Canadian Light Infantry came into being.

As a thank you for this honor, Princess Patricia designed and sewed the first regiment flag. It became affectionately known as the Ric-A-Dam-Doo, which is the phonetic translation of the Gaelic saying: cloth of thy mother.

Over several years, one battalion became three, plus a fourth of reservists. Much of the Second Battalion trained as paratroopers, while another group became sniper specialists of very high regard. During the Second World War several highly skilled soldiers of the second battalion took part in a joint effort with the United States to assemble an elite fighting group. The world's first Special Forces unit became better known as the *Devil's Brigade* or the *Black Devils*.

Canadian Special Forces teams were put together from these returning soldiers after the war. One highly trained crew called themselves the Snow Devils. The Princess Patricia's Canadian Light Infantry and their elite unit has worked for many years with NATO and continued as peacekeepers all across the globe for the United Nations.

I've taken some dramatic license and created the Snow Devils – a fictional Special Forces unit. I apologize for any mistakes I've made in military procedures.

The following is an excerpt from the unofficial marching song of the Snow Devils Special Forces unit:

The Ric-a-Dam-Doo, pray what is that?
'Twas made at home by Princess Pat.
It's Red and Gold and Royal Blue.
That's what we call the Ric-A-Dam-Doo,
Dam-Doo, Dam-Doo, Ric-a-Dam-Doo!

Old Hammy Gault was the first PP,
And he led this band across the sea.
He'd lose an arm, a leg or even two,
Before he'd lose the Ric-A-Dam-Doo,
Dam-Doo, Dam-Doo, Ric-a-Dam-Doo!

Jimmy Hawthorne, the Colonel Grand,
Is commander of this noble band.
He'd go to Hell and charge right through
To save our beloved Ric-a-Dam-Doo,
Dam-Doo, Dam-Doo, Ric-a-Dam-Doo!

Johnny Andrews is our Lieutenant dear,
He always buys us rum and beer.
Whene'er there's trouble in a mile or two,
You'll find him there with the Ric-a-Dam-Doo,
Dam-Doo, Dam-Doo, Ric-a-Dam-Doo!

Dance with Snow Devils and you'll get burned.
Fire and brimstone is all you've earned.
So stay on the path that's right and true,
Or you will deal with the Ric-a-Dam-Doo,
Dam-Doo, Dam-Doo, Ric-a-Dam-Doo!

CHAPTER 1

Five Princesses

1800 hours, June 21, 1987

Zadar, Yugoslavia

Dark clouds brewed over the Adriatic Sea to the south. The waves in the harbor roiled black and choppy. The impending storm would hit the seaside city in less than an hour.

A lone military vehicle pulled up to the deserted building at the end of dock five. Battle hardened bodies emptied out of the Humvee. They silently assembled in front of the truck. Hand signals sent one man patrolling around the large building. The remaining four entered the unlocked metal door at the front of the retired freight terminal. The lead two soldiers split off left and right with guns ready. The meager light that fought its way in through streaky glass and haphazardly boarded-up windows bounced off the once polished concrete floor casting a ghostly pallor, as if the building was filled with fog.

A battered green Vespa rested heavily on a rusty stand just inside. There may have been an office area just beyond the entry door once, but it had long since been gutted. A small mountain of old pallets and crates looked more like they had been poured, rather than stacked, in the corner of the cavernous warehouse. The two remaining men followed fresh drag marks that had recently plowed a trail across the dusty floor. In the rear of the dark building they found a woman sitting on a wooden crate looking through binoculars. There was an excellent view of the entire harbor through a newborn gap in the window slats. She was aware of their presence but had given no such indication. The lead soldiers quietly rejoined their comrades, nodding an all-clear signal to the other two.

"Lieutenant Andrews of the 2nd Battalion, Princess Patricia's Canadian Light Infantry, reporting as requested, Ma'am." The group of soldiers came to attention. Andrews, the tallest of the four, could see that her focus appeared to be on a ship, moored about half a kilometer down the harbor, at the next dock over.

"I requested a US Navy Seal team or an Israeli Assault squad," the dark-haired woman stated with a faintly British accent. Turning around finally, her intense eyes assessed the group in front of her. During the past couple of years she had in fact run operations with Mossad, SAS and Seal teams. "I most certainly did not request four Canadian Princesses."

"Five, Ma'am."

"Oh, there are five of you!" The British accent becoming stronger as the sarcasm increased. "Well then, that makes all the difference, doesn't it now?"

"Perhaps you could brief us on the mission, Ma'am." The Canadian soldiers received reactions similar to this from time to time. They were aware that most people knew very little about the Canadian Armed Forces and fewer still had any idea that there were Special Forces teams from the great white north.

After climbing off the solidly-built crate, agent Janet Porter paced back and forth for two full minutes saying nothing as she weighed her options. She glanced out at the ship that would soon take two dozen young women away from everyone and everything they knew.

"Fubar!" she said under her breath. This was her new favorite word. The petite brunette had picked it up from a US

Navy Seal team a few months earlier. FUBAR is the acronym for fucked up beyond all recognition she'd found out. The word seemed appropriate right now. She'd never even heard of Canadian Special Forces. Canadians played hockey, ate mounds of pancakes swimming in Maple syrup and wore beaver-skin hats.

It was crunch time and a judgment call needed to be made. It had taken her two frustrating weeks to find the operation here in Zadar and another week to properly study the operation. And now, as far as she could tell, they were closing up shop and moving somewhere else. She had no clue where or when they might surface next. Janet desperately wanted to save some of these women. Should she put their lives at risk in order to save them from a certain and horrible future? These lean men didn't look like they ate too many pancakes...

Andrews watched as a look of determination swept over the woman's face. She'd come to a decision. Despite standing only about five foot two, Andrews noted a strong presence about her.

"You and your men will just have to do, Lieutenant Andrews." The woman offered her hand to the soldier. "Agent Janet Porter, Interpol," she introduced herself, and gave him a brief business-like smile.

"Here is the situation," she glanced at her watch, "in the next half hour a group of large, gun-toting men will be loading approximately two dozen kidnapped young women onto that boat." Agent Porter handed him the binoculars and pointed at the docked ship.

"If it leaves the harbor with them upon it, their loved ones will very likely never see them again."

"Understood, Agent Porter," Andrews said, as he passed back the binoculars.

"Mankowski, on the roof," he ordered.

"Yes, Sir!" the sniper specialist double timed it back out to the Humvee to retrieve his McMillan Tac-50 rifle and a case of low drag ammunition.

"Reese!"

"Yes, Sir!" The smallest of the soldiers stepped forward.

"I want eyes on that ship, ASAP."

"Ric-a-dam-doo!" he responded eagerly, and was gone.

Janet wondered what the hell Ricka Damn Do meant. Maybe it was like Fubar? She decided to ask later.

"Sergeant Johansen, find St. Jean and take up positions on either side of that dock." Then he added, "Wait there for my signal."

"Yes Sir!" Johansen followed after his comrades.

Janet had to admit that the Canadian soldiers seemed to know what they were doing.

"What else can you tell me about who we are up against, Agent Porter?"

"A few months ago word got passed to the Agency that a large number of girls were being smuggled through Croatia. They are taken from Slovenia, Serbia, Bosnia, Kosovo and further away. Most end up in the sex trade, shuffled from city to city around the world. I was able to trace one part of the operation to here."

"Nice work," Lieutenant Andrews commented.

"This is just the tip of the iceberg." Janet brushed the compliment aside. "It is a huge and well-funded operation. I, we, that is, Interpol is determined to tear it completely apart."

Andrews got the impression that this was more than just an assignment to the passionate agent in front of him.

"I have observed them bringing twenty to twenty five girls here every two days for the past week," she reported. "Four large SUVs with two armed men each, deliver the girls to six more machine-gun-toting guys from the ship. The men appear to be well acquainted with each other, and no money has been exchanged, so I assume they are all part of the same organization."

"How long did the men stay after the exchange?"

"Half of the group always left immediately," she answered, "and the remaining four guarded the dock until the ship pulled away."

"I'm on board, Lieutenant," Sergeant Reese reported through the radio attached to Lieutenant Andrews' hip.

Janet grabbed her binoculars off the crate and scanned the deck of the ship.

"Situation report, Sergeant Reese," he responded, while pressing the button on the mike attached to his shoulder.

"I count twelve crew and six hostiles, so far. The crew is readying for departure, Sir."

"Keep your head down for now, PB." Andrews told his comrade.

"How did he get up there so fast?" Janet was astonished, still searching for signs of Reese on the ship.

"You won't be able to spot him, Agent Porter," the Lieutenant told her. "The bad guys won't either, until it's too late."

"PB?" she asked.

"It's kind of a nick name," Andrews shrugged, "you'll have to ask Sergeant Reese..."

He pressed the mike button again. "Report in."

"In position," Mankowski reported.

"Johansen and I are less than one minute out, Sir!" Sergeant Bobby St. Jean buzzed in quietly with a slight French accent.

Lieutenant Andrews pressed the mike button twice. The short static bursts let everyone know he had heard them. He turned to join his men.

"You can observe from here, Agent Porter."

"That's not very fuckin' likely, Princess! This is my Op!"
She stood toe-to-toe with him. "Let's go!"

"Only, if you stay behind me!" he blurted out, already
too late. Andrews shook his head and smiled as she ran ahead
towards the exit. The smile quickly disappeared when he was
forced to triple time it just to keep up. The woman could move.

Soon they were crouched behind cover on dock four.
The first sprinkles of what would soon be a hard driving rain
began to fall. Minutes later, just as Janet had predicted, four
large SUVs pulled up across from the main gangway to the ship.

A few moments after that, six armed men appeared at
the top of the gangway. The SUV doors then opened in unison.
Armed men, followed by twenty-four blindfolded women, all
got out of the trucks. The men roughly herded the frightened
women toward the ship.

As soon as everyone arrived at the bottom of the
gangway, the kidnappers on the ship started down. Unlike the
previous deliveries, all eight of the men from the trucks
continued to help move the women.

"Usually, half the guards have gone back to the truck by
now," Agent Porter told the Canadian soldier.

"We'll have to take them on the gangway." Andrews
whispered into his mike. "How is your view, Mankowski?"

"Maybe sixty percent, but it is getting worse, Sir." Billy
Mankowski looked up at the sky as the rain began to fall harder.

Janet overheard the exchange between Andrews and
Mankowski. She looked back towards the rooftop where
Mankowski was positioned. She could barely see the building,
let alone him in the worsening conditions. She shook her head
hardly believing that the sniper would be of any use from that
range in this weather.

The women were fed onto the narrow gangway in single
file. At the top of the ramp, five of the kidnappers headed down

to guide their captors, while the men at the bottom prodded the confused girls upward.

Not wanting to lose the use of one of the world's finest snipers, Lieutenant Andrews decided sooner was better than later.

"Stay here," he told the Interpol agent. "I mean it!"

Though unhappy about it, Janet gave him a reluctant thumbs up acknowledging his order and stayed behind cover.

"Ric-a-dam-doo, Ladies!" he shouted into his mike and leapt out from cover.

Things happened fast. From a quarter mile away Mankowski calmly pulled the trigger on his sniper rifle several times in rapid succession. Four hostiles dropped before any of them knew what hit them. The marksman had taken out the men closest to the women. That left four on the upper portion of the gangway and six at the bottom, with the girls now loosely sandwiched between. Mankowski quickly fired several more shots, persuading the men closest to the women to keep back.

Janet watched as four of the men on the ramp crumpled mid-step. She didn't hear the shots from the rifle until after the fifth man went down. The remaining hostage takers yelled at each other and shot blindly towards the echoing rifle reports. The three soldiers on the ground closed toward the group at the bottom of the gangway from all sides.

With the sudden chaos breaking out below him, the guard at the top of the ramp did not expect an attack from behind. A clean hip check that would have sent a sturdy Boston Bruins' defenseman flying into the arena boards had a similar effect on the guard, knocking the wind out of him as he toppled over the ship's railing. The startled guard was still fighting to recover his breath as he silently entered the dark cold water. Displaying the incredible speed that had once made him a top National Hockey League prospect, Reese flew down the ramp. The gun in his hand was purely for battering purposes at the moment. He couldn't shoot at the kidnappers for fear of hitting the girls. He barreled into the closest man, crashing him into the remaining two. A hard knee to the face of that man, as he tried to regain his feet, incapacitated him and the soldier took the fight to the next man in line.

Lieutenant Andrews had the same shooting issue rushing in from the rear. Johansen and St. Jean, however, had green light targets as they approached rapidly, shooting from each flank. The remaining hostage takers panicked at the sudden attack from all sides. Their bullets blazed wildly. During the ensuing melee, two of the kidnappers, their guns already empty, managed to break away. They raced towards the SUVs.

Out of the corner of his eye, Sergeant Mankowski saw the two hostiles sprint away but couldn't do anything about it. He was still busy encouraging kidnappers to stay away from the girls. By this point, the rest of Canadian Special Forces team were all engaged in hand-to-hand combat.

Janet also spotted the two escapees and jumped out of hiding, trying to cut the runners off. She ran hard, emptying the clip of her 9mm Walther as she closed the gap. Amazingly, she hit the man in front. He went down. However, the other runner turned toward her, saw that her gun was also empty and charged.

Once his team had the gangway mostly under control, Mankowski turned his scope to find the runners. He found the dead one first. The second one wasn't at the trucks. He looked up from the scope, but the rain and distance rendered unassisted sight useless. Vision continued to get worse through the viewfinder, but he carefully swung the rifle in widening arcs. Finally he located the runner, but could not get a shot away. The Interpol agent was in his line of fire. She was doing a good job of evading her large attacker's kicks and punches, but the man was getting closer and closer to her with every passing second.

"Don't let him get hold of you," he said aloud, but his unheard warning wasn't heeded. The man had latched onto the agent's arm and began reeling her in. Mankowski didn't want to see the woman get hurt. Just in case he got an opportunity for a clean shot, he forced himself to watch. Much to his surprise, less than five seconds after the man grabbed her, he was writhing on the ground begging. She had his hand and arm twisted at a painful-looking angle.

"I don't believe it." Mankowski recognized her technique as Brazilian Jiu Jitzu. "That was quite impressive. The girl has skills." The sniper was often stuck alone somewhere and he had a habit of talking to himself in these situations.

A few seconds later, Andrews and then Reese arrived to assist. They helped secure the big man who was now sporting several broken fingers.

"How are the women, Lieutenant Andrews?" Porter asked.

"All accounted for," he answered. Then added, "They're scared and confused but unharmed, Ma'am."

"Peanut Butter?" she asked, as Sergeant Reese pulled the kidnapper to his feet.

"Pardon me?" the Sergeant asked.

"You know, as in Reese's Peanut Butter Cups," the Interpol agent explained. "Sergeant Reese, isn't it? The PB stands for peanut butter, right?"

PB looked at Janet as a bolt of lightning lit up the dock and her eyes. Damp hair clung at odd angles to her face. She was beautiful, even soaking wet. "You can call me anything you want, Ma'am." Lieutenant Andrews rolled his eyes.

"My name is Janet." She had a newfound respect for this Special Forces team.

"Janet," Reese replied, the respect in his voice mutual. Sparks were flying between the two.

"Will one of you please explain to me just what in the hell a Ricky Dammy Do is?" she asked, as they guided their prisoner back towards the others.

"It's just something we Canadian Princesses like to say," Sergeant Reese teased her.

"I deserved that!" Agent Porter laughed and decided that she wanted to work with these Princesses again, especially the cute sergeant in front of her.

Janet and the Snow Devils spent the rest of the day making travel arrangements for the rescued young women. In most of the cases, a family member had hopped on a plane immediately to escort their lost daughter or sister home. The Canadian team used their connections to arrange military transport for the remaining few who didn't.

That night, as the young Interpol agent wrote her reports, she could not stop thinking about Sergeant Reese. She felt an immediate connection to him and wondered if he felt it too. The whole Canadian team had impressed her. The respect and caring they'd exhibited to the women, including herself, that day, was above and beyond. They'd insisted that she join them for dinner and she'd enjoyed the time spent with them a lot more than expected. The huge egos she'd encountered on other Special Forces teams seemed to be missing with this group. They were good at their jobs and they knew it, but they didn't flaunt it. They treated her like a part of the team and told her to contact them whenever she needed assistance in the future. She intended to do just that. After just one operation with this team, she didn't want to work with any other.

Janet spent the next morning convincing her boss to pull strings and call in favors, if required, to get this group on speed dial. The agent failed to mention the growing crush she had on one of the Canadian soldiers.

Interpol Case Supervisor Bill Matthews was startled to get a call less than an hour after making a few enquiries about the squad, from one Colonel James Hawthorne. The head of the Canadian Special Forces Division had already received a mission report that detailed the great work being done by Interpol on the human trafficking front. He agreed to make his team available in this important endeavor whenever logistics made it possible.

For Janet Porter this would prove to be a match made in heaven, in more ways than one.

CHAPTER 2

Life is Good

The present
Green Valley, Arizona

A soft voice interrupted the lively Terri Clark tune flowing through Janet's ear buds. "Five minutes remain."

"Thank you, Nano!" Janet replied out loud as the music returned, her voice raspy from physical effort. This was her favorite part of running. The last few minutes.

Though tired, her strides lengthened. She had set a goal time of forty eight minutes within the Nike program on her IPod Nano. However, half way through the run this morning she'd changed her mind. Janet's new goal was to finish the six mile distance under forty five minutes. With less than half a mile to go the former Interpol agent pushed harder.

Windless, seventy degrees, it was another perfect morning for running through the pecan groves. A few wispy clouds hung over the Santa Rita Mountains on PB's left.

"Ten minutes remain." An identical MP3 player to his wife's reminded him and he slowed his pace some. No rush, PB thought to himself. Janet would grab the water bottles and meet him at the corner. She preferred a longer cool-off walk than he. Since they liked to run at different paces, the Pecan

Groves just east of town worked perfectly for them. Multiple pathways crisscrossed through the trees. This allowed them to start and finish together. On warmer summer mornings the shade that the leafy trees provided was more than welcome.

He didn't need the shade this morning. With a mile and a half to go the sun felt great as it began to break through the thinning clouds, warming his left side. Morning exercise was the ex-soldier's cup of coffee. This morning, an eight mile run filled the bill. Tomorrow tennis... The next day, who knew? He glanced over at the Santa Rita's. Maybe a hike up to Josephine's Saddle? Retirement was good. Life was good. His pace quickened again. He couldn't help it.

"I was born in a cross-fire hurricane," PB sang along with Mick, as another Rolling Stones song began. He had to smile to himself. A few nights earlier, he'd commented to Janet about the high number of popular singers that had come from his home country. To make his point he offered and subsequently made her a mix of music from several Canadian artists including: Shania Twain, Michael Buble', Bare Naked Ladies, Sarah McLachlan, Crash Test Dummies, Celine Dion and others. Janet had patiently listened to him brag, as she also threw together a mix of British music for him. The greatest hits of the Beatles and Rolling Stones. He could have run for hours and not heard the same fantastic song twice. She won, hands down.

Retired for six years already, the couple had bounced around from country to country, place to place, looking for a location that suited all of their needs. Maintaining a low profile was a must for the couple. They had made more than a few enemies around the globe. One of which had put a sizable price on Janet's head, vowing revenge from the prison he'd been put into. Unfortunately for the Reeses, the threat of retaliation had already cost them two retirement locations.

Beautiful Mataro, Spain, on the coast of the Mediterranean Sea had been retirement attempt number one. Janet introduced her husband, from the land-locked prairies of Canada, to the exhilarating sport of windsurfing while there. PB loved it. Exploring the coast and zipping across azure waters filled their days.

Until one afternoon, when they happened into a remote cove and encountered a yacht under siege. The rescue of a British diplomat and his special friend from pirates had gotten headlines all across Europe. PB shuddered slightly as he thought of the man's scorned and outraged wife, the Countess of Barrowford. The cheating ex-diplomat had been mercilessly raked over the coals by her and the media. Leaving him to the pirates may have been more humane.

A week later, while dining in a street-side café, a drive-by-shooting attempt on the Reese's lives alerted the couple to the consequences of being good Samaritans. While the shooters may have been bounty hunters, alerted to their presence by the media attention, they never found out for certain. Dead pirates also have grieving and vengeful families, just like anyone else. Janet and PB emerged unharmed; however, three innocent people had been injured in the shooting. Spain and the Mediterranean had been hard to leave, but for their own peace of mind and the safety of those around them, they moved as far away as possible.

They managed to call Adelaide, Australia's pretty 'City of Bridges', home for a little more than a year. Janet was especially fond of the city and the charming cottage they were renovating; she settled in quickly. PB began playing tennis at the local courts and soon made some good friends. The Reeses were enjoying the outgoing and fun-loving Aussies.

Twelve months passed without incident. Then Bobby St. Jean, Princess Pat turned treasure hunter, stopped in to visit his friends. He happened to be in the area following some wild theory that the fabled treasure of the Templar Knights had found its way to Australia. Once back on his quest, St. Jean got involved with some unsavory people he should have left alone and soon found himself being chased across the desolate Outback. Janet and PB intervened. Once again, unwanted notoriety attached itself to them. Soon, other treasure hunters from around the globe amassed in the area. Concerned that their faces might be seen by the wrong people, the Reeses said goodbye to the house that had just begun to feel like a home and to their new friends.

Flights were booked to South Africa, an apartment rented in Johannesburg and boxes labeled 'fragile', but actually filled with junk, were shipped ahead to the African nation. With the help of a certain Special Forces unit, the couple was secreted away to a different continent all together. While a small military jet landed at Luke Air Force base in Arizona, a soldier matching PB's description, flying with a false passport, sat next to a reasonable facsimile of Janet Reese on a Qantas airliner, as it flew under the outer rim of the South Pole. Once they arrived at the new apartment in South Africa the pseudo couple separated and disappeared.

Climate, recreation, and population density were all major considerations in the search for a retirement community. Ironically, it was PB, the boy that had grown up on a farm near a tiny remote community, who wanted to be near a major center which offered all the amenities. While Janet, the girl from London, was looking for peace and quiet. Their time in Australia gave the Reeses an appreciation of the desert. The active couple had been surprised to find themselves spending less and less time at the beaches, in favor of exploring the Outback.

Janet and PB toured the Mojave and Sonoran deserts in the southwestern corner of the United States. They drifted around New Mexico, the interior of California, and Utah before settling on a location near Tucson, Arizona. The parks and trails near Moab, Utah had captivated them, as had the beautiful red rocks of Sedona. However, they felt that both small communities hosted too many tourists for the security-minded couple.

After more than three years in the quiet cozy town of Green Valley, the Reeses had begun to put down some strong roots and made some good friends. Several of their old friends had even managed to visit without raising alarms or starting small wars. It was beginning to feel like home, despite the apprehension of getting too attached. Acquiring property and material things became a risk they were willing to take. They relaxed, but remained vigilant. Vigilance wasn't just an option for the unusual couple, but relaxation was. They slowly began to appreciate the casual and laid back lifestyle offered by the region.

Janet was PB's Achilles' heel and he would never totally relax as long as there remained a price on her head. He knew that he'd give his life for hers the first night they'd met all those years ago. That had never changed. Theirs was a marriage of equals. They'd even discovered that their IQ scores were exactly the same. Since Janet was the smartest, most capable person PB knew, he hadn't been surprised when she scored 140 on the comprehensive test they had taken one quiet afternoon. He had been genuinely surprised by his own score, though.

PB never tired of her company, whether it was in the bedroom, having a meal out, or hanging from a cliff -- Janet was it for him. It was not a weakness in her abilities that concerned him. Far from it. In a fight, his wife could handle herself as well as any Special Forces soldier. But, he knew deep down that he could be compromised to protect her.

PB had spent his whole life building up his strengths and correcting his flaws. As a boy, he had practiced his slap shot for hour after hour, gaining complete control of it. He'd skated on the frozen creek that wound through the farm until he could navigate its twists and turns at full speed, frontwards and backwards. But he didn't know how to fix this, and it had eaten at him. If it had ever come down to choosing between his wife and any of the other Devils, he'd have chosen her. Thankfully, it never had. He felt guilty just the same. He would die for his brothers without hesitation, but PB couldn't sacrifice Janet for anyone or anything.

When he arrived at the corner, Janet was already there stretching her legs. She stood upright and gave him a high five as he passed, already slowing his pace. PB shut down his Nano just as it began congratulating him for achieving his goal time of one hour.

"Forty-four, fifty-seven," his wife reported with pride, as he turned back toward her.

"Not bad for an old gray-haired broad," PB teased.

"Hey, watch it Mister," Janet said, absently touching her graying mane. She'd decided not to color her hair, to better fit into the retirement community. Besides, her husband had sworn that he loved the new look.

"Seriously though, that's excellent! I told you it wouldn't take long to get your legs back under you." PB took the water bottle she offered and kissed the top of her damp head.

"I'm getting there." Janet had broken a couple ribs six months earlier while mountain-biking the trails at Elephant Head Rock. It had been difficult for the fifty-four-year-old, former Interpol agent to be completely inactive for three months, and then limiting herself to non-strenuous activities for another three, while she healed. She was anxious to get fit once more.

CHAPTER 3

Red, White and Blue

Eleven hours later
Nogales, Arizona

The rusty red 1984 Ford F-150 half ton carried a load that
defied the imagination of most people. Stacked above the
special cargo was a giant heap of old furniture including a
complete dinette set, a threadbare recliner, two white
refrigerators, several bicycles, a few cardboard boxes and an
assortment of floppy mattresses, all magically held together by
bailing twine. Had it not been for the fact that the truck was
approaching the international border, on its way to Mexico, one
might have assumed it was headed for a garbage disposal site.
Instead, it was returning home, as it did every few weeks, from
the swap meets up north in Tucson and Phoenix. One man's
junk is another man's treasure proved especially true when you
crossed the border with it into Mexico. Unlike the other
bargain hunters' trucks, the load this one carried back would
potentially be worth millions of American dollars.

The battered-looking old truck was well-known to the
permanent check-stop of the border patrol. They had unloaded
the junk more times than they cared to remember, over the past
few years from this truck and several others like it. Raul even
knew most of the border guards by name, and never failed to
offer them some sort of mystery treat prepared by his wife, just

for these trips. The patrol officers had a secret lottery among them -- guessing what day they would find the old heap on the side of the road with the plates taken off and steam still rising from the burnt-out engine. They were certain that Raul and Juan Carlos had to rebuild half the truck each trip just to make sure it could return home with such a load.

The only thing they ever found of value, during their many searches, was the tool chest that occupied almost half of the space in the box. If you lifted the lid it appeared to be full of rusty tools, old chains and random engine parts. It was the same tool box that a dozen years earlier the Red Devil gang, in another lifetime before the big cartels, had fashioned a false compartment to carry drugs northward across the border.

Today, however, the rectangular metal box smelled of expensive shampoos and borrowed perfume. The only modification necessary had been several drilled holes to let some air in. Teen-aged American girls were the cargo of choice these days, and there was just enough room for two of them in the space that had once carried a dozen bundles of marijuana. Juan Carlos knew just how to position them. The way they laid together often reminded him of the yin and yang figure that dangled from the rearview mirror. He especially liked it when they grabbed girls with different hair colors. He enjoyed how they looked, and would snap a picture of them in their fetal-like position, just before he closed the lid of the tool box. Mr. Morales and Raul didn't have to know about the pictures. They were just for him.

The junk shook violently but held together as the truck went across a pair of railway tracks. Raul glanced at the cracked rear-view mirror to make sure nothing had shaken loose that he would have to pick up and retie. He chuckled to himself as he remembered the idiot border cops looking down their noses at them.   For what they had in the tool box, he'd earn more than all four of those *pendejos* would in a year.

He was, on the other hand, happy to be across the border and that much closer to Rosa and his brand new Escalade. It was the nicest vehicle he had ever owned. Big and beautiful and comfortable; the moment Raul had sat in the driver's seat he'd been sold. His back wasn't as good as it had been twenty years earlier and he really appreciated the infinite adjustments of the butter-soft leather captain's chair. He also felt a bit naked without the Escalade's bullet-proof glass and door panels. Northern Mexico was getting to be a dangerous place these days, ever since the arrival of the big cartels.

Two loud bur-rump, bur-rump noises, accompanied by her head bouncing up and down on metal roused Emma Morrison from her drug-induced sleep. Her tongue was dry and she had trouble getting any liquid to form in her mouth. She tasted copper, like she'd been sucking on a penny, and by the way her throat felt as she struggled to pull enough air in through her nose, she must've swallowed a dollar's worth.

What sounded like a vehicle motor hummed a loud steady rhythm nearby. She managed to crack open an eye, but couldn't see anything. Emma tried to move but her arms and legs wouldn't budge. She felt pins and needles where her hip bone supported most of her weight and she instinctively tried to roll onto her back to relieve the sensation, but her shoulder immediately bumped into something hard.

As the high school junior's faculties and senses slowly returned, everything about her situation felt wrong. Her eyes flew open and then shut again. Open, shut, open, shut -- the result was exactly the same: total darkness. Fear chased any chance of comprehension away. A scream erupted from deep inside, but couldn't get past her lips. Full panic set in. She struggled to move. Her shoeless foot hit up against something hard and flat when her uncooperative leg finally straightened, and she pushed against it. The top of her head bumped into another hard surface. More screams tried to get through the tape across her mouth, until hyperventilation mercifully put Emma back to sleep.

Juan Carlos looked through the passenger side mirror. The lights of Nogales were fading away. He started to relax. It had been a long stress-filled day. He much preferred the days when he actually set up a table at the meet and sold his handmade merchandise. The old cowboy enjoyed the camaraderie of his fellow vendors and he made a tidy little profit to top it off. Raul, on the other hand, treated the trips north as a necessary evil to keep up their cover. It was his job to fill the truck with junk for the return trip home and he did just that. Since most of the cargo would end up at the bottom of a pit anyway, he bought for bulk rather than resale value. Raul's purchasing prowess was not well respected by his peers at the meet. But since he was back every week or two buying more of the stuff they always passed up, he must have a market for it.

Today he had been even hastier with his purchases and had filled the truck in less than an hour after the swap meet had opened. Their targets would be at the Park Place Mall that afternoon. Casing the mall and laying plans for the grab was the main priority.

An hour and a half later, Raul had located the two most likely mall entrances that the girls would use when they arrived. Juan Carlos and Raul then joined the other bored husbands smoking outside the mall entrances as they waited for wives and daughters to finish shopping. No one gave either of them a second look or noticed them glancing at each teen girl who entered the building.

Finally, after a long three hours, the target teens strode past Raul. Juan Carlos got a phone call from his partner. Raul had spotted them as they passed under the G sign attached to a light standard in the southwest section of the parking lot. It was Juan Carlos' responsibility to disable the parking lot cameras that pointed out towards parking area G and then move the truck over to that location, while the younger man kept tabs on the girls inside the mall. Then they would trade off every half hour, one watching the girls and one ready at the truck at all times.

The grab had gone flawlessly. It had been Raul's turn in the truck when the girls finally exited the mall. Once they had passed the light standard, with Juan Carlos right on their heels, Raul pulled the truck between the teens and the mall. One of the girls dropped something and they both bent down. Juan Carlos hit two jean covered buttocks with the fast acting tranquilizers while Raul had flipped open the hidden compartment on the side of the truck. They had the girls stowed away in seconds. Raul pretended to tighten the ropes on the load as he checked to make sure no one had witnessed the event, while Juan Carlos picked up the girls' belongings and dumped them into the cab.

A minute later they pulled out of the mall and headed for Juan Carlos' favorite meal in the whole world. He and Raul had a tradition at the end of every trip to Tucson. On their way out of town they'd grab Sonoran hot dogs from the El Guero Canelo on Twelfth and a couple cold beers from the Seven Eleven down the street. After the long hot afternoon he'd had, both had tasted particularly good that day. Juan Carlos decided that another beer or two would go down pretty nicely right now, but he knew better than to suggest it to Raul. There would be cold beer waiting for them at the ranch. He'd just have to remain thirsty until then.

Sometime later, the box bounced up and down a few times. Again, Emma began to stir. She awakened as she slid up against something. Suddenly aware that her face and body was mashed against another person, she stiffened. *I'm not alone!*

Emma's mind raced with questions. *Who is it? How did I get here? Why don't I know where I am? My brain hurts.* Then she recognized the faint scent of perfume in her nostrils -- the other body was Monica's. Emma relaxed. Finally, she knew something for sure. *I'm not alone. Monica is here with me.* Their bodies swayed slightly in unison. She realized they were moving and that the soft rhythmic beat that surrounded her was a car motor. They were in a metal box that was being driven somewhere. *How did we get in here? Ow! Thinking hurts!*

Monica's body felt like a life raft in an ocean of dark, and she melted against the warm softness. She laid, void of thought, for a long while. Her mind was a swirling mist, dancing to the steady hum of the well-tuned engine. Then she noticed a new noise. The fog thinned as her consciousness stirred again. She recognized the gritty sound. It was tires on gravel. *We're not in the city anymore!*

Where are they taking us? Who is doing this? Why us? We didn't do anything to anybody. She could feel the fear rising and threatening to take over, once again, as she contemplated her situation. *Why is this happening to me? Come on Morrison, don't panic. Keep it together. Think of something else. Anything... Dad, Daddy. Yes, this is helping.* Emma remembered the huge smothering hug her father had given her, a few weeks earlier, right after she'd lost the state tennis final. She felt so safe and protected in those arms. *Daddy are you looking for me?*

Fragments of that afternoon and evening began to emerge. The girl's last memories before waking in a dark box continued to assemble.

Oh no! The party... Monica... Grandma Rita... Oh God, I was on the phone lying my ass off to Grandma Rita. Dad's going to be pissed. I'll be grounded. That's okay Dad -- ground me for life if you want. I'd give anything to be at home in my room right now! Mom, I miss you so much! I'm sorry for being mad at you. It wasn't your fault. I felt so betrayed when you died. I know that you loved me and Dad. I love you, too!

The mall... Monica and I were at the mall! We'd spent all afternoon shopping. Blue jeans, I bought a pair of jeans and some perfume.

Then memories of walking through the parking lot toward the car came forward.

They had just met those cute boys in the food court and were invited to a party. The taller one was cute, but Emma knew that Monica always fell for tall guys, so she resigned herself to the idea that the shorter one's eyes were nicer, and she had caught him checking out her legs. She wanted to give them their numbers and make plans to see them another time, so she wouldn't have to lie to her grandmother. Monica was doing her best to convince her to meet up with the boys as they neared the car.

"I don't know Tucson well enough," Emma remembered having argued. "We'll end up getting lost."

"I have GPS on my phone, silly," Monica countered.

"I promised Grandma Rita we'd have her car back by seven."

"Call her and say we've decided to go to a movie," Monica had said. "If she says okay, we'll go check out the party. If it turns out to be lame then we'll leave and actually catch a flick."

"That new Zach Ephron movie started yesterday." Emma remembered hoping the Zack Ephron reference may actually convince Monica to forget about the party altogether.

"Good idea, use that." She had smiled at me, pleased that I now appeared fully committed to the plan.

"Okay, okay," I'd said, caving in.

Her memory spit out the last few bytes of information it contained.

We were at the back of Grandma's Mini and I was on the phone lying to one of the nicest people in the world, about going to a movie that I really want to see, so that we could meet up with some boys that we don't know. I can be such a loser sometimes! I'm so sorry Grandma! Hey, my head is starting to feel better. Keep thinking, Emma. I was struggling with the phone, the shopping bags and the car keys. I dropped the keys. That was her last memory of the outside world. *Okay, I dropped the keys, then what? There has to be more!*

Emma's head bumped the end of the box as the vehicle came to an abrupt stop. Then the engine noise stopped. It was suddenly very quiet. She could hear Monica breathing. Slow and steady, in and out, her friend remained unconscious. Car doors slammed. She felt the truck shutter with each impact.

Faint voices filtered into the box. They were deep men's voices. She strained to hear what they were saying. The voices were fast and muffled. They weren't making any sense. Then she recognized a couple of words, "Las Niñas". Whoever they were, they were speaking Spanish. *Why are they speaking Spanish?* Nothing about this whole situation made any sense to her.

Scraping noises on the other side of Monica alerted Emma that something was happening. She burrowed her head down behind Monica. Fresh cool air washed in as the far side of the box fell away. In one second, Monica was snatched from beside her and her own body unconsciously filled the void left behind. Even with Monica gone, it seemed as though her arms and legs barely fit in the cramped space. Yellowish light reflecting off the ground gave Emma a glimpse of the metal coffin surrounding her. Then gnarled brown fingers reached into the box. Emma shrank back from them. She wedged herself as far from the opening as she could manage. A face filled with wrinkles and lines appeared. Dark eyes stared in at her.

"This one is awake!" Juan Carlos shouted in Spanish, startled to see open eyes staring back at him.

"Don't let her see your face!" Raul shouted back. The younger man immediately pulled his t-shirt up over his chin to his eyes, but his bulging muscles didn't leave room and it snapped back into place, leaving him exposed. He quickly turned around, facing away.

"It's too late." Now that he knew she had seen his face, Juan Carlos took a few seconds to examine her. Beautiful, athletic and perfect teeth, he could always tell the difference by their teeth. Where he came from, the girls couldn't get their teeth fixed, so they took what they got. If their teeth were crooked or one was broken, that's how it stayed. There was never any money for luxuries like fixing teeth and noses and other parts, but the Gringas did. Red, white and blue -- red hair, white teeth and blue eyes. That had always been his image of perfection. This one had two out of three, and the hair color was the easiest to fix. In the seconds that he was reaching into the box to pull her out, he let himself dream that he could keep this one for himself.

"Morales is not going to be happy about this." Raul had a way of throwing cold water on any of Juan Carlos' daydreams. Just mentioning the boss would be pissed at him turned the beads of sweat on the back of his thick neck to near freezing. The boss's wife scared him even more. He'd been around long enough to know that the help only pissed her off once. He no longer felt like having a beer. A couple shots of whiskey might help though...

He blinked himself back to reality and clenched his vice-grip hands onto Emma's bicep and yanked her close enough to turn her around so that he could grab the other arm from behind. He knew from experience that the pretty white teeth were nice to look at, but the deep scar on his left hand would always remind him that the red, in red, white and blue, could be blood, too.

CHAPTER 4

Agent Janet Porter

Aprox. four decades earlier
Birmingham, England

Millicent (Millie) Porter ran a tight household. The medium-sized home she lived in was kept clean, except for, occasionally, her two sons' bedroom. Dinner was always on time. Having been born and raised in London, it had taken her a while to warm up to Birmingham. An Arts major in college, she fell in love with an Engineering student, Edward Porter. They married right after graduation. He quickly landed a job designing auto parts with British Leyland at the Castle Bromwich Assembly Plant in Birmingham. Now, after living here for fifteen years, Millie thought of herself as a Brummie and didn't want to live anywhere else.

A part-time position at the Hippodrome, home of the Birmingham Royal Ballet and the Birmingham Opera Company, was a dream coming true for Millie. Her boys took after their father and were more interested in football and martial arts. But Millie held out hope for her youngest child, Janet. Her ten-year-old daughter had started ballet at the age of five and had progressed quickly. She now danced with the twelve-to-fourteen-year group. Millie marveled at how graceful and light on her feet Janet had become. Her daughter's Arabesque was the strongest and steadiest of all the girls. Several instructors told her so. Mrs. Porter finally had a willing partner to take to the opera, theater and museums.

Janet Porter greatly valued the time she spent with her mother. She even enjoyed ballet, especially at first. However, Janet loved rough-housing and hanging around her older brothers and their friends even more. Her rigorous ballet training had given her strong legs and many hours of stretching had made her extremely flexible. All in all, she was an excellent athlete and the younger girl was never picked last when neighborhood football teams were chosen. By the age of eleven, much to the dismay of her mother, Janet left ballet and joined Tai Kwon Do. Her rigorous dance training did not go to waste. The small girl excelled at the martial art. Her discipline, strength and flexibility soon had her competing at high levels.

Janet Porter never lost her interest in the Arts, though, and accompanied her mother to an event or opening at least once a month. She blossomed into a very pretty young woman. Her brother's friends no longer viewed her as one of the guys, even though she could still compete with them athletically.

By the time she entered secondary education, it was obvious that Janet was also the academic star of the Porter siblings. She found herself interested in just about everything. History, geography and the political sciences were of special fascination to her. Miss Porter's academic talent was noticed by a guidance counselor and she was placed into a pilot program at Cambridge University that would eventually become known as Pre-U.

Janet flourished in this environment. She had always been more comfortable around people older than herself. A degree in Sociology was followed by a year in West Africa helping develop a large irrigation project at Lake Chad. During her time there she came into contact and had a brief affair with an Interpol agent. The agent was in the region investigating the poor working conditions of many African diamond mines.

When Janet returned to the UK she applied to Interpol. Her education and background made her an excellent candidate and she was accepted. After the intensive training program, it took her only two years to advance to Field Agent status. She found herself drawn to crimes against women. It astounded her to learn that forced prostitution and slavery were alive and well in this day and age. It went on right under our noses in every country, not just in the poor and underprivileged areas.

Human trafficking is a big, ugly business. Interpol estimated that there are more than two million victims at any given time. Approximately eighty percent are exploited for sexual slavery and are predominantly women and girls. The odds of escaping or being rescued from this life are one in a hundred.

Agent Porter vowed to improve those odds by tearing down the organizations responsible. It would not be easy work, but she wasn't the type to back down from a challenge.

Within three years, the tenacious agent had closed several small trafficking rings. The first of which was right in downtown London, and then others in the Philippines, Africa and Mexico. Her arrest and conviction rates were astounding.

Meticulous notes and great instincts were the reason for her success. She left little to chance. Like many Interpol agents, she worked alone until it was time for the arrest. Then she would turn to local law enforcement for assistance or Special Forces teams -- if the bad guys were extremely tough or very well-armed. She especially liked working with US Navy Seals. During all three of the take downs she had paired up with them, they had been fast, professional and capable.

An SAS squad from her home country had worked with Agent Porter on one of the cases. While they were very good, two female victims had died during the raid. It hadn't seemed like such a success to Janet. The Mossad team she'd worked with had been extremely capable, but there seemed to be a trust issue. They hadn't trusted her judgment and the feeling became mutual.

Finally, after years of chasing small players in the human smuggling business, Janet got wind of a large one in Eastern Europe. Though she didn't know it at the time, Agent Porter was on the trail of the largest, most successful, trafficking ring in modern history.

She was soon in Bulgaria. Alarming numbers of young Eastern European women were disappearing. The promise of a better life in North America, the United States in particular, proved to be very tempting. Once they were lured away from home, their parents and loved ones never heard from their daughters or friends again. Life expectancy in the sexual slavery trade is very short, often less than five years.

Janet spent weeks following weak leads and, often times, mere rumors. She eventually landed in the coastal city of Varna which sported a slightly better economy than most of Bulgaria. Restaurants, bars and clubs were surviving. There was some tourism, but the harbor generated most of the business through imports and exports. A break in the case came from an unlikely source. An independent prostitute that Janet had spoken with briefly, a few days earlier, called her. Most threw the Interpol agent's card away before she had moved more than ten steps away. English speaking Lady Gwendolyn hadn't.

That evening when Janet returned to her hotel room, the message light was blinking on her phone. It was most likely the London office wondering why she'd been in Bulgaria for a month and had nothing to show for it. She decided London could wait while she unwound from another day of pounding the dreary streets of the Eastern European city. She ordered curry from the restaurant next door and took a quick hot bath. The very hot, clean water was easily the thing she liked most about this particular hotel.

Forty-five minutes later, clean and partially fed, Porter called the front desk to retrieve her message. "I've got something for you. Meet me at Payolee's Bar at eleven tonight. L G."

A glance at her wrist told the rejuvenated woman that it was already 10:30. Janet threw on the clothes she'd just removed and ran out the door. She got lucky and there was a taxi waiting at the front door. The first she'd seen there. The twenty-five minute ride seemed to take hours. She would be a few minutes late. The Interpol Agent prayed that Lady Gwendolyn would wait for her.

Entering the dimly-lit establishment at a run, Janet scanned the bar and then the row of deep booths along the side wall. There was no sign of her contact. She looked behind her. The taxi had already gone back to a safer part of town. Janet ran her fingers through her still slightly-damp hair and discovered that it was too badly tangled to get a comb through it. Janet smoothed it down, by hand, as best she could. It would have to do. She was surprised to discover that Payolee's had a pleasant atmosphere. Soft lighting, comfortable booths and blues music in the background gave it an American feel.

Two patrons and one of the bartenders were at the far end of the bar watching football highlights on a small color television. They were excited about the prospect of the Bulgarian team joining the world group for the next World Cup. Apparently they'd been very close this year. Janet felt a sudden pang of regret. It had been far too long since she had gotten together with her brothers to watch Manchester United play.

After a month in the country, Agent Porter had picked up some of the language. She could follow some conversations, especially if she had an idea what they were about. Speaking it, though, was another matter. Another month in Bulgaria, perish the thought, and she'd be conversational or better. She already spoke five languages fluently.

At the nearer end of the bar, three businessmen laughed about something. She had no idea what. The other bartender delivered drinks to a young couple, in the second from last booth, who looked very much in love.

Two other booths were occupied and everyone seemed to be enjoying themselves. Janet went to the nearest empty booth and slid in. The roving bartender came right over. She ordered a Mojito. Happily, he knew what that was and headed back to the bar. Janet had become addicted to them while in Mexico. She'd spent some vacation time there after a successful raid with a certain Navy Seal. A week of beaches, Mojitos and Allan had been just what she needed. It had been fun but hadn't turned into anything serious. By the time her drink arrived, she'd decided to try and organize another getaway with the handsome soldier.

One sip later, Lady Gwendolyn appeared from the rear of the bar. Janet assumed the toilet facilities were back there. Almost every male eye gawked as she entered the room. Immediately after spotting Agent Porter, the strikingly beautiful woman signaled the bartender to bring one of whatever the other woman was drinking. She sauntered over to the booth and shimmied in, her evening dress very tight in all the right places.

"Sorry I'm late," Lady Gwendolyn began, "one of my regulars needed a date for a high profile business dinner."

"You look fantastic," Janet complimented, "Lady..."

"Call me LG," the woman cut her off. "My friends call me LG." These were, in fact, the initials from her real name.

Lucy Gordon had fallen in love with the wrong guy many years earlier. A teen runaway from a small town near Idaho Falls, she'd made her way to New York. She met Brad practically right off the bus. He was so nice and helpful, not to mention good looking. Weeks later she met his boss, a brute who was nothing at all like Brad. Her life spiraled down quickly from there. Sometime later, Lucy's father came to town looking for her. When he began to get close, the small town girl was shipped off to Eastern Europe. Lucy defied the odds and surpassed ten years in the life. Strong character and a tough mid-western constitution had allowed her to slowly and stealthily wean herself off heroin. When an opportunity arose, the intelligent woman slipped away and eventually set up shop as an independent, hundreds of miles away in Varna. She still had some self-respect but not enough to believe she could go back to Idaho after the life she'd led.

"LG," the Interpol agent replied, "thank you so much for contacting me."

"I wish someone like you had..." LG paused and stared briefly into space, before getting to the reason for their little meeting. "Well anyway, one of my special friends," she fingered quotation marks around the word friends, "works down at the docks. He told me that there are strange comings and goings at a deserted warehouse near his office."

The roving bartender set a glistening Mojito in front of LG and then whisked away with a tray full of drinks to the next booth.

Janet lifted her glass and tilted it slightly toward the other woman, "Salute."

"Salute," LG replied and took a sip of the minty mixture. "Oh, this is quite good."

"It is, isn't it?" Janet smiled as they both took another sip. "It's called a Mojito."

"Mojito," LG repeated, "I'll try and remember that."

"You were saying something about strange comings and goings," Janet prompted.

"Yes," LG said, putting the tasty drink down. "Curiosity got the best of my friend and he crept over to the building and peaked inside." She looked around to assure herself no one was listening before continuing. "The windows were all blacked out, but he managed to get a look inside. He told me it looked like an opium den. You know with mattresses and old sofas scattered around the place. Except every one of the drugged out people turned out to be scantily or half-dressed young women."

"Were there any guards?" Janet asked.

"He told me that he'd spotted a couple of guys carrying pistols," she answered. "Then he got the hell out of there."

"Did your friend give you an address?" Agent Porter inquired.

"No," LG smiled. "But he told me that he could see the building from his office and I know where that is."

An hour later they were at the docks.

"That's his office," LG pointed at a third floor window, "up there."

Janet looked at it, then turned one hundred eighty degrees and scanned the mostly dark dock area that the window faced. One derelict building stood out. It was approximately a quarter mile away. Janet produced a small pair of binoculars from her handbag. Closer inspection revealed a large dark-windowed SUV sitting on the street out front of the building. Janet adjusted the focus until the view was crystal clear. The driver's window was cracked open a few inches. A few seconds later a puff of smoke escaped through the opening, revealing at least one occupant.

"That's it," she pointed to the building. "LG, I can't thank you enough."

"You can thank me by helping those girls."

"I'm going to do my best," Janet promised.

"It's Lucy," the woman from Idaho reached out and reintroduced herself, "Lucy Gordon."

"It is my great honor to meet you, Lucy Gordon." Janet shook the offered hand. "You have helped me immeasurably today. If there is ever anything I can do for you..."

"Just be careful," Lucy warned. "The men who do these things are heartless, soulless bastards."

"Yes they are," she agreed. "You have put yourself at enough risk already, Lucy Gordon. You should go before you're seen."

"What about you?"

"I'll be here for the rest of the night," Janet explained. "I have a lot to do."

Janet hugged the taller woman and they said their goodbyes. LG turned and started walking back to the car she had borrowed.

"Lucy," Janet softly called her name, stopping her. "I can arrange to have you relocated anywhere in the world."

"Idaho Falls," Lucy whispered reverently to herself, before turning around. The same beautiful place she couldn't wait to leave all those years ago.

"Anywhere," Janet assured her. "Think about it."

"I've got your number." Lucy said, and quickly turned back around before the tears began to flow. Maybe, just maybe, she could go home again. Keeping her back straight, she marched back to the car. Once inside, the flood gates opened as she thought of her mother, father and two younger brothers.

Agent Porter spent the rest of that night and much of the next three days documenting the movement of girls and men through the abandoned warehouse. This operation was much larger than any she'd previously found. It was a human processing center. Twenty to twenty-five girls were brought there every day, while a similar number of other girls were shipped out. To where, the agent didn't yet have an answer. The girls were guarded by three shifts of eight. None carried automatic weapons that she could see. She was reasonably certain they were all equipped with handguns, although she only saw a few.

Janet contacted the London office to arrange assistance on the raid. Her first priority was freeing the dozens of girls being held right now. She hoped more answers could be obtained through interrogations of the guards. Since there were no Special Forces teams readily available nearby, and the Agent on the Ground - Janet, had not reported heavy arms, local LEOs (Law Enforcement Organization) were called upon for assistance.

The raid was planned for dawn the next morning. She was to meet with Bulgarian Police at 6:00 am the next morning and brief them. They would handle the raid. She was not to be involved, once the operation began. This wasn't unusual, as the locals usually wanted to take credit for the bust. Janet didn't care about that. She cared about the girls. She went back to her hotel, ordered in, took a hot bath and enjoyed a good sleep.

She was at the meeting place by 5:00 am. Right away she could tell something wasn't right. The guard car was gone. The place seemed deserted. Janet left the well-hidden observation station she'd fashioned from old wooden boxes and discarded pallets and worked her way down to the building. A side door hung wide open. In her heart she already knew they'd been tipped off and were gone. She glanced inside to physically confirm the emptiness of the building. Disappointment consumed her. She'd managed to save no one. These girls needed her help and she'd let them down. A small scream of desperation escaped her lips.

It was followed by thuck, thuck, thuck. The door frame splintered around her. She dove into the building. Half a second later the sound of three gunshots echoed down to the building. Someone shot at her. Janet scrambled away from the door. Without thinking about it, her trusty Walther PPK had the safety off and a bullet chambered before she got three steps. Within seconds she'd gotten to a blacked-out window. It was covered with tar paper. The Interpol agent tore a small peak hole and looked out.

Coming across the yard were three policemen. The biggest of them sent each of the others running around the perimeter with a pair of nods, before continuing confidently towards the door the woman had ducked into.

Janet looked around for cover. She could see nothing substantial in the huge warehouse. Then she spotted a staircase in the far corner. She raced toward it, leaping the mattresses and avoiding the threadbare furniture that still lay about. As she got closer, she could see the stairs led into a lower ceilinged area, perhaps a storage mezzanine of some kind. The wide stairs, composed of heavy rough-hewn lumber, had smooth treads from the many boots that had climbed them before her. Janet flew up, three steps at a time, disappearing through the hole in the ceiling just seconds before the large cop poked his head through the doorway.

Even darker up here than on the main floor, it took the agent's eyes a few moments to adjust. The mezzanine turned out to be larger than the woman had imagined. During days long past, it appeared to have been used as a receiving area for pallets of goods. Janet had seen setups similar to this at the British Leyland factory where her father worked. A large metal table sat below an eight-foot-by-eight-foot door that swung inward. Above the table, attached to the ceiling, a sturdy stationary crane ran between the table and a trap door, where it would lower the pallets of goods down to the main level. Mumbled voices from below increased the urgency of finding a way out.

Agent Porter climbed onto the dusty table. Three sliding metal bars secured the big door. The top bar slid back easily. The middle bar wouldn't budge. The bottom one moved with considerable effort. Janet slammed her shoulder against the door hoping to loosen the remaining bar. The old door jiggled but the bar was still stuck. Janet could see that time and moisture had warped the door. Maybe with the help of a lever of some kind she could move it. Behind her the stairs creaked, as someone slowly climbed them. A pretty good marksman, the Interpol agent laid down on the dirty table, rested both elbows in front of her and looked down the sights of the 9mm semi-automatic. Only twelve meters away, Janet could shoot the O's out of a can of Coca Cola from this range.

A brown woolen cap appeared slowly, followed by swarthy dark eyes and a hooked nose. He searched along the floor. His head swiveled back and forth. She waited patiently. Not much of Janet was visible from his low vantage point. He took a tentative step up. Then his eyes locked onto Agent Porter's. He swung his revolver towards her and instantly the bridge of his nose collapsed into his brain. The crooked cop crumbled instantly and tumbled heavily back down the stairs. Angry shouting was followed by a dozen shots fired randomly though the floor of the mezzanine. One bullet ricocheted off the crane and another hit the underneath of the metal clad table, but didn't have the force to go through. She could hear arguing below. Janet managed to pick out a few of the Bulgarian words. It sounded like neither remaining man wanted to be the next to venture up the stairs.

While they argued, Agent Porter noticed a short but chunky piece of lumber beside the nearby wall. It wouldn't work as a lever, but would be a suitable battering ram. She slid off the table and grabbed it. Janet slammed it against the handle. The bar didn't move, but the noise turned out to be much louder than she expected. She put all her weight into the next shot. Success, the bar moved an inch. Four more quick slams and the door popped open. The arguing stopped. She assumed one or both of them were on their way up. She looked out the door. A rotting conveyer belt extended outward about forty meters to a loading dock. The rusty frame didn't look all that stable anymore. Plus, she'd be an easy target if caught on it. She had an idea. Janet swung the door open. Light from the rising sun flooded in.

The top of Andreas' bald head and then his beady eyes slowly poked through the opening in the floor. The bright opening in the wall caught his attention immediately. He did not wish to meet the same fate as his buddy Petr, so his head managed a three hundred sixty degree visual sweep of the bright room. The bitch that had killed his friend was nowhere in sight. Carefully he climbed the rest of the stairs.

Now, certain that his prey had fled, he walked quickly over to the open door. The door hung about four inches above the table. He could see the beginning of an old conveyer belt from where he stood. He'd need to climb onto the table to get a better view.

He grunted with exertion as he pulled himself up. The Bulgarian cop peaked around the door frame. The conveyer was empty. He hung his head out and looked up, down and all around. He couldn't see the troublesome woman anywhere. She had to be either climbing down the wall, or had reached the ground already. As he stepped onto the shaky conveyer, for a better view, the man shouted something over his shoulder.

There was an angry response from down below followed by heavy feet pounding on the long stairway.

It's now or never, Janet realized. Besides, her cramping fingers and toes would not cling to the sliding bars on the back of the door much longer. Silently, she dropped onto the table. She put her shoulder to the heavy door and pushed with all her might. At first it seemed to move in slow motion, but once she had momentum it began to accelerate. The creaking sound of the dry hinges alerted the dirty cop. Lunging at the rapidly closing door, he might as well have been trying to stop a charging NFL lineman. Janet barely felt the impact that sent him tumbling backwards. The side of the building shook as the door slammed home.

The top half of the third policeman's body cleared the opening in the floor at the same time that Janet slid the top latch into place. He was about ask his partner how could the woman have disappeared, when he realized the shadowy form half way across the room was the Interpol agent, not his partner. He swung his handgun upward, the index finger tightening on the trigger.

Janet turned from the door and the big cop came into view. Thunder filled the room, and the metal platform below her bounced slightly as a heavy bullet slammed into it. The Interpol agent dropped to her hand and knees as the other hand gripped the gun at her hip. Staring into the rising barrel of the big forty-five, it looked like a cannon to her. Janet watched helplessly as his finger flexed again. Her own nine millimeter, now out of the holster, was still travelling into position.

Millie Porter's only daughter thought she was dead. She wasn't -- not yet. The second blast travelled high, singeing a few brunette hairs on its way past.

Police Sargent Ilia Pushkavorkin angrily added his left hand to his pistol for support. He would not miss again. As he zeroed in the front sight, there were six quick pops, which sounded like a string of firecrackers going off compared to his big gun.

Janet emptied her clip. Her first shot caught a shoulder, but the remaining five formed a tight cluster in the center of his chest.

Ilia had been dead wrong about not missing again. His final shot crashed wildly into the wall as he tilted sideways. He knew he'd been hit. Strangely though, it reminded him of his childhood days when his older sister used to poke him on the shoulder and chest with her finger just to get a rise out of him. Ilia smiled. His sister's pretty face was the last thing that drifted through his mind as he joined Petr at the bottom of the stairs.

Janet flicked the empty clip out of the Walther, pulled another from her holster and rammed it into place. As her hearing cleared, she began to notice muffled shouting from beyond the loading door. She walked over to the stairway and cautiously moved down a few rungs until she had a view of the warehouse. Satisfied no one else had entered the large building, she returned to the table. The shouting sounded desperate.

Once again on the platform, the agent undid the latch and cracked open the door. Peaking though, the conveyer appeared empty. The frantic voice came from below the tattered rubber walkway. She swung the door open and ventured out. The conveyer creaked with her added weight.

"Ilia, help me, I'm down here." That much Bulgarian she could understand. He had heard the shooting and probably thought that his partner firing the last shot meant victory for their team.

Janet peaked over the side. There, the second cop clung to a strip of belting. His surprised reaction, at the sight of her, caused the belting to tear slightly. He dropped a few inches and went perfectly still. Immediately, she saw his dilemma. Whenever he tried to pull himself up or even move, the weather-worn belt tore. The old belt could break at any moment. Though the ground was only thirty feet below, the side yard of the abandoned building had become a dumping ground for those still in business at the docks. Hunks of concrete, rusty metal of all shapes and sizes, busted windows and a couple of broken toilets waited patiently for a new companion to join their miserable existence.

He said something to her in a pleading voice and put on his best puppy dog face. As soon as he smiled, Janet recognized him. She'd documented him, along with several other men, who had visited the warehouse on a daily basis. Most likely, sampling the merchandise had been a part of the dirty cop's compensation package. It was possible he knew where the women had been taken.

"Do you speak any English?" she asked as she positioned herself above him. He slowly shook his head.

"Parlez-vous français?" This was met with another negative shake.

"Habla usted español?" Once again, her question was met with a negative response.

"Sprechen sie deutsch?" Janet asked. With only Russian in reserve, her language options were running thin.

"Da, sie deutsch," he responded, nodding his head just a little. A barely audible tearing sound resulted. The man went very still again.

"Where are the women?" She asked in German.

"I don't know," he responded carefully.

"That is a shame," Janet told him as she stepped back from the edge. Her abrupt movement caused the once sturdy contraption to shake. Though the belt was a meter wide, it suddenly felt much narrower. The bolts in some of the conveyer's braces had corroded completely away. Sustaining the weight of two people was a lot to expect of the unmaintained equipment. A louder rip resulted.

"Please help me," he pleaded, "I have a wife and children."

"Children?" she asked with an implication for additional detail.

"A boy and a girl," he told her and then elaborated, "thirteen and fifteen."

Rage and disgust filled Janet. Most of the young women taken were not much older than this piece of filth's children. How could a parent do this to someone else's daughters? She calmed herself.

The Interpol agent stepped slowly into view. "Where are they taking the girls?" She could see the internal struggle taking place, as his dark eyes flashed back and forth while he considered the consequences of saying nothing or squealing on the powerful organization he was a part of. Janet holstered her gun and produced a jackknife from her pocket. He watched anxiously as she pried the largest blade from the handle. When he still said nothing she knelt down and put the blade near the tearing piece of belt.

"Zadar," he said quietly.

"What was that?" she pressed the knife blade down.

"Zadar," he told her more loudly. "They are moving the operation up the coast to Zadar. The girls were sent there."

"Give me an address," she demanded, "or a name. Anything that might help me find them."

"The harbor at Zadar," he said, "that's all I know."

The Interpol agent decided that the man hanging below her didn't look like he'd been the brains of the group. "I believe you," she told him and closed the knife. Janet stood up and walked to the loading door. "Good luck with the landing," she called over her shoulder, to the man who would have killed her given the chance, "you miserable, cheating bastard."

"Wait, don't leave me!" Janet heard him pleading through the door as she forced it shut again. She slid the top bar into its latch and left.

Janet found a telephone at a nearby operational warehouse. She called the London office, apprized them of the situation and had them alert the Bulgarian Police that they had officers down. She went back to the hotel where there was a message waiting from Lucy Gordon. The Interpol agent took a hot bath, packed her bag and joined Lucy at a restaurant near the airport.

After some discussion with Lucy, Janet called Interpol and made arrangements for Miss Gordon to fly to Paris for a debriefing and then on to the United States. Once the American was safely on a plane, the Interpol agent then booked herself passage on a ship to Zadar, Yugoslavia. The next morning she went back down to the harbor, careful to avoid the hive of police activity at a certain abandoned building.

Tucked under her arm, was the Varna Daily paper. The faces of Varna's *finest* plastered the front page along with a factually vacant story extolling the heroic efforts of three local police officers, two of which lost their lives, while the third suffered a broken leg, several cuts and a couple of bruised ribs, in a valiant effort to stem the flow of illegal drugs into their fair city.

CHAPTER 5

Tennis Anyone?

Present day
Green Valley, Arizona

P B came in from the garage, returning from Sunday morning doubles league.

"How was the tennis this morning?" Janet asked.

"It was okay. Ben wasn't there, though."

Ben Morrison, six foot two, slightly overweight, had played Division One tennis for the Minnesota Gophers back in the mid-seventies. He still maintained good strokes including a blistering forehand and deceptively-angled crisp volleys. A once-mighty serve had been reduced to a shadow of its former self, due to fused vertebrae in his lower back. Ben was one of the few players in the region capable of pushing PB around on the court. Not to mention that he was an all-around nice guy. Ben and his wife, Rita, had been over for dinner several times in the past few months.

"Did he hurt his back again?"

"I don't know. He just didn't show." PB shrugged as he set down his racquet bag.

"That's not like Ben." Janet felt a chill run down her spine. "Something must be wrong."

"Doug Stedman happened by and had his racquet in the car so he joined us."

"PB, I think you should call him."

"I will. Right after I have a shower."

The phone rang as PB sauntered past the kitchen island. He snatched it up. Nothing showed on the caller ID.

"Hello?"

"Hello PB, it's Ben," the familiar voice sounded tired.

PB glanced over at Janet and nodded.

"What happened? Did you sleep in, you old fart?"

"Emma is missing," Ben said, weakly. "We think she might have been taken last night from the Park Place Mall in Tucson. Rita and I have been here for hours."

Janet watched PB's demeanor transform from happy retiree to Special Forces commando within a few moments. She knew that something was terribly wrong.

"What can we do to help, Ben?"

"Probably nothing PB," his voiced cracked. "You and Janet..." There was a pause. "Well, it's just that Janet used to be in law enforcement of some kind. We were hoping... I'm just so frustrated."

"Of course," PB assured his friend, "we'll help in any way that we can. What do the police have to say about the situation?"

"They finally sent over a couple of detectives," Ben answered. "Apparently the girls haven't been missing long enough for the police to take the situation seriously. Emma wouldn't just stay out all night without contacting her father or us."

Janet watched her husband's face for clues as he listened to more details. The mention of police had her on high alert. Her husband was hard to read, but something bad had happened -- that much was clear.

"I'm sure everything will be alright," PB tried to assure him. "You and Rita hold on. We'll be there as soon as we can."

PB set the phone back down on the counter.

"Emma and her friend Monica didn't come home after shopping last night." PB tried to sound calm, but deep down his gut was telling him that Ben and Rita's granddaughter needed help.

"Oh, my God," Janet's shoulders slumped as her mind instantly imagined several scenarios, most of them not good. She'd only met Emma once, but the teen had seemed pretty level-headed. Not the type to stay out all night.

"Let's not jump to any conclusions until we have more facts," PB added quickly, trying to convince both his wife and himself. "The girls' phones are both shut off and Monica's father swears that it would take an act of Congress to get his daughter to power her phone down."

Their eyes locked, recalling the cruelties they had witnessed during their battles against human traffickers. Neither wanted to think about the possibility of losing the latest lifestyle they'd been cultivating in southern Arizona. Getting involved could do just that. There was really no choice in the matter. They were in. Both knew it.

"They found Rita's car in the Park Place Mall parking lot," PB reported, "but not the girls."

Janet walked over and traced the faint scar on his forehead with her finger. PB gazed across the back yard at the gorgeous view of the Santa Rita Mountains, then leaned down and kissed his wife.

"You're right, let's not jump to any conclusions. They're teenagers, after all," she said, forcing a smile. "Have a quick shower and let's go help find these girls."

The Park Place Mall is much like any modern mall in a North American city. It is large and bright, clad with attractive marble floors and walls. A maze of long hallways filled with specialty shops, anchored here and there by large department stores, a large multi-theater cineplex and a food court that offered any kind of fast food you could think of.

PB sat with Ben and Rita and their son Robert in the mall manager's office going over what they had learned from a police contact.

"The police aren't very concerned at this point, but at least they did go through mall security footage." Robert Morrison spoke slowly, both looking and sounding a little like a zombie. Lack of sleep, fear and frustration were all taking their toll. Clearly not accustomed to the Arizona heat, his clothes were wrinkled and sweat-stained. "They are trying to identify and locate a couple of boys that the girls spoke with in the food court." Emma's father then added, "The police just want to talk to the boys. It appears from the tapes that the girls left the food court alone and continued shopping. The boys headed off in a separate direction, a little while later, with two other girls."

"Maybe the boys told them about a party?" Ben offered. Rita reached over and grabbed his hand.

"That's a police theory," PB confirmed. "There is a BOLO out on the car the boys were driving."

"Rita let Emma use her Mini Cooper to go shopping with Monica," Ben said. "The girls had promised to have it home by 7:00 pm."

"Emma called me at about 6:30 to ask if they could stay out longer and go to a movie," Rita said, her voice shaky. "I agreed, but now that I think about it, she sounded a little strange on the phone."

"How do you mean?" Janet asked.

"I don't know," Rita said, shrugging. "She just didn't sound like her usual self. I should have told her to come home right then..."

"This is not your fault," Ben told her, wrapping his sobbing wife in his arms.

.   .   .

Janet left PB with the Morrisons, to take a look outside.

In the southeast corner of the mall parking lot, Rita's cute red Mini sat alone. The mall had been busy when the girls had gotten there Saturday afternoon, but most of the shoppers hadn't arrived yet today.

The police, now seeming more serious about the situation, had found footage of the girls pulling up, parking and walking to the entrance. Half an hour later, two of the parking lot security cameras had mysteriously been repositioned. One of which had been pointed at the southeast corner, where the car was clearly visible. The other located next to it had provided coverage to the southeast exit. Both cameras now pointed at the northeast section of the parking lot. The perpetrator or perpetrators had to have been on the roof to gain access to the cameras. Despite the rising heat from the naked desert sun, Janet felt a chill. This was not good news at all.

Janet had Rita's spare car keys. She wore gloves and was careful not to contaminate what she knew in her heart would eventually become part of a crime scene. She found nothing in or around the car, not even the bags of merchandise that the girls had been carrying through the halls. The mall cameras had clearly shown the girls exiting with bags. The natural thing to do, especially if you were going out to a party, would be to stow the bags away.

"Where are the bags?" Janet wondered out loud. She wandered toward the rear of the mall and looked in the giant trash receptacles. Empty. The garbage truck must have come by earlier this morning. It had been a long shot anyway. The former Interpol agent decided to do like the popular game show *Who Wants to be a Millionaire* and call a friend for advice. She took out her phone and made an international call to the smartest person she knew. After a short greeting she got down to business.

"There is clear footage of the girls arriving and parking early yesterday afternoon," she spoke into her cell phone. "Shortly after they go inside, two parking lot cameras were purposely repositioned away from their car."

On the other end of the line, Sarah Woodrow, an Interpol Intelligence Officer based in the London office, listened carefully.

"The police were able to track the girls as they moved around the mall for the next four hours or so," Janet continued. "At six twenty pm the girls exit the mall carrying a few small shopping bags and, shortly thereafter, disappear out of camera range as they head towards their car."

"It sounds to me like your girls were specifically targeted," Sarah stated to her former colleague. "Most likely the perpetrators had eyes on them all afternoon. They must have been waiting for them at the mall," she continued. "This could explain how they knew which cameras in the lot to disable."

"These girls don't know anyone here in Arizona," Janet pointed out.

"Social media," Sarah explained. "One or both the girls likely twittered or face-booked their plans for the day."

"I hadn't thought of that."

"Text me their phone numbers," Sarah told her. "I'll have my department search for digital records."

"I'll get them right to you," the former agent responded.

"Is one of the girls from a wealthy family?"

"Monica's father is a CEO," Janet answered. "Castle Homes is the name of his company, I believe. Why do you ask?"

"We investigated a nasty group in that part of the world a couple of years ago," Sarah reported.

"Do you have reason to think they are involved?" Janet asked.

"It's far too soon to tell," Sarah quickly replied, hearing some alarm in her friend's voice. "I just recall that their victims were taken in pairs. I'll pull the files and take another look at them."

"Thanks."

"I do recall that we had identified most of the suspects in that case," Sarah added, "but just couldn't find any evidence to connect them."

"There is still a chance these girls will just show up safe and sound," Janet countered, "but things don't look very good right now."

"Listen, I have to run, Janet. Meetings coming out my ears."

"I remember them. My condolences," she replied.

"I'll do what I can from here," Sarah stated. "Keep your chin up, my friend."

"Thank you for helping with this, Sarah."

"We're forever in your debt for saving Duke Barrowford, the cheating putz," Sarah reminded her. "All the British MI agencies were asleep at the wheel on that one. When word leaked out that you were ex-Interpol, we looked like heroes here in the UK, while you..."

"Well, PB and I appreciate the help, just the same," Janet admitted. "Talk to you soon."

"Ta ta," Sarah replied and was gone.

Janet slid the phone into her pocket and headed towards the mall entrance, now more certain than ever that these girls were in very serious trouble!

An hour later Janet received a quick call from Sarah confirming that, at approximately 8:10 pm Friday evening, Monica Arthur had tweeted about the girls' plans for shopping at the Park Place Mall Saturday afternoon.

"I need to get a close look at the security tapes," Janet told her three companions. Ben and Rita had joined her and PB at the food court to discuss the proceedings. Robert was lying down on a sofa in the mall manager's office.

"This won't be easy to hear," PB looked across the table, into his friend's eyes. "Janet and I think that Emma and her friend may have been kidnapped."

"Why?" Ben's eyes filled with tears.

"The intentionally-disabled parking lot cameras," PB explained. "Plus, we believe that the kidnappers knew the girls would be here from a tweet that Monica sent out to her friends Friday night."

"Does that mean they were after our girls?" Rita asked fearfully.

"We think it's a strong possibility," Janet put her hand on Rita's shoulder, "And if so, they were almost certainly after Monica and Emma just happened to be with her."

"Maybe they'll just let Emma go," Ben proposed.

"Maybe," PB tried to sound optimistic, "but just in case, we're going to look for some proof that will get the police motivated into action."

Tears spilled down Rita's cheeks. Janet moved over, knelt in front of her friend and grabbed both of her hands. "We'll do everything in our power to help get Emma back." Rita nodded and managed a brief smile. "We have a clue to go on that we didn't have before."

"There is a pretty good chance the kidnappers got here early and cased the place," PB took over the explanation. "It doesn't sound like much, but if we can find footage of them or their vehicle, it would get us and the police pointed in the right direction."

"What can we do to help?" Ben stood.

"You guys should go home and get some rest before you fall over," PB instructed them. "Janet and I will let you know as soon as there are any developments."

After a little more convincing, the exhausted Morrisons reluctantly collected their son and drove home.

As soon as they left, the Reeses went directly to the mall manager's office.

A roundish man with girlish hips, Albert Fisker had been relatively good looking, many years earlier. A divorce and too much alcohol had been tough on him. Pretty good at his job, the mall management firm he worked for had taken full advantage of his marital status and transferred him around the country, dangling the carrot of a regional management position for his hard efforts. The Park Place Mall was his fourth location in the last three years. One of the few perks to his job was the large number of attractive women who managed the shops and stores in malls. Fisker met personally with each and every one of them, too. Unfortunately for him, so far, none had been terribly interested in sharing their life with a balding forty-year-old who looked like he was closer to fifty. He tried to remain hopeful. At least he was almost certain the promotion would be offered any day now. If not, there would soon be another group of shopkeepers to get to know.

"I'm sorry," Albert told the couple in front of his desk, "I can't just hand over security footage. Besides this is a police investigation."

"Look Mr. Fisker," Janet began, "the police are following a completely different avenue of leads. We won't bother or hinder their investigation in the slightest."

"Even so, I just can't..." he started to respond.

"If these girls end up hurt or worse," PB interrupted him, "there is going to be a lot of negative publicity coming your way."

Albert Fisker didn't need this pressure. The promotion was so close he could almost taste it. It was just his luck, wasn't it? Why hadn't those stupid little bitches gone to the Tucson Mall instead of here?

"If we find anything," PB tossed out a bread crumb, "we'll bring it back to you first."

"Then I could alert the police personally," Fisker picked up on the idea.

"No one would have to know we were even involved," PB told him. It was a win/win situation, since the Reeses didn't want their involvement made public anyway.

Albert made an executive decision and went against policy. "Okay, for the safety of these girls, you can look at the footage."

"You're doing the right thing," Janet assured him.

"No one can know about this," Fisker warned. "Wait for me in the food court."

As soon as they left his office, Albert called the security room. "Alicia, would you please make me copies of our security footage for the past twenty-four hours and bring them up to me, ASAP."

Two hours later, Albert Fisker had detectives in his office. He explained how he had taken it upon himself to do some investigating of his own. Then he showed them footage of a beat up old Ford half ton truck, with faded unreadable plates, circling the mall yesterday morning. Then just before the girls went missing the same rusty, battered truck, only this time carrying a giant load of furniture, entered the parking lot and drove directly towards the spot where the girls were parked. Not coincidentally, this was the exact same area where the cameras had already been disabled. Six minutes later, the truck came back into view and then exited where it had entered only minutes earlier.

The police finally jumped onto the kidnapping bandwagon. The boys had been found and questioned. They had texts from the girls that said they were coming to the party, but the girls never arrived nor had they answered any further texts from the boys. Two dozen officers and a crime scene unit were soon crawling through the mall and parking lot, searching for clues. Since it was now being called a kidnapping the FBI was called. With Mexico so near, the Feds sent a cross-border specialist.

Albert Fisker became the man of the hour. Many were calling him a hero. A local news team interviewed Albert in the food court. For the first time, a couple of the shopkeepers noticed what a great smile he possessed.

CHAPTER 6

Los Diablos Rojos

Thirty years earlier
Northern Mexico

When Hector Morales was four years old, his mother ran away with a travelling salesman to escape her alcoholic, abusive husband. Her last words to Hector were, "I'm sorry that I can't take you with me, Baby. Be strong and you will be alright."

For the remainder of his childhood Hector lived occasionally with his father, but more often with his grandmother. He soon learned that Daddy had inherited his mean streak from her. Both Hector and his father referred to his estranged mother as the Bitch and his grandmother as the *Witch* (but only when they were well outside the range of the older woman's incredibly keen hearing).

Hector was small for his age, but he became tough as nails. Hector was indoors only to eat, sleep and sporadically attend school. His grandmother hadn't spent even one day of her life in a classroom and certainly didn't care if *the boy*, as she called him, did homework.

Since Hector was the only kid in town that would stand up to the school bully, Nemo (the Giant) Suarez, they soon became friends.

The boys left school and their troubled homes by the time they were fourteen and lived on the streets full time. At twenty years old, the David-and-Goliath pair were respected by the other hoodlums and tough guys in the region and were certainly feared by all the ordinary folk living in and near the small city of Hermosillo.

Hector ran a small but effective crew that stole mostly cars and cigarettes, dealt drugs and shook down local businesses for protection money. With Nemo, now six-foot-six with huge bulging shoulders that often forced him to step sideways through doorways, as his enforcer, the gang met little resistance. Hector's operation grew to include the surrounding towns from Guaymos in the south, all the way north to the border town of Nogales.

It wasn't long before Hector was the most feared man in the region. Nemo was definitely the toughest, but he mostly just did as Hector told him. Neither had any compunction about ending the life of anyone that got in the crew's way. People in the area began referring to Hector as *el Pequeño Diablo* or the Little Devil and Nemo as *el Grande Diablo*. Like the popular song lyrics suggested, "You don't tug on Superman's cape, or spit into the wind," and you didn't mess with either the Little Devil or the Big Devil if you knew what was good for you. They began calling their little gang, *Los Diablos Rojos*. The Red Devils continued to grow, expelling or absorbing any other drug traders in the area.

Nogales became the main focus of Hector's operation. Soon he was smuggling large quantities of marijuana across the border. His higher than average IQ and street smarts more than made up for a lack of education. He loved the challenge of outwitting the American Border Patrol and whatever current task force that was trying to slow the flow of drugs into the USA. A well-trained crew and innovative smuggling methods quickly made Hector one of the wealthiest men in the Sonoran Desert, on either side of the border.

Hector decided to build himself a large estate in the coastal town of Puerto Penasco where he could get away and relax. He started thinking of himself as a businessman and entrepreneur. He even started wearing suits and carrying a briefcase.

Nemo, on the other hand, spent all of his money on fast cars and even faster women. He never stopped being a bully. He enjoyed inflicting pain and proudly bore his many scars.

As large and homely as Nemo had become, his younger sister, Maria, had grown into a slender and beautiful woman. You would never, in a million years, pick them out in a group of people as being siblings.

Maria became the only female who Hector ever cared for since his mother left him. He grew to love her more than life itself, which surprised everyone including himself.

After a short courtship, and Nemo's indifferent blessing, they were married. A beautiful home and a loving wife he adored, Hector could never have imagined such a good life for himself. However, the same day Maria found out that she was pregnant, was nearly her and her husband's last day on this earth.

The Sinaloa Cartel, quickly becoming the largest in Mexico, had taken notice of Hector's booming business and decided to add it to their collection. The cartel studied his operation and attacked it with military precision.

Even if they had been prepared for the attack, Los Diablos Rojos would have been no match for the much larger crime syndicate. The cartel swept through Hector's compounds and properties, killing everyone they came across. Only those fortunate enough to be away during the attack survived. Hector was on the east coast taking care of some personal business. Nemo had driven his sister to Hermosillo for a doctor's appointment and two others were in Tucson on a drug run. Twenty-two men and women lost their lives that day, only three of which were cartel members. Subsequent negotiations with the Cartel had not gone very well. The Cartel kept his compounds, his equipment, his inventory, and his entire territory. In exchange for all that, plus a promise to stay out of the drug business forever, he, his wife, and his few remaining men were allowed to walk away with their lives.

For several months the Morales gang laid low, licking their wounds and watching their backs. Hector discovered how much he enjoyed staying home with Maria. With a baby on the way, he began looking for a new career. He was even considering some legitimate ventures.

Ironically, it was Nemo that got them started into the business that would keep Hector in the lifestyle that he wanted for Maria.

Keeping a low profile was difficult for Nemo. Retaliation was all the big man could think about for the first few weeks. After miraculously surviving a suicidal raid that first night, it took plenty of urging and pleading by his sister and brother-in-law to keep Nemo away from the cartel. Eventually, his rage subsided and the big man returned to the fast night life he had enjoyed when he was the king of the streets. Only now, Nemo had less money to throw around and the women didn't seem quite as easy since he was no longer the biggest player in town.

One night, at a bar a little further down the coast, Nemo got very upset after a pretty tourist continually rebuffed his advances. When an opportunity presented itself, he simply grabbed the girl and spirited her out the back. He hogtied, gagged and blindfolded her and started driving back to his place.

After he calmed down, Suarez realized what he had done. Kidnapping a tourist was not smart. He had forced himself on a few local girls back home, but this could have serious consequences. Nemo drove up and down the coast for a couple hours trying to figure a way out of the situation. He thought about killing her and throwing her body into the ocean. However, in the end, he did as he had always done. Nemo went to Maria and Hector to get him out of trouble.

A few hours later, Hector, Maria and Nemo were all in agreement. They would need to dispose of the young woman and send Nemo away. At least until they could determine if the police had any leads to tie him to her disappearance.

The girl, who had been lying quietly on the sofa, became agitated as she slowly translated the conversation. She wriggled until she got the gag dislodged from her mouth. She jabbered in English. Maria went over to quiet her. The next words that came out of her mouth changed everything.

"Pour favor, mi padre, ah, ah, mucho pesos, sil vous plait!" Her combination of Spanish and French was good enough to get her point across. Maria stopped in her tracks. Several thoughts ran through her mind at once. She realized their big problem had just become a major opportunity. It just needed to be handled right.

A week later, the girl was exchanged for a large sum of cash. Since the girl had seen his face, Nemo was sent to live, at least temporarily, on the eastern coast of Mexico.

What remained of the el Diablos Rojos gang, got into the kidnapping business full time.

CHAPTER 7

Shining Armor

The present
Tucson, Arizona

Monday morning, FBI SSA Roger Novak pulled up to the Park Place Mall as if arriving on a shining white stallion. Sun gleamed off his dark sunglasses as he stepped out of the specially prepared Federal Bureau of Investigation's Mobile Command Unit (MCU). He had arrived to save the day. A visible, have-no-fear-the-FBI-is-here, attitude emanated from him as he strode into the mall.

Within minutes he made it clear to everyone involved that he was now in charge. Novak sat down in the Mall Manager's office chair and rested his elbows on the desk in front of him. He regarded the small group gathered in the office, Monica Arthur's parents and Emma Morrison's father and grandparents. The FBI agent recognized the red-rimmed eyes and pasty tired skin he had seen on the families of just about every kidnapping case.

"I'm FBI Supervisory Special Agent Roger Novak," he began. "I'm part of the FBI's Cross Border Kidnapping Task Force or CBKTF as we like to call it."

"There is a task force for this?" Mrs. Arthur cut in.

"Cross border kidnappings happen quite often," he answered. "Most cases are much simpler than what happened here with your girls." He paused for a moment. "Often the kidnappers simply hang around near the border and watch for Americans getting out of nice cars or those wearing expensive clothes and grab them while they are shopping. The more brazen ones don't wait for them to cross the border."

"What makes you think our girls were taken by Mexicans?" Rita Morrison asked. "Tucson is forty miles from the border."

"The M.O.," he slowed for a second to explain the abbreviation. "Modus operandi in this case is similar to several others that have happened in Albuquerque, Phoenix, Palm Springs, Yuma and several other southwestern cities," he told them as he squirmed, trying to get comfortable in the cheap office chair. What a hideous office, Novak realized as he took a closer look at the décor. Two mass produced prints in glossy white plastic frames, no doubt purchased at one of the chain stores, hung on the wall. The lone window had a great view of the dumpsters in the loading bay. The beautiful marble floors of the retail area had been downgraded to plain flat squares of white ceramic. Well, at least the cheesy picture frames kind of matched the floor. The toilets out in the public area of the mall would be more attractive and spacious than this office, Novak realized. He turned over the photo of two little pug-faced children that had been staring at him from the corner of the desk. This office would not do.

"I said," Ben Morrison repeated himself, "have you dealt with these kidnappers before?"

"Oh, sorry about that," the FBI agent regained his focus. "Yes, if this is the group that I suspect, several times as a matter of fact." He stood up. "Come with me. The MCU should be ready for us."

Novak led them out of the mall to the forty-four-foot-long motorhome. The bright white Mobile Command Unit commanded attention, adorned with six foot tall navy blue lettering centered on each side that simply read FBI. While the Supervisory Special Agent had been inside the mall, the large vehicle had transformed. Several small satellite dishes had popped up on the roof and stabilizing legs now extended to the pavement at the front and back of the large vehicle. The biggest change however was the width of the MCU. The sides of the bus had each extended outward three feet. SSA Novak walked directly to the nearest giant letter B and punched in five numbers on an electronic key pad. An almost invisible door hissed open and steps smoothly extended out below it.

After the stark white exterior, Ben had expected the inside to be a sterile work area. He couldn't have been more wrong. Rich mocha hardwood covered the floor. On the right side as he entered, towards the front of the MCU, was a full kitchen with granite counters and a large side-by-side refrigerator. Beyond the kitchen lay geek heaven. One wall was covered by a massive video screen displaying, rotating, live satellite images of the mall and parking lot. The visiting group realized that the images were live as they watched people pointing at the big white vehicle while they wandered past. The rest of the area was filled with smaller monitors, server towers, as well as, a bunch of other electronic gadgetry. Plus two very well-equipped work stations at which two young men worked busily.

"Those are my techies, Agents' Ted Wright and Randy Jenkins." Novak waved a hand towards the agents without looking in their direction. Both men looked up briefly and nodded, then got right back to work. Novak, the senior agent in both age and rank, directed the group into a lavishly furnished lounge area. The group took seats on the soft leather sofas and chairs while Novak grabbed several ice cold waters for everyone from the stainless steel fridge.

Beyond the lounge area was a handsomely-appointed office area. And past that, there was a closed door to yet another room. With the slides out, the luxurious bus felt as large as a house inside.

"That's better," he sighed as he dropped into one of the chairs. "As I said, I have worked several cases like yours before. I understand their playbook. These kidnappers will return your daughters once they have received the agreed-upon ransoms."

"What about a rescue attempt?" Rita Morrison asked.

"Yes, why can't we just send in the Marines or the Navy Seals?" Abigail Arthur agreed.

"I'm afraid it doesn't work like that," the SSA explained. "First, they are being held in a foreign country and governments don't like it when we send armed men across their borders. Second, we don't know where the girls are being held or by whom. Mexico is a big place. They could be anywhere."

"What are we supposed to do, just sit around and wait?" Robert Morrison asked indignantly.

"That is all we can do, at this point," Novak replied, in a calming tone of voice. The agent looked at his watch. "We shouldn't have to wait long, though. I expect they will contact us with *proof of life* within the next couple of hours."

"Proof of life?" Rita asked timidly.

"This is a good thing," Novak assured her and the others. "We'll get a call directing us to a live website where they will show that the girls are alive and as yet unharmed."

"As yet unharmed -- what does that mean?" Ben was first to voice the question that flew through the others' minds.

"I'm not going to lie to you," the SSA told them. "The FBI has been involved with seventeen, now eighteen, of these cases over the past two and a half years. During that time several of the hostages were beaten, a few severely, some of the girls were raped, three weren't returned and one of the hostages killed."

"Oh my God," Ben Morrison gasped, as tears flowed from several eyes at this news.

"There is some good news, however." Novak raised his hands to bring back everyone's attention. "I have personally worked on eight of these cases, and have been able to successfully negotiate the safe release of seventeen hostages."

"Excuse me, Sir," Agent Jenkins interrupted.

"What is it, Randy?" Novak called to the other end of the MCU.

"The kidnappers have made contact," he reported. "We'll have video any second."

By the time everyone had moved to the front of the MCU, the satellite view of the mall had been replaced by a video of the girls huddling together in a bland white room. To the relief of all involved, the girls looked scared but unharmed. After a minute the feed quit and the screen went black.

"Could you trace it?" Novak asked the tech agents, already knowing the answer.

"No," Agent Wright answered. "The video was scrubbed and bounced to several public locations before putting it into the Cloud, just like the others. There is no way to find the source."

"Now we know the girls are okay," Novak stated. "At least that's a start."

Walter Arthur cleared his throat and spoke up, "What happens now?"

"The video confirms that we're dealing with the same group that I suspected," Novak informed them. "The good news is these people are professionals."

"They're animals," Abigail Arthur interrupted Novak and choked down a sob, "if you ask me." The group nodded in agreement. Her husband reached over and squeezed her hand.

"Yes they are," the FBI man acknowledged and then got back on track. "However, we'll negotiate with them, agree upon a ransom and get your girls back safe and sound."

"You make it sound easy," Ben Morrison commented.

"I'm sorry if I gave you that impression. This is not going to be easy at all. Not for me and most certainly not for you." Novak looked him in the eyes and then to each of the others in turn before continuing. "The next three or four days are going to be the worst of your lives."

Abigail Arthur sobbed again.

"I promise that we'll get through this," SSA Novak spoke soothingly, "if we work together." His posture indicated that the meeting was over. "Now, if you'll excuse me, I have a lot of details and preparations to attend to before next contact." Roger guided them back through the MCU and back outside into the harsh desert sunlight.

"We should hear from the kidnappers in approximately eight hours," he informed the group as they exited. "I'll contact you once that happens." Novak was about to turn and go back inside when he heard his name being called.

"SSA Novak!" Detective Daniel Jiminez shouted, as he rounded the corner of the MCU. He was waving a shiny DVD disc as he walked quickly over. Trailing on the heels of the Tucson Police Department's finest, were a man and woman Novak hadn't seen before. They veered off and went directly to the Morrisons, while the detective came to Novak.

"Sir," Jiminez began excitedly, "we may have isolated some footage of one of the kidnappers."

"Are you sure, Detective?" the FBI agent didn't think it was likely since that had not happened in any of the other cases.

"We think so," Jiminez handed the DVD to Novak and glanced past him into the MCU. The local detective was desperate to impress the FBI agent and planned to ask about employment opportunities within the agency when the right opportunity arose.

"The man appears to be stalking the girls. We managed to isolate a clear image of his face."

"We'll take a look at this," Novak said, distracted by the civilian couple that had joined the Morrisons. There was something unusual about them. He couldn't put his finger on it, but he had a strange feeling about them. Despite the graying hair, the man had a very capable look about him. He'd never seen them before; he was certain of that. Roger was very good with faces. The woman had been staring at him, but broke contact when his eyes met hers. He'd seen eyes like those only once before. He decided to go over and introduce himself to the couple and find out what involvement they had to the case, if any.

"Great work, Detective," he handed back the DVD and stepped down from the doorway onto the radiating pavement, "take this into Agent Jenkins and have him run facial recognition."

"Yes Sir!" Jiminez jumped at the chance to go inside the FBI's Mobile Command Unit.

CHAPTER 8

Birth of a Snow Devil

20:27 , February 24, 1982
Baffin Isaland, Canada

Private Donavon Reese fired two shots over his shoulder as he scrambled away from the campfire into the icy darkness. The young soldier knew he would not survive the arctic night without the parka or bedroll he had left behind. Once certain that his pursuer quit chasing him, Donavon came to a stop. He blew hot breath onto his quickly freezing bare-hands. The Private turned around and headed back to confront his attacker.

Thirty-nine hours later

Originally called Helleland by Viking explorers, Baffin Island had been discovered by Erik the Red more than a thousand years earlier during his first trip to the new world. Located within the Arctic Circle, above Canada, the huge island is more than double the size of Great Britain. As cold as Hell, the island is still less than affectionately called Hell Land by the Canadian Special Forces teams that reside there, during training maneuvers.

A twenty kilometer per hour breeze carried eddies of dry snow across the frozen tundra. An impotent ball of fire hung limply in the grayish, empty sky. The sun seemed incapable of producing any heat this close to the North Pole. Despite this, the temperature registered a balmy minus ten degrees Celsius. This just happened to be the most pleasant day the Special Forces team had experienced during the past two weeks of exercises.

Colonel James Hawthorne paced slowly back and forth at the edge of the temporary survival training facility. The drone of twin diesel generators drowned out the constant howling winds that never took a rest this time of year. The faint smell of diesel exhaust had permeated the entire area, both outside and inside the tents. One or both of the generators operated constantly to provide light and heat.

Hawthorne could not break camp and leave this God forsaken place until the last Special Forces recruit arrived. It would take several hours to pack up all the camp equipment and the half dozen large tents that housed the only humans this far north. The northern most Inuit village was located 140 kilometers south on the west coast of the island.

Three days earlier four recruits and four veteran Special Forces soldiers had been dropped at various locations around Hell Land. Each man supplied with winter gear, a sidearm, a knife, a compass, a meager supply of rations, and a map showing the co-ordinates of base camp. They had been instructed to find and return to camp by noon today.

Only the best of the very best make it onto the elite Alpha and Bravo units of the Canadian Special Forces teams. The Bravo unit operated officially as a part of the Canadian Expeditionary Force Command. Based at the Canadian Maneuver Training Center at CFB Wainwright, in Alberta, they are deployed on highly-planned missions like most other Special Forces teams around the world. The Alpha unit operated under the umbrella of the Princess Patricia's Light Infantry 2nd Battalion. Rovers or floaters, they travel from 'hot spot' to 'hot spot' across the globe to help out, if or when things start to get out of hand. The Bravo team referred to them as 'Babysitters', but most would jump ship given the opportunity.

Both units had a personnel opening. They'd started out with twenty-five applicants and had ground them down to four. Petty Officer 1st Class Raymond Wilkins had come to the exercises highly recommended by Rear Admiral Dockins. The navy man had not disappointed, either. Big, strong and smart, Wilkins was on or near the top of both teams' lists. To Hawthorne's great surprise the greenest of the recruits, barely a year out of basic training, had worked his way up the list and was neck-and-neck with Wilkins. Passing the survival training portion of the program was mandatory and the Private hadn't returned yet.

Hawthorne knew it had only been two or three minutes since he last looked, but he pulled back the sleeve of his parka and checked his watch anyway. 11:27, three more minutes gone and still no sign of the last man. Noon approached rapidly. He kicked a lump of snow. It didn't help relieve the frustration he felt. He scanned the horizon through his field glasses. The pacing started again.

The other seven men had trudged into camp at various times earlier that morning, tired and hungry. One recruit hobbled in with an ankle sprain and another with a mild case of frostbitten fingers, but otherwise none the worse for wear. Wilkins had been the first to make it back, another checkmark in his favor.

Lieutenant John Andrews, an eight year veteran of the Special Forces Alpha unit and the second to return that morning, appeared from the mess tent and walked over to his Commander. His boots made a crunching sound with every step on the frozen powder. Even wrapped with a blanket around his shoulders, the lieutenant looked fiercely strong.

Andrews had pulled a lot of strings to get the first year infantryman into the Special Forces program. He'd first met the former hockey phenomenon while Donavon Reese played for the Regina Pats of the Western Canadian Hockey League. Named after the Princess Patricia's, the hockey franchise gave free admission to members and veterans of the armed forces, and treated the real *Pats* like a part of the team.

The Special Forces soldier went to as many games as his schedule allowed; in 1978 that had been only one game. The Medicine Hat Tigers played host to the Pats that night. It had been a good game with the playoff-bound Tigers prevailing. Reese had been named the third star of the game. He'd scored two goals and an assist in the losing effort. Later that evening, on his way back to base, Andrews recognized the Regina Pat team bus which was stopped at a restaurant. Dressed in his Lieutenant's uniform, the hockey fan went in and spoke with several of the players, including the humble new star of the team, about the history and lives of the other Patricia's.

A few months later, Donavon Reese was drafted by the Minnesota North Stars of the National Hockey League. Everyone who'd seen him play knew that Reese would be playing with the big boys of hockey, sooner or later. No one expected his meteoric rise to end so quickly.

Andrews hadn't realized the impact he'd made on the goal scorer, that night at the restaurant, until he had bumped into Private Reese a few weeks earlier at the Canadian Forces Base at Edmonton, Alberta. Donavon Reese had given up his blossoming and very lucrative professional hockey career to enlist with the Princess Patricia's Canadian Light Infantry.

The NHL's leading rookie scorer had found his fast new lifestyle hollow and lacking. Even though many professional hockey players were very generous with their time and money, visiting hospitalized children and forming charities, most spent their spare time drinking, gambling and chasing women. Charities were a great thing, but Donavon Reese wanted to be more proactive. The Minnesota North Star rookie shocked his agent, his teammates and the hockey community at large when he decided not to sign the new, much larger, contract being offered at the end of the season. Donavon wanted to do something more with his life. He chose the armed forces. Specifically, the Princess Patricia's Canadian Light Infantry, which the soldier he'd met at a restaurant two years earlier had spoken so passionately about.

"Don't worry about Reese, Sir. He'll be here." Andrews assured his boss.

"I hope you're right about him, John." The Colonel knew his second in command was high on the inexperienced recruit.

"The kid's C.O. told me that Reese is the most capable young soldier he's ever trained," Andrews added.

Hawthorne continued to worry, though, and resumed pacing. Reese had proven himself to be more than just promising over the past few weeks. However, Hawthorne had witnessed other very good candidates get scrubbed from the program, or worse. Five years earlier a pack of arctic wolves had taken the life of an injured recruit. That had haunted him, even more than losing a man on a mission. There are many more dangerous hazards here in the Arctic besides wolves. Sudden deep crevices could appear in glaciers, avalanches, blizzards and the world's most powerful land carnivore, the Polar Bear, prowled these parts.

He lifted the binoculars and scanned the horizon once again. Then something caught his eye. He adjusted the focus. "Son of a bitch!" he muttered, stopping in his tracks. "Son of a bitch!" the Colonel repeated loudly as he shook his head in disbelief.

"What is it, Sir?"

He handed Andrews the binoculars and pointed directly east. Andrews gently swung the glasses back and forth before settling on a muted white blob. It looked out of place in the stark sea of snow and ice. It also appeared to be moving. For a few seconds the soldier thought he was looking at a Polar Bear in the distance. Upon second glance he realized that something wasn't right with the furry white creature.

"What the fuck? Pardon my French, Sir." He let go of the blanket so that he could adjust the focus. It was a long way out but the image sharpened. A cheer erupted from Andrew's throat as he handed back the field glasses.

The Special Forces teammates looked at each other. Already the worry lines began to fade from Hawthorne's face. Suddenly, Hell Land seemed more hospitable. The Colonel decided that breaking camp could wait until the next morning.

"Well, Ric-a-Fucking-Damn-Doo!" said Hawthorne, exhaling deeply.

The relief Lieutenant Andrews heard in his friend and commanding officer's voice was quite evident to him. John had never doubted the amazing Donavon Reese, but even he hadn't expected anything like this.

He yelled to the mess tent, "Guys, get out here! You are going to want to see this!"

Twenty-nine minutes later, with four minutes to spare, the Special Forces candidate strolled into camp wrapped in Polar Bear furs.

The whole camp had turned out to witness the spectacle. Reese removed the strip of fur that covered most of his face as he made his way to Colonel Hawthorne.

"Private Donavon Reese reporting as ordered, Sir!" He saluted.

"At ease Soldier," Hawthorne saluted casually and then glanced over at Reese's other hand, which held what was left of the soldier's backpack. His eyebrows raised a little.

"A souvenir, Colonel." He smiled and pulled out a huge white bear paw by the gleaming black claws. Each claw extended out of the thick fur at least three inches. Reese handed it to his commanding officer.

He turned from the Commander and looked over at his fellow recruits, "I thought you boys might be hungry, so I picked up some takeout."

Reaching around Reese produced the hind leg of a caribou that he had strung across his back with a strap from the same ill-fated backpack. He tossed twenty pounds of half-frozen venison to Sergeant St. Jean.

The company's resident chef already had a recipe in mind as he caught it.

Amid back slaps and congratulations the whole camp began to chant "Polar Bear Reese, Polar Bear Reese, Polar Bear Reese!"

.   .   .

The Alpha Unit commander couldn't sleep as he lay in his cot. He recounted the events Private Reese had shared during his debrief.

On day one of the mission, at approximately 20:30, an adult Polar Bear attacked Reese's camp. It had probably been drawn to the smell of the roasting caribou that the recruit had managed to take down earlier in the afternoon. Reese fired several shots at the beast as he hastily retreated into the darkness away from the bear and the campfire. He must have hit the bear with one or two of the rounds because the beast became incensed and tore up Reese's abandoned supplies, including his overcoat and bedroll.

Private Reese had circled around and waited for the bear to settle down and begin eating again, then crept up behind the giant, from downwind. He got as close as he dared, about ten meters, carefully aimed the Colt semi-automatic to where he estimated the animal's heart to be and fired two quick shots. A fortuitous weight shift and dense, heavy ribs saved the creature. Not seriously harmed, and angered once again, the bear spun around and reared up to his imposing height of ten feet. The next shot bounced off the bear's thick skulled forehead barely stunning the creature. It roared and lunged at Reese. Only about ten feet away now and closing fast, the young soldier managed to get away one more round. That bullet travelled through the giant bear's left eye, dropping it instantly. The creature's huge paw landed on Reese's left foot, tearing a hunk of leather from the heavy boot with one final spasm.

"Son of a bitch," Hawthorne said aloud one more time.

Arriving at camp, Donavon Reese had been the least physically impressive of the four recruits. Five foot nine and no more than a buck sixty-five soaking wet. The other recruits out-weighed him by an average of at least thirty pounds. However, Reese had quickly shown great adaptability and character. Clever, fast and incredibly agile, Andrews had been right about him! This kid was something special. Polar Bear Reese! That was what the men were calling him now, even the Special Forces team veterans.

It had taken years, but Hawthorne knew in his heart, he had finally found a man to round out the unit when he left the field. Twenty years as the leader of the Pat's elite Alpha unit was plenty. Nights like tonight, sleeping on a narrow cot, reminded him that he was ready to spend more time at home with his family. Andrews was more than ready to take over the unit, no question. The difficulty had been finding someone able to fill Andrews' shoes. That rare individual who can handle anything and everything asked of him. Private Donavon Reese had made a believer out of him. Not an easy task.

He checked the luminous dial on his wrist -- 02:37. Tomorrow would be a big day. Tear down the camp, get back to Edmonton and then the real training would begin. Private Reese's name stood alone at the top spot on the Alpha unit list. Tomorrow there would be a new Snow Devil.

"Son of a bitch," he chuckled. Colonel James Hawthorne closed his eyes and forced himself to sleep.

CHAPTER 9

Batman, Robin Hood and the Red Devil

The present
Puerto Penasco, Mexico

The sunrise Tuesday morning was gorgeous. Breakfast on the patio had been another of Maria's great ideas. It had become a Morales family tradition. When weather permitted, which was generally more than half the time, breakfast was served on the main patio, overlooking the harbor. The gorgeous backyard made breakfast seem just a little more special. A cold front had forced the Morales family indoors for more than a week, but this morning felt much warmer. The whole family was in great humor.

"Ali, did you finish your science project?" Hector asked his son.

"Not yet, Papa, but I still have four days until it is due," eight year old Alejandro Rafael Morales, named after both his grandfathers, answered without concern.

"You know what they say," his father reminded him.

"Don't put off until tomorrow that which can be done today," the boy recited the lesson he had been told on many occasions prior. "I'll finish it right after school."

"Good man, good man," Hector praised his son and glanced over at Maria who was smiling at the exchange.

"Excellent! If you get it finished before dinner, I'll take you and your sister into town for pizza." Maria added some extra incentive for the procrastination-prone boy.

"And ice cream, too?" five-year-old Gabriela asked her mother, excitedly.

"Of course, we'll have ice cream!" Maria confirmed and smiled at her daughter, then turned to Hector. "Your father has a busy day today, but maybe he will join us for pizza."

"Can you, Papa?" Gabriella pleaded. "Can you?"

"Oh, Pumpkin, I will try my best to be there," Hector answered. "But just in case I can't make it, could you do me a big favor?"

"Yes."

"It won't be easy," he told her, gravely.

"I'll try, Papa!" Gabriela sat forward in her chair.

"You will have to guard it with your life."

Gabriela nodded seriously.

"Try to save me just one slice of pizza before your brother eats the whole thing!"

"Okay, Papa!" She looked over at Ali and stuck her tongue out.

"You're right about that Papa," Alejandro laughed, "it won't be easy!"

.   .   .

Hector drove his sleek black Porsche Panamera S to his legitimate business, Morales Metal Works. He went upstairs to his office to take care of a few pressing issues. The boss man then made his way down to the shop area and spoke briefly with each worker. He then slipped into the locker room where he pulled aside the last set of lockers, revealing a hidden passage.

He stepped inside and slid the lockers back into place. LED rope lights lined either side of the tunnel floor, providing a trail to navigate along. Building secret tunnels was just another of the skills Hector and his crew had picked up during their days in the drug trade. The tunnel travelled about thirty-five meters underground until it emerged, across the alley, into the bathroom of an abandoned building that had once been a rival machine shop. Through a dummy corporation, Hector also owned this building.

He quickly changed from his suit into jeans and a t-shirt. With his suit hung carefully on the coat tree in the corner, Morales unlocked the bathroom door and stepped through. Cheap sunglasses, a tattered ball cap and a convincing fake mustache completed the transformation from successful business man to local working stiff.

Inside the building he kept a sun-faded old Datsun pickup truck for such trips to visit his other, very far from legitimate, business. The Datsun's tiny four cylinder engine had been replaced with a high performance straight six, from a 280Z sports model. The engine purred when he started it.

Hector pulled away slowly and soon mixed into the traffic. He and his little truck immediately blended in with the hard working blue collar people on the road. He drove eastward, away from the beaches.

Hector really enjoyed this part of the kidnapping game. He became el Diablo Rojo and thought of himself as a cross between Batman and Robin Hood. Like Bruce Wayne, he lived in a mansion and would sneak off to his hidden lair where he would put on a disguise and do battle against the evil villains to the north. And like Robin Hood, he took money from the rich, who lived their decadent lives beyond the walls and fences that separated the two countries, and brought it down to poor old Mexico. He felt good about what he did. He was good for the economy. Like Bruce Wayne, no one could or would know what a hero he really was. No one knew, except Maria of course. She was his Alfred and Maid Marion combined.

After a few miles he stopped at a roadside diner for coffee. He chatted with the waitress and another patron -- all the while carefully watching for any indication he was being followed.

Twenty kilometers further down the road he took a right turn onto a single lane dirt road that wound through some hills before ending at an abandoned farmhouse. Hector got out of the truck. From this vantage point, he could see the entire trail and a good portion of the highway leading up to it. When he was certain that no one had followed him, Hector got back into the truck and drove back down the trail. When he got back to the highway, the Datsun crossed over onto a two lane gravel road that headed north.

Five minutes later he pulled into another run-down yard, but this one wasn't abandoned. Chickens milled about everywhere, scratching and poking at the ground. There were some goats and sheep in a pen, near a large barn, at the back of the yard. A few cows and horses grazed in a small pasture beyond the barn.

A thirty-year-old woman appeared on the porch of the house. Rosa Torres looked the part of a poor farm wife, dressed in a faded cotton dress with a matching kerchief on her head. In reality, the longtime girlfriend of Raul was the computer whiz of the operation. She set up the untraceable video feeds, tracked the whereabouts of potential targets on social networks, set up the security for the operation (you could not approach the farmyard from any direction without her knowing it) and was generally in charge of the operation when Hector wasn't there.

"Good morning, Rosa," Hector called as he got out of the truck.

"Good morning, Mister Morales. Raul is in town getting some supplies. Juan Carlos is down at the barn keeping an eye on things," she reported.

"How is the new stock?"

"Grade A condition." They were always careful not to say anything incriminating while out in the open.

"Excellent work Rosa, as always!" She returned a smile at his praise. "Have you run the numbers?" he asked, referring to the estimated family worth of the girls.

"Oh yes, and they look very good."

"Great, I'll be in to look them over shortly," he told her, and then added, "Why don't you and Raul join Maria and me for dinner tomorrow night?"

"We'd love to," Rosa gushed at the invitation. She had never been invited to the mansion before.

"Excellent," Hector smiled, as he headed to the barn. It never hurt to throw a bone to the help every once in a while.

In the barn he found Juan Carlos braiding a rope that he would likely fashion into either a halter or a bridle. It was a hobby the older man used to pass the time and a good cover for crossing the border. Hector headed directly to his friend and gave him a pat on the shoulder.

Juan Carlos Medina, like Hector and Raul, had managed to survive the Sinaloa Cartel attack. Fiercely loyal, the tough old cuss had been with Hector for more than twenty years.

"How are you my friend?" Hector asked, not expecting much of a reply. Juan Carlos did not speak much, he never had.

"Good, good."

Hector picked up one of the many halters lying on the nearby workbench. The craftsmanship was superb. What had started out as scrap pieces of baling twine was now both beautiful and functional. Many more halters and bridles hung on hooks around the barn walls. Medina sold them at the big swap meets in Tucson and Phoenix. They were quite popular, he'd been told. Hector did not know how much money the little side businesses brought in for his men, nor did he care.

Every week or so, Juan Carlos and Raul would cross the American border, at Nogales, with the halters. They would return at the end of the day with a truckload of old furniture and other junk that they would sell in Mexico. This was a common practice at the border town checkpoint. They were, however, the only ones smuggling people into Mexico. The girls were hidden in the special compartment under the furniture. The border guards would occasionally make a show of emptying one of the first trucks coming through. Juan Carlos and Raul were always careful, especially when they had a special payload, to position themselves near the back of a long line of returning trucks and had always crossed without incident. Though they had been unloaded a few times over the years, the hidden compartment had yet to be discovered.

"I'm glad to hear it!" He set down the halter and walked over to the false wall at the rear of the barn, pressed a button disguised as a knot and a hidden door popped open slightly, becoming apparent amongst the gray lapboard that covered the walls.

Hector stepped inside and shut the door behind him. To his right was a video studio, complete with cameras and a large blue screen that covered the far wall. On his left was a three-by-three-by-three meter concrete block cube that served as the holding cell. A single metal door adorned the center of the nearest side. There were no windows or peep holes. A heating and cooling unit sat humming on the top of the cube. Four hidden cameras in each of the upper corners revealed almost every square inch inside the cube.

Hector went directly to a desk which had a four-way split-screen monitor and sat down. Rosa also monitored the holding cell from the house. The shivering girls sat huddled together on one of the two cots. At the front of the cell a four-foot-by-four foot block wall provided just a little privacy for the porcelain commode behind it. He flipped a switch on the microphone in front of him. Hector spoke clear English into it.

"Good morning, my Pretties," his words reverberated back to him through the monitor speakers, modulated into a robotic cadence. The startled girls jumped and screamed, bringing a wicked grin to his face. El Diablo Rojo became the Wizard of Oz, an all-powerful, faceless voice in a strange world.

.   .   .

Once certain that Mr. Morales was busy with the girls, Juan Carlos got back to work on his latest weaving project. He retrieved it from under the work bench where he had quickly stashed it when the boss walked in. Almost finished, he had fashioned a doll in the likeness of Emma Morrison. It had blonde hair, white skin, little blue eyes and was wearing a red dress. The old cowhand had to admit that her soft straw-blonde hair was growing on him. He no longer imagined her as a redhead. When Emma became his wife, she would always wear a pretty red dress. He smiled broadly to himself as he tied the last knot. She would love his gift, he knew it.

Immediately after he and Raul had secured the girls into the cubicle, Juan Carlos had gone up to the loft, where he lived, to count his money. For years and years, he had simply thrown all the American money he got from his trips up north into a wooden box in the corner. He lived pretty much expense free. It cost nothing to live in the loft. His meals were provided. The old truck was his, but Hector paid for all the gas and maintenance on it. He didn't even pay for the twine that he made the halters out of. He just ordered it and the bills were taken care of up at the house. He bought himself a bottle of tequila every month and paid his share of rounds at the bar when he and Raul occasionally stopped on the way home from the swap meets. They never drank more than one beer each on the other side of the border. For one thing, it was against one of Maria's rules and, for another, alcohol was so expensive up there.

It had taken him almost an hour to count and double check all one hundred eighty-eight thousand nine hundred and fifteen dollars. Money didn't mean much to the old cowboy, but he knew this was quite a lot. There was more money in a bank account that his paycheck went into. Rosa had set it up for him. He'd have to ask her how much was in there since the well-paid farmhand had no idea. Juan Carlos guessed that he was wealthy by most Mexican standards.

If Mr. Morales wouldn't give him the girl, Juan Carlos felt confident that he could buy Emma from him. A thrill ran down his spine at the thought of marriage. He'd been a bachelor long enough -- too long, he told himself. There was something about this girl. She was special.

CHAPTER 10

Two for the Show

The present
Green Valley, Arizona

The morning sun, now fully visible in the eastern sky, warmed the Reese's backyard. Details of the Santa Rita Mountains were filling in where only minutes ago they had been just a silhouette against the lightening sky. Only Mount Wrightson, the tallest and center-most of the range had snow left on it. Likely, by the end of the day that would be gone as well. The warmth of the last few days in the surrounding desert had melted most of the small accumulation of the white stuff from earlier in the month. The small southern range didn't get whitecaps every year. The residents of Green Valley would be sorry to see the snow vanish so quickly. Snow is especially wonderful to look at from a distance.

Both Janet and PB spoke into their cell phones as they paced around the winding brick pathways of their backyard. PB finished his call first and shut down the gas-fire pit they had been using to keep the early morning chill at bay. Most Tuesday mornings at this time they would be on their bikes headed for the Las Compañas Activity Center to lift weights. This wasn't a typical Tuesday.

PB had been on the phone with Ben, who was quite upset. Monica's father, Walter Arthur, the founder and CEO of Castle Homes, was demanding and receiving most of the FBI's attention. Neither Morrison nor his son could even get in the same room with them this morning. Even the police detectives had become tight-lipped around Ben and Bob. He'd been unable to get any news about the mystery stalker from the mall surveillance tapes. PB glanced over at Janet and hoped that she was having better luck with her Interpol contacts.

"Thank you, Sarah. I owe you big time!" Janet poked the screen of her phone a few times and held it up for her husband to view. PB rushed over to get a good look.

"This is Raul Nunez. The FBI has indeed identified him from the mall tapes." Janet turned her phone back and manipulated the screen again. "He is a known associate of one Hector Morales." She showed PB a picture of Hector. "Apparently, the Mexican Federales have quite a dossier on Morales. Hector ran the Los Diablo Rojos, a criminal gang that mostly smuggled marijuana across the border. He was forced out of the drug business by the Cartels in 2004 and then suspected of getting into the kidnapping and human trafficking business sometime soon after."

"Can't they just go in and arrest Morales?"

"Not without some proof. He runs a legitimate business in Puerto Penasco. It's a small city on the coast, also commonly called Rocky Pointe by American tourists."

"I hate this," PB clenched his fists in frustration. "These people can't be allowed to destroy so many lives with impunity."

"It gets worse," Janet continued, as she scrolled to another picture. "This is Nemesio Suarez, enforcer slash brother-in-law of Hector Morales."

PB looked at an arrest mug shot of the man. He took note that the top of the man's head went a couple of inches past the top of the two meter height chart in the photo. "He's a big boy."

"Some of the returned girls reported being beaten and raped by a terrifying giant," Janet stated. "Sarah also attached a brutal video clip of a huge, hooded man killing one of the girls."

"Let's take a look," her husband decided. "We need to see what we're dealing with."

The clip was only ten seconds long. It showed a very large muscle-bound, hooded man flinging a girl off his back and then grabbing her like a doll and throwing her head first into a concrete wall. The angle of her head looked unnatural as she crumpled to the floor. The poor girl's last moments alive were spent in absolute terror. The final seconds of the video showed the enraged giant's wild eyes.

"He's got a temper," PB observed, making a mental note for future reference.

"Apparently, they have the entire video in the big FBI van," she explained. "It is several minutes long."

"The FBI is running the show now?" PB asked after pacing for a few seconds.

"Agent Novak, out of the San Diego office," she reported. "He's on the FBI's Cross Border Kidnapping Task Force. Apparently, he has worked a number of similar kidnappings."

"That's encouraging," PB said. "What else did you find out?"

"They call this type of kidnapping, *One for the money, two for the show.*"

"What does that even mean?"

"According to Sarah, these kidnappers have a history of taking girls in pairs. Almost always, one of the girls is from a wealthy or powerful family. A very large ransom will be demanded for the girls. If the negotiations aren't going well, they pretend to randomly pick one and then make a show of roughing up, torturing or raping," Janet paused, "and in, at least one case, killing the less-privileged girl. They kidnap one for the money, and the second is used as incentive."

"In this case, Ben and Rita's granddaughter will be the girl for the show," PB stated.

"They'll be forced to watch," Janet's voice not much more than a whisper now, "an untraceable video feed of beatings and possibly worse."

"The Morrison family will be devastated," PB said, shaking his head.

"At a certain point, the wealthy family will generally pay anything to save their daughter from sharing the same fate as her friend."

"What happens to the show girl?" PB was almost afraid to ask.

"It can become sort of a bidding war against the human traffickers. A young pretty, blue-eyed blonde like Emma is a sought after commodity in the sex trade and could be worth almost a million dollars, as you know."

"Ben and Rita still have a mortgage and I don't think Robert is rolling in cash either. How much time do they have?"

"This group works fast," she reported the bad news. "Usually no more than a week from taken to never heard from again."

"Will Interpol help us with this?"

"Sarah said that their hands are tied," Janet explained. "About a year ago, working with the Mexican authorities, they raided Hector Morales' home and business. They were unable to find one trace of evidence that proved he was involved with the current kidnapping, or any previous ones. Local authorities professed outrage on behalf of their beloved benefactor, all the way to the Capital. Since then, the Mexicans have shut Interpol out of further investigations."

"What about the FBI?" PB asked.

"On the west coast they work successfully with the Baja California Anti-kidnapping Group in these situations," she explained, "but there is no such organization in this part of Mexico to assist them on the other side of the border."

"There should be," her husband added in frustration.

"Yes," Janet agreed, "it is a growing problem that needs to be addressed. The local Mexican authorities have their hands full dealing with cartels."

"Morales is using the border like it's a giant security blanket," PB complained.

"Unfortunately, everyone's hands are tied up by government bureaucracy," she complained. "Law enforcement from both sides will not cross the border."

"Well, our hands aren't tied," PB pointed out. "We're just a couple of average Joes and we can go where ever we want to or need to."

PB's phone rang, as if on cue. It was Ben and he was frantic. The ransom demand had come in. It was ridiculous. The kidnappers wanted twenty million dollars for each of the girls. Ben doubted that including himself, his son, and his son's in-laws, they could raise even half a million. PB tried to calm his friend down by explaining that the first number given by the kidnappers was always very high, just to make subsequent numbers seem more reasonable during negotiations. This helped a little, but PB could tell that Ben was still pretty freaked out when the call ended.

"Pack your bags, Honey, we're taking a trip to Mexico," PB said to his wife.

As Janet headed into the house, PB got his friend back on the phone, "Ben, Janet and I are going out of town for a few days."

"Right now?" he asked with a hint of abandonment in his voice.

"It's just that we have an idea about the girls that we want to follow up on," PB informed him.

"What are you going to do?" Ben and Rita were the only people in town that knew even a hint about the Reeses' past. And only that they'd met in Eastern Europe while they were on some sort of military-type task force together. PB and Janet had not shared mission details with anyone outside a courtroom.

"I don't want to say just yet. Besides, it may not amount to anything," PB answered truthfully. "Let's keep this between us, Ben."

"No problem," Ben promised. "Be careful my friend."

"I'll check in with you soon," PB signed off and joined Janet in the house. They packed lightly, bringing only one handgun each, tucked into hidden compartments in their overnight bags. Janet went online to book a room while PB loaded the Range Rover. Within half an hour they were on the road to Yuma. Tens of thousands of tourists cross the border there into Los Algodones, mostly for the extremely reasonable dental procedures and eyeglasses. They left their car in long term parking and joined the queue of tourists crossing into Mexico.

Once they had cleared customs and security, the couple rented a small car and continued on to Puerto Penasco.

The pretty resort town bustled with activity. Located just one hundred kilometers south of the Arizona border, it sits on the Sea of Cortez, a beautiful piece of the Pacific Ocean, sheltered by the Baja California peninsula.

Sandy beaches, parasailing, sunset harbor cruises and fishing charters are just a few of the many recreational choices available to visitors. Puerto Penasco had started life as a fishing village. The seafood trade is still alive and well in the area.

Savvy visitors return home with coolers and ice chests filled with shrimp and the catch of the day.

Excitement and energy filled the air, as the restaurants and bars overflowed with tourists during the long weekend that was just beginning. Janet had been lucky to find a room on such short notice; a one bed/one bath condo unit had become available due to a last minute cancellation. Las Gaviotas was a smaller and older resort right on the beach. Most of the other similar resorts had been torn down and replaced by large luxury hotels or fancy estates. The dark, burnt-orange walls inside the condo were softened somewhat by pale yellow kitchenette cabinets, lacy curtains and a matching bedspread. Thankfully, everything was very clean. A spectacular view from the third floor balcony more than made up for the lack of décor updates and an elevator.

Reconnoitering down the beach, along with the many other tourists, revealed that they were less than two blocks from the Morales home. The beach-front property had a prime location with a glamorous pool and grounds rivaling those of the large resorts. Above the pool, on a grand patio, a maid was making some final adjustments to a large bouquet of flowers that sat in the center of an ornate marble table.

As the pair casually circled one of the most spectacular houses they had ever seen, Janet couldn't help but ponder the many lives ruined by the man who lived in it. On their second loop past the property, three women were now seated at the patio table. PB and Janet edged closer without being obvious.

"That's Maria Morales," Janet whispered excitedly, as she brought up the beautiful woman's picture on her phone to confirm her suspicion. The other two women on the patio weren't in the photo array of Hector's known associates that her Interpol friend had forwarded.

Maria looked casually stunning in an embroidered Dolce & Gabbana sleeveless dress that would have been right at home at a red carpet function in Hollywood. A matching lace shawl protected her bare shoulders from the elements.

The oldest of the three women looked very classy in a long-sleeved, Yorkshire-cream-colored dress with a long string of pearls and matching earrings.

Wearing a simple knee-length black dress, the youngest of the group was a fine looking woman, but hardly noticeable in the company she was keeping that evening. Rosa Nunez sipped her wine and smiled often as the other two women chatted up a storm about designer collections and other society dribble she had no knowledge of or interest in. But it was an evening out, away from the ranch. She knew that Raul wasn't enjoying himself too much, either. Maybe they would stop at a cantina later, for a little dancing. Her man could definitely cut a rug!

Hector Morales stepped through an open French door at the rear of the house.

PB had the urge to jump the low fence, run up onto the patio and beat the location of the missing girls out of Morales. Janet sensed this and put her hand on her husband's tense shoulder.

"We can't tip our hand yet," Janet reminded him. "It could put the girls in immediate jeopardy."

"I know," PB agreed, "but it would be very satisfying."

A heavy-set man stepped out behind Hector and nodded appreciatively at the view, his eyes lingering on Maria perhaps a moment or two longer than they should have. PB recognized him and told Janet about the mayor's photo in a tourism brochure back at the hotel. They could see the outline of a third man standing inside the house, but couldn't make out his features. The women rose from the table and the whole group moved indoors.

"We won't likely get any more worthwhile intelligence here," PB stated. "We know where Morales lives and at least some of the company he keeps."

The sun was dropping fast and a hint of winter chill tinged the air.

"Tonight might be a good time to take a look around Morales Metals," Janet indicated, as she zipped up her light jacket.

"Yes, but first let's get something to eat; I'm starving."

"You're always hungry!" she slapped his firm flat stomach. "I don't know where you put it all."

"All the sex keeps me thin." He put his arm around her and squeezed her butt cheek. "Obviously, it works for you, too!"

"What about all the weights, running and biking?"

"That just keeps us in shape for the sex," he laughed, as he gave another squeeze.

"You're incorrigible!" She swept his hand away.

"Maybe, but you love it."

"Yes, I do!" she admitted and leaned over to kiss him passionately. There was still plenty of heat between the two of them. Janet and PB headed back down the romantic beach arm in arm.

.   .   .

The fish tacos had been every bit as good as the front desk clerk at their resort had promised. The ice cold cervezas at Cocodrilos Bar and Grill had washed them down perfectly. The busy restaurant was just a few minutes from the Las Gaviotas condo. The two-for-one coupon hadn't hurt either. With one of their appetites satisfied, they headed back to their room to take care of the other. They had some time to kill while the night continued to darken.

A couple of hours later, neither the single security guard, with his attention glued to a regional soccer game, nor the pad-lock on the rear man-door of the Morales Metal building kept the couple from searching the place.

The large shop area was filled with drill presses, big sheet metal laser-cutting machines, cranes and forklifts, racks full of large pieces of metal and bins for the smaller pieces. It certainly looked like a legitimate metal shop. They focused on the offices. Just like Interpol, a year earlier, they turned up nothing of interest, other than some financial sheets revealing moderate profits. This business alone could not possibly provide the Morales family with the lifestyle they currently enjoyed.

Disappointed that not a single clue of the whereabouts of the girls had been uncovered, Janet and PB headed back to the condo.

At least they now had the layout of the building and property. They made surveillance plans. Janet, whose dark hair and deep tan could blend with the local population better, would follow Morales in the morning. If he went to work, she'd position herself where she could see both the front of Morales Metals and into Hector's office window. A nook behind some bushes, at the side of a building a few doors down and across the street, provided such a view.

PB intended to get to the metal shop early enough to watch the workers arrive, then settle in and keep an eye on the rear of the business. Their best chance of finding Emma and Monica was to have Morales lead them to the girls' location.

CHAPTER 11

The Real Fun Begins

The present
Puerto Penasco, Mexico

Bright and early Wednesday morning, Janet watched PB head out on foot towards Morales Metals carrying a backpack loaded with water bottles, snacks, binoculars and his favorite gun, a Canadian-made Para Ordnance Fourteen 'S'. The .45 caliber Stealth model with marbled ebony grips had been a gift from the Alpha unit after his final mission as a Snow Devil. Janet tossed a similar pack into the tan Kia Rios they had rented for the week, except the former Interpol agent's pack contained her tried and true Walther PPK nine millimeter. The little Kia was a popular car on the Mexican side of the border. The inexpensive rental also looked right at home in the bargain condo's parking lot.

Dressed in a pant suit with her dark, slightly gray-streaked hair pulled back, Janet looked like a local heading off to work. Ten minutes later she was parked with a good view of the Morales mansion. Half an hour after that, she discretely followed Hector and his big black Porsche to work.

"He's at his desk," Janet reported into her cell phone. Invisible from the street, she was in the previously-scouted location that gave her a good sightline into Hector's office.

"And so the real fun begins," PB answered sarcastically from his hidden location at the back of the building.

Two hours passed before Morales got up from his desk and disappeared from Janet's view.

"We have movement," she informed her husband.

"Nothing happening back here yet," PB responded.

The pair was on high alert waiting for Morales to come out of the building on one side or the other. Neither took any notice of the old Datsun truck that left from the building across the alley. By lunch time, when he hadn't returned to his desk, the couple knew he had somehow slipped away.

.   .   .

Actual business at Morales Metals had delayed Hector that morning. A contract to supply all the steel for a substantial new pier would keep the machine shop at full production for the next six months. A small bribe to the mayor had secured the bid. Hector just realized he would have to add a second shift at work to keep his current customers happy. His cover business was starting to show very good profits. A few more contracts like this one and he could go legitimate, if he wanted.

Hector was in a very good mood when he arrived at the ranch. He popped in to see Rosa first, as usual.

"Good morning, Mr. Morales," she greeted him with a light hug and small greeting kiss to the cheek. Right away she could sense his good cheer.

"Yes, it is a very good morning indeed, Rosa."

"I have some news that will please you," Rosa told him as they passed through the farm house kitchen. Rosa unlocked a door that lead into a room at the back of the house. "The FBI has assigned Agent Novak to the case."

Could this day get any better? Hector glanced at the bank of eight security monitors that lined the far wall. Four of the monitors displayed the girls, while the other four showed the farm grounds in each direction. There was no movement happening on any of the monitors.

FBI Special Agent Novak and Hector had negotiated several successful ransom exchanges together. They had a certain understanding. Hector would not have to waste valuable time convincing some new agent that he meant business. In fact, this would be the eighth negotiation with Novak since the Turtledove Wines ransom exchange four years prior. That one would have been Hector's largest payday at the time, at five million American dollars. However, it had turned into the worst job of all.

Before the incident, Special Agent Novak had been a real prick to deal with so Hector had flown Nemo in to help motivate things. His brother-in-law, dressed in his devil costume, would scare Freddy Kruger.

That day, Nemo was supposed to rough the girls up a bit, especially the friend, Tabitha Winger. Somehow, during the demonstration, Tabitha had gotten loose and jumped on Nemo's back, biting and scratching. Nemo had gone crazy, brutally killing the girl with his bare hands and most likely would have killed the Turtledove girl, too, if they hadn't turned the hose on him.

That was also the last time they broadcast a live feed. The families had witnessed the entire event. It had been an ugly situation, but he and Novak had hammered out an agreement. The Turtledove girl was home. Hector got paid. FBI Agent Novak got a promotion. Everybody ended up happy. Well, not everybody... Not the Winger family. Tabitha Winger was the only friend's name, from any of the previous pairings, that Hector could remember.

"Let's go right to graphics package number three for today's video," he instructed Rosa. "Agent Novak might as well earn his paycheck."

"Okay Mr. Morales. It will take Raul and Juan Carlos about half an hour to dress the set."

"I have some calls to make," Hector said, looking at his watch. "Let me know when everything is ready."

"Of course, Mr. Morales," she responded as he walked out.

Twenty minutes later, Rosa found her boss sitting in the Datsun, on his cell phone, with all the doors wide open, trying to catch what little breeze the late morning provided. In two or three hours the air would truly be hot, but for now it was bearable. She carried with her a plate of Chile en Nogada -- chilies in a walnut sauce. Mr. Morales loved her traditional cooking and this dish in particular. She stood and waited for him to finish his call. When he did, she handed him the plate.

"The set will be ready in ten minutes," she told him.

"Very good," he answered. "This smells great, Rosa."

"I thought you might be hungry." Rosa blushed at his compliment.

"Thank you, this was very thoughtful." He took a forkful and rolled his eyes to let her know how wonderful it tasted. "I'll be back for another plateful when we've finished the video."

"I made plenty," she confirmed, letting him know he could have as much as he wanted.

"I have one more quick call to make," he told her, "then we can get started."

"I'll have Raul bring the girls out," Rosa responded and headed back to the house and her video control suite.

The girls stood together, arms around each other, on the end of what appeared to be a strip-bar runway, when Hector arrived. They were blindfolded, scared and confused. Raul and Juan Carlos stood off to the side. They each had a low voltage electric cattle prod within easy reach and a table loaded with large mugs of colored water that looked like beer beside them. Perfect, everything looked as it should.

Hector sat down at the work station. Three cameras gave different views of the girls and the large green screen behind them. Rosa controlled the cameras and did the editing, with his approval, of course. He spoke into the microphone on the desk.

"Good afternoon, my Pretties." He could tell that they recognized his metallic voice from the previous day. "You will do everything I tell you to or there will be consequences." Morales nodded to Juan Carlos and Raul.

Dressed like Matinee Cowboys, with big black hats and red kerchiefs covering their lower faces, they picked up the cattle prods and zapped each of the girls in the buttocks. The prods were on the lowest setting, but stung just the same. They were great motivators.

The girls jumped and screamed in unison.

"As I said, there will be consequences unless you do exactly as I tell you!"

Juan Carlos and Raul didn't need to be told to pull the cattle prod triggers again for effect. They knew their parts by heart. The girls screamed on cue.

"Nod, if you understand," Hector told them.

Both girls nodded. Tears filled their eyes and ran down reddened cheeks. They looked perfect.

"When I say action, and not before," he instructed them, "you will remove your blind folds and slowly remove your shirts and pants. Then you will walk to the end of the runway, turn around and walk back. Do you understand?"

Neither girl moved as they processed what was being asked of them. Electricity arced near their heads. Amid sobbing, they nodded enthusiastically, not wanting to feel the harsh electric jolts again.

"When I say action, you will begin," he reminded them. This was followed by a couple more nods.

The green screens on his monitors suddenly came to life. It appeared as though the girls now stood in the middle of a rough and dirty-looking strip club. The bright set-lights came on. The studio filled with raunchy music and the sounds of men jeering and laughing.

"Okay girls, action!" Hector's mechanical voice ordered above the din.

Once again cattle prods zapped the girls' rears, eliciting small screams and reminding them to get started. Their arms untangled and they reached up to remove the blindfolds. The set lights practically blinded them. Glassfuls of warm tea started hitting them in the face and soaking their clothes. Monica wiped the tea and tears from her eyes and began to pull off her tee-shirt. Raul and Juan Carlos, blending in perfectly with the green screen rowdies, groped the girls' legs as they peeled off their wet clothes and slowly moved down the runway.

Hector shook his head in amazement. The scene had gone seamlessly. He had done this enough times to know how it would look to scared parents. Hector had them do one more take just to be safe. Rosa sometimes found errors he couldn't see. The addition of Rosa to the team had been a Godsend. At last night's dinner party, he'd asked Raul and Rosa how the couple had met. They told him it had been at a Hitchcock film festival. Raul had sat next to her at a showing of *North by Northwest* and they'd been together ever since. Neither Hector nor Maria had even known that their longtime employee enjoyed classic movies. Other than he'd been very capable, Hector realized he didn't truly know much about Raul.

.   .   .

Janet and PB spent a long, hot, frustrating afternoon with nothing to do but wait. Just before quitting time, Hector surprised them by walking out the front door and climbing into the Porsche.

"He just came out the front," Janet texted her husband. "I'm on him," she informed her husband, heading quickly back to the Kia.

A few seconds later, her phone buzzed, indicating a reply message. She took her eyes off the Porsche for a second and peeked at her phone.

"Moving to pos 2," PB had responded. On foot, he would begin the journey to the mansion. He'd approach from the beach side.

The afternoon's frustration continued for Janet as she followed Hector straight home to the mansion where the Morales family stayed in for the night. When the last of the lights finally went out in the large home, PB joined Janet in the car and they drove back to their condo, muscles aching from inactivity.

"I heard from Ben this evening," he reported as she drove. "The ransom demand was lowered to fifteen million each."

"Ouch, that's still pretty high."

"They received a video, too."

"Oh no, was it bad?" She could see from the look on her husband's face that it had been.

"Pretty bad, the girls were taken to some seedy underground club and forced to strip down to their underwear in front of a very unsavory crowd. Ben said the girls looked terrified and were crying the whole time," PB took a pause before continuing. "He told me it had been very hard to watch."

"I can't even imagine..." her voice trailed off.

"On the positive side," PB tried to sound upbeat, "Ben said that even though the FBI guy is a pompous ass, he appears to know what he is doing."

"How do you think Ben and Rita are holding up?" Janet asked, fearing the worst for her friends.

"Ben sounded pretty beat up by the whole affair. He said that Rita wasn't doing very well." PB's voice betrayed his deep concern for their friends. "Ben believes that the Arthurs are just about ready to give in to the demands."

"We need to find those girls soon," Janet stated, as she steered the car into the resort lot. PB nodded solemnly. Janet could sense the frustration growing in her husband. She was feeling it, too. There wasn't much else for them to do at this point. All they had, so far, were suspicions.

As she stepped out of the car, Janet looked up at the star-filled sky and was reminded of a happier night many years earlier.

CHAPTER 12

Hi Hoe, HAHO

February 10, 1994
Rayong, Thailand

Three hours after the successful raid on a shipment of Ukrainian girls that arrived in the coastal city of Rayong, the Pats were unwinding with beers under the thatch-roofed patio of a local pub. The popular tourist drinking hole overlooked a wide, white-sand beach.

"It says here that Rayong province is renowned for its pristine beaches, spectacular waterfalls and shopping." Billy Mankowski shared the information from the tourism brochure he was perusing. Mankowski did not fit the usual lone wolf mold of the typical sniper. He was the most social of the group and a big hit with the ladies.

"Well, they certainly weren't exaggerating about the beaches," St. Jean chimed in, as the group spotted a group of young, bikini-clad Thai women wandering past. The emerald water lapping at their toes.

"Sand, sun and surf," Captain Andrews said, raising his beer. A second later it was joined by four others as the heavy glass tankards clinked together above the table. John Andrews was the only married man in the group. And while he'd rather have been on his way back home to see his wife and three year old son, he recognized that the unit could use a little R and R. The team had earned a few days in the sun. He swallowed the last of his beer and waved at the pretty barmaid, whose English language skills were quite good.

"Another round for my friends," he indicated the three guys on his left, and then looked at the man to his right. "Oh, what the hell, you can bring one for him, too!"

Everyone laughed as PB punched his buddy in the shoulder. Reese enjoyed the close-knit camaraderie of the guys in the unit and did not for one minute regret his decision to leave the NHL and join the Patricia's. Despite being the youngest and newest man on the team, his extraordinary abilities had earned a lot of respect from everyone. In truth, while Captain Andrews was the coach and play caller of the team, PB had become the *go to* guy in the field. The team was stronger since he'd become a part of it and everyone knew it.

"This is pretty good beer," Reese turned the label towards himself and read the brand-name out loud, "Singha."

"It is pronounced Sing," a familiar woman's voice interrupted from behind the group. "The 'h' and 'a' are both silent," Janet pointed out as she strolled up, wearing a short-sleeved white linen blouse and khaki shorts. She slid into the empty chair waiting beside Reese.

"On top of everything else, the woman even knows her alcohol," St. Jean said, winking at Janet. "This girl is a keeper, PB."

PB leaned over and gave her a welcoming kiss. "Tell me something I don't know."

A full-fledged romance had developed between PB and Janet over the past two years, despite the limited time spent together. PB was head over heels and pretty certain Janet felt the same.

Captain Andrews gestured to the waitress to make it six beers.

"How'd the interrogations go?" PB asked his girlfriend.

"We got a solid lead on the Austrian." This got the table's attention. The man known only as the Austrian was believed to be the brains and leader of the human trafficking ring they'd been chasing.

"Did you get a name?" St. Jean asked on behalf of the group.

"No, but we got a description and his location," the British agent reported.

"Good work," Andrews patted her shoulder as the beers arrived.

"Not good enough," Janet explained to the group. "He's staying in a villa twenty kilometers outside of Izmir Turkey, but twelve hours from now he'll be in the wind, again."

"Let's go get the bastard!" St. Jean pounded his fist on the table.

"I wish it was that easy. I just spent an hour and a half trying to arrange transportation. It is impossible to get to Izmir from here in time."

"These beaches don't look that pristine." Mankowski crumpled up the brochure and tossed it at Johansen with a devilish smile.

Reese touched the ring box he was carrying in his left pants pocket. A waterfall might have provided a great place to pop the big question, he thought, with a touch of regret.

Johansen snatched the crumpled paper out of the air. "I hear that Turkey is lovely this time of year."

"Didn't you all hear me?" Janet asked. "I can't get us there in time!"

PB put his arm around her shoulders. "We can get you there, though."

"High hoe, hey hoe, it's off to work we go!" Bobby St. Jean sang a line parodying the Sleeping Beauty classic. This brought a few chuckles around the table. He raised his frosted mug toward the sky and the guys quickly followed suit.

"Hey hoe!" the soldiers repeated, before taking a swallow of Thailand's best beer.

"Hey hoe," Janet was just a beat behind, as she brought the frosty mug to her lips. Then she noticed everyone grinning at her. "What?"

"H A H O stands for high altitude high opening," PB explained to her. "It is a parachuting term."

"Oh," she replied before fully understanding the ramifications of his words. She was taking a deep pull from her ice cold beer when it sunk in.

"Oh, no, no, no!" She shook her head violently. "Me, jump out of a plane?"

"Jumping out of an airplane never hurt anybody," Mankowski started the old joke.

"It's the landing that kills them!" Janet filled in the punch line, morbidly.

"Don't worry," PB assured his girlfriend, "we'll be right there with you the whole way."

.   .   .

Fifty-one minutes later, her briefcase and overnight bag in hand, Janet was staring at a small jet. The Bombardier Challenger 601 was a permanent loaner to the team from a very grateful Canadian Provincial Premier whose son had been liberated from an Iranian prison, where he'd been facing trumped-up drug trafficking charges. Originally designed as a small passenger commuter, this particular plane had undergone two major renovations -- the first of which turned it into luxury transportation for the Premier and up to nine other dignitaries, plus two staff.

The second set of renovations had customized it further for the Canadian Special Forces squad. An additional fuel tank had been added. Some seating had been removed to make a rear storage room for rapid deployment equipment. The six leather seats, that remained, reclined flat for sleeping or additional seating space. The exit door had been removed and a taller, wider one installed. The cockpit, the small well-equipped galley kitchen and upgraded lavatory had all been left unchanged from the first renovation. The exterior of the small jet was painted flat black. A small Canadian flag adorned the tail, while a Royal Canadian Air Force emblem was displayed on the nose just below the pilot's windshield. The white identification numbers displayed on the engine, plus the six small darkened cabin windows were the only other things visible on the fuselage.

Air Force Major Hank Avery walked up to Captain Andrews from the back of the plane. He had just finished the visual inspection. The tall thirty-four-year-old man looked trim and very handsome in his perfectly pressed uniform. The Aviator glasses he wore above a neat brown mustache reflected the setting sun as he arrived.

"She is fuelled and all the necessary arrangements have been made, John."

"Thanks, Hank." Captain Andrews then introduced their extra passenger to the major. "Major Hank Avery this is Interpol Agent Janet Porter."

"Major Avery, it is very nice to meet you," Janet began.

"Call me Hank, everyone else does." His handshake was warm and genuine.

"Alright, Hank, you can call me Janet."

"So you're the one that the boys are always going on about."

"Tell me Hank, just what do these boys say about me when I'm not around to defend myself?" She turned and shot a stern look at the soldiers.

"Many terrible and awful things like: you shoot like Wyatt Earp, swear like a drunken sailor, fight like Bruce Lee, you're smarter than a German rocket scientist and you look like a movie star."

"I don't swear like any damned drunken sailor," she retorted, as her face reddened.

"Wyatt Earp probably wasn't that good of a shot," St. Jean piped in, "and if I'm not mistaken, Bruce Lee died, so he's not much of a fighter anymore..."

"And by movie star looks, we were talking about Clint Eastwood," Andrews added.

"She has more of an Ernest Borgnine look, don't you think?" Johansen asked, as he framed her face between his thumbs and fingers in the classic director pose, bringing a round of guffaws from the rest of the guys.

"Okay, okay, you guys," Janet laughed along with the group. The embarrassing moment passed by.

Hank indicated his approval of Janet holding his thumb up while she was turned away and managed to squeeze in a wink to PB.

"Hank is our transportation specialist-extraordinaire," PB explained. "He gets us wherever we need to be, by land, sea or air."

"And even more importantly, Hank always gets us back out and safely home," Captain Andrews pointed out and brought the focus back to the time-sensitive mission. "PB, you give Janet a quick tour of the plane and then set her up in my seat. I'll fly up front with the Major. Billy and Rick do an equipment check. Bobby, the galley is yours."

Half an hour later the Bombardier jet was twenty thousand feet above the Indian Ocean and rising.

Captain Andrews appeared from the cockpit and made his way to a plastic-coated world map attached to the wall in the rear of the cabin. All eyes fell to him. He grabbed an erasable marker and put an X on the shore of Thailand.

"We're taking a mostly water route to our destination." He drew a line that curved well below India then back northward through the Arabian Sea. "Hank got permission to fly through Yemen and Egyptian airspace, but not Turkey. We don't want the Austrian tipped off. Therefore, Turkish authorities have been left out of the loop for security reasons," he explained as the marker's thick line continued through Yemen, up the Red Sea, and through the Mediterranean Sea and past Turkey. "We'll deploy at twenty-eight thousand feet, ten kilometers off the coast near Izmir." He added another X at the drop zone.

"Clear skies, with a light eight kph breeze out of the southwest are projected at drop time. This will give us the ability to land up to five kilometers past our target, if the need should arrive." He marked an X on the target location. "Deployment will be at 04:20 local time. Hang time will be approximately fifty minutes, give or take. I'll drive the train. Reese, you and Janet will be tandem on the caboose. Our extraction point will be one kilometer north of Izmir on the coast at 10:00 hours. The Major has made arrangements for a commercial fishing boat to take the team and any guests we may have accrued, from there to Athens. Are there any questions?"

None were voiced, as a few eyes wandered over to Janet for her reaction. She nodded her approval to the plan.

"Good," the captain said, then looked over at St. Jean and raised his eyebrows.

"Chow in 20 minutes," Bobby answered the silent question and the briefing was over.

WAYNE A D KERR

After an amazing meal of seasoned sockeye salmon served over a stir-fried medley of seasoned yellow and red peppers, onions and summer squash, most of the team settled in for a few hours of rest. PB was fitting Janet with jump gear in the equipment room.

"Do you guys eat like that all the time?" Janet asked.

"Bobby can cook," he answered. "Though, I think he was showing off, just a little, tonight."

"That was the best tasting salmon I've ever eaten," Janet marveled.

"Don't say that too loudly; he'll get a big head."

"Too late," Bobby said, poking his nose into the equipment room. "I'm brewing some tea if anyone would like some."

Both declined the offer and went back to outfitting Janet.

PB inspected the thermal jump suit Janet was wearing. "How does that feel? It looks like a pretty good fit."

"The arms are a bit too long."

PB rolled up the cuffs for her, then grabbed a size small helmet and face mask from the rack and helped her put them on. After a few adjustments he was happy with the fit. He then attached a small hose.

"We'll be breathing pure oxygen for the first half of the drop," PB explained, while he showed her the regulator dial. "You don't have to worry about the adjustments; I'll take care of them."

"We'll really be travelling almost thirty kilometers at night without getting lost?"

"These airfoil-style chutes are very easy to steer. With the right coordinates, an altimeter and compass, John could land us on a proverbial needle in a haystack. We'll be dropping in, what we call, stack or train formation with John in the lead.

The rest of the boys will follow about thirty meters apart, one behind the other."

"What about us?"

"We'll be just a little further back. Our chute is both larger and slightly slower. But, we'll be close enough to maintain visual contact. Plus, we'll have radio communication with everyone."

"What about..." Janet started to ask.

"The chutes and our jumpsuits, as you can see, are all black," he said anticipating her next question. "We'll be virtually invisible from the ground at night."

PB explained the entire drop to Janet, step-by-step, to help her feel comfortable with the impending jump.

Not surprisingly, Janet was unable to get any sleep during the flight. Her policy had always been not to jump out of perfectly good aircrafts. At 03:30, Turkish time, the cabin lights came on and Captain Andrews entered from the cockpit.

"Saddle up cowpokes!" he ordered.

Thirty-five minutes later PB had checked and rechecked Janet's gear a few times. She was now securely attached to PB. The small jet dropped to twenty-eight thousand feet and slowed significantly. Andrews swung open the custom door, then reached above the opening and touched a framed photo of his grandfather -- the first Captain John Andrews, and then a cloth replica of the original company flag, sewn by Princess Patricia. He shouted "Ric-a-Dam-Doo" and jumped through the opening. At four second intervals the others followed, each repeating the same ritual as they exited.

Captain John Andrews, the first, had been an early volunteer in Hammy Gault's little army -- that would eventually become the Princess Patricia's Canadian Light Infantry. During World War II the experienced soldier had been sent to Fort William Henry Harrison near Helena, Montana to train with hundreds of other Canadian and

American soldiers. The men that made it through the rigorous training became a part of the world's first Special Forces team. Their original purpose was to disrupt and terrorize the German troops.

They were good at it and would soon become better known by a couple of other names: *The Devil's Brigade* or *The Black Devils*. All modern American, Canadian and British Special Forces units can trace their heritage back to these brave souls who dropped behind enemy lines, wreaked havoc and disappeared into the night.

Ahead of Janet, St. Jean performed the ritual and added "Yahoo" as he jumped. She wanted to take a step forward but her feet wouldn't listen. Four seconds passed in the blink of an eye. PB shouted "Ric-a-Dam-Doo" over her shoulder and literally swept Janet off her feet. Suddenly, she found herself outside the plane freefalling into the night.

Janet couldn't see a thing, nor could she feel PB behind her. Everything was black. She fought against the idea that she was all alone. The five second long freefall seemed like an eternity. Finally, with a lurch the parachute opened and she could feel PB and gravity, once again. A strong hand squeezed her shoulder and the moments of panic faded away.

Captain Andrews' voice filled her helmet. "On target," he reported, "with conditions as expected."

As each of the others checked in, PB pointed them out to Janet. She was soon able make out four large rectangular black chutes against the slightly less-dark-black beneath them. The top of each double-layered chute had a small gray arrow pointing forward. The arrows were all aligned.

"This is Caboose confirming that I have a visual of the entire train." Then he added a confirmation, "the train is on track." After he spoke, PB pointed upward at the sky.

Janet looked up. It was as if she could see every star in the universe above her. "It's so beautiful," she gasped. They floated through the peaceful sky for several minutes in silence.

PB pointed to a faint glow in the distance. The chute arrows were pointed directly at it. "That is the city of Izmir up ahead. It's the Captain's first and easiest flight path reference."

"Even St. Jean could find that one," Billy's muffled voice cut in, followed by some snickering.

"Now I'm not even sorry about putting Salt Peter on your fish tonight, Billy," St. Jean piped back.

"When we get over land, we'll observe radio silence and you won't have to listen to these knuckleheads," PB stated for everyone's benefit.

"Do we have to wait until we're over land for radio silence to begin?" Janet laughed.

"Hey, I resent that," St. Jean sputtered and again laughter followed.

The glow from Izmir was getting brighter. Soon individual lights would become visible.

An inspiration hit PB. He decided that the time was right; he didn't need a waterfall. It was such a beautiful night and he had the woman he loved right in front of him. He felt like it was now or never.

"Janet," he paused collecting his thoughts, "I've never felt about anyone the way I feel about you. I love you with all my heart. I know that we are living crazy lives right now. You live in London and I'm in Canada, when we aren't hanging over the coast of Turkey or chasing bad guys across rooftops or through sewers. The logistics aren't exactly ideal and I'm not sure how we would make it all work..."

A few very quiet seconds drifted by as he decided how to proceed.

"Just pop the damn question," Captain Andrews cut in. "That's an order, soldier!"

"Yes, Sir," PB answered and then asked the million dollar question. "Janet Porter, will you marry me?"

"Well," she answered slowly, "you've put me in a very awkward position Sergeant Reese."

"Oh, no," slipped out of Bobby's mouth before he could stop it.

"Because, I really want to kiss you right now!" she added.

All five men let out a collective sigh of relief.

"Of course, I'll marry you! I love you with all my heart, PB!"

After several congratulations were exchanged the Captain brought the focus back to the mission. The shoreline was no more than a mile ahead. "Let's get back to the job at hand everyone."

"Once we land, I'll set up shop on the hilltop north of the house," Mankowski reported. This location would afford the sniper good sightlines of the rear of the house and the outbuildings, including the large detached garage on the property, provided their Interpol intelligence was accurate. It would take him less than a minute to get his rifle and sight assembled, locked and loaded.

"Johansen and I will flank the perimeter of the property and get quietly acquainted with any guards we meet. Then, we'll rendezvous at the back door to assist with retrieval," St. Jean added.

"I'll make entry at the rear of the house, taking care of any bogeys in that area. Then find our target and escort him out the way I entered," Reese stated his part of the plan.

Janet had been on enough missions with the team to know that her new fiancé was usually first in. He seemed to have the ability to melt into his surroundings and then all of a sudden appear just where he was needed. If he hadn't already had a nickname, they'd probably have called him Houdini. The whole team was in awe of the ninja-like stealth he possessed. PB took the point on most missions.

"Agent Porter and I will secure the garage," Captain Andrews said, ending the final run-through of the plan. "We'll appropriate suitable transportation and meet you at the house."

"Radio silence will begin in one minute," he reminded everyone.

PB and Janet had drifted a little behind the others but were well within sight range. He squeezed his arms tightly around his fiancé.

"The train is still on track, Sir," he reported as the shoreline approached. The remaining few minutes of the descent was spent in silence.

Janet had never in her wildest dreams imagined a night like this. Everything was happening so fast. Part of her wanted to keep sailing through the stars, forever. Part of her wanted PB to turn their chute and find a secluded spot so she could tear his clothes off... It was more than just physical, though. He was the strongest, kindest, gentlest man she'd ever met. For a person with only a high school diploma, he was well-read and intellectually stimulating. This had surprised her more than almost anything. They could talk for hours. Well, if she was honest with herself, their first kiss had been electrifying. She'd felt it right through to her toes. And the first time she saw him without his shirt... Had it been love at first sight? Maybe? He'd certainly caught her attention right away. He was the one! She'd known that for quite some time.

Another part of her wanted to keep going with the mission; she'd never been so close to her goal of catching the Austrian. She'd been obsessed with closing down his cruel organization for the past three years. The slippery son-of-a-bitch had ruined the lives of thousands of young women and men, not to mention tens of thousands of their loved ones.

She said yes! PB felt like the luckiest man on the planet. He marveled at the circumstances that had allowed a boy from the Canadian prairies to meet a girl from London, England, in Eastern Europe. Somehow, he'd fallen for her on that first rainy night in Yugoslavia. He'd never met a woman like her before. She was tough as nails, yet so compassionate. Her dark flashing eyes and smile captivated him. He loved that she could take a ribbing from the tight-knit team and fire it right back in spades. PB never tired of talking to her. There were several things he never tired of doing with her. With Janet he'd learned the difference between sex and making love. Sex had always been good, but sex with the person you're in love with was ten times better! Janet made him feel whole.

The Special Forces soldier realized they were drifting a little. He reluctantly let go of his fiancé and brought them back on line. He would kiss Janet and properly present the ring once their mission was completed. With only a few minutes until touchdown, he began something that he could do as well as anyone alive. PB brought his complete focus to bear on the task at hand. For the next few hours his fiancé, Agent Porter, would simply be a part of the team.

CHAPTER 13

The New Boyfriend

The present
The Morales Ranch, Mexico

The masked kidnapper stared strangely at Emma as he handed her the morning platter of food. His eyes never left her even while he passed the other platter to Monica.

Monica sat on the end of her cot and looked at the food. In the bowl was a scrambled egg mixture with beans, peppers and green salsa.

"Haven't you people ever heard of granola or yogurt," she turned, looked at the door and asked loudly. "What would be so wrong with a waffle or even a bowl of corn flakes?"

The masked man back-stepped to the door without acknowledging her comments.

"Emma's got a new boyfriend," Monica teased, once the cell door had been closed.

Emma didn't laugh. She stared at the small doll she had found wrapped inside the napkin beside her plate of beans and eggs. Twelve inches tall and made from small colored ropes, it managed to be both creepy and impressive at the same time. Emma lost what little appetite she'd had. She set the plate and doll down at the foot of her narrow cot and shimmied back across the thin mattress away from it.

"Monica, this is serious!" She could tell that the older of the guards had been looking at her oddly even through the masks he wore. It had been him who delivered her the doll.

"Relax girl," Monica rolled her eyes. "I'm just teasing. Besides they aren't going to hurt us. That video they made of us was a joke."

"I was scared."

"Not me," the Arthur girl proclaimed. "I just went along with the whole stupid thing to speed up the process."

Emma knew better. They had both been very scared. Monica screamed just as often and loudly as she had. Emma decided not to contradict her friend; there wasn't much point.

"The cameras, the lights, the big green screen, it was all just for show. If they really hurt us, they won't get paid," she continued confidently. "And Daddy will pay them whatever they're asking. Then we'll go home."

"Don't forget," Emma countered, "I've seen both their faces."

"That doesn't matter," Emma's friend tried to sound assuring, but was secretly concerned about her friend's safety. At the same time, Monica was extremely relieved that she hadn't seen any faces. Not sure what else to say, she wiped the few remaining beans from her plate into her mouth with her finger.

"Then why do they still wear their masks whenever they're around us?" Emma countered. "That's just for your benefit. They aren't going to let me go. They can't afford to."

"Don't worry about it, Ems, we're a package deal. I won't leave without you," Monica smiled sympathetically. "We'll be home soon, I promise."

"I hope you're right." Emma didn't sound convinced.

"Are you going to eat that?" Monica asked, eyeing the unattended plate of food on the other cot.

"Go ahead, I don't want it," Emma told her. She was too worried to even think about food.

The dark-haired girl rose from her cot and sat down on the foot of Emma's narrow bed. In one minute flat she had scooped and licked the paper plate clean and then tossed it like a Frisbee into the corner to join hers. Monica picked up the doll. The Emma replica was solidly made and had some heft to it.

"This is Mini You," Monica exclaimed, marveling at the craftsmanship. The tightly woven braids were smooth to the touch. "Shoulder length blonde hair with baby blue eyes."

"I figured that much out myself," Emma replied unhappily.

"Oh My God!" Monica said, using Valley Girl slang. Her eyes widened, while her fingers traced across the doll's chest. "It's anatomically correct!"

"It is not!" Emma argued.

"Two little bumps," Monica said, glancing down at Emma's late blooming chest while she continued to rub her fingers across the doll's bosom.

"Stop that," Emma cried out, suddenly feeling very uncomfortable. She lunged for the doll in her friend's hand. She wasn't quick enough. "Give it to me!" she commanded.

The girls wrestled. Finally Emma got the better of Monica and took possession of her likeness. She retreated into the corner to protect it.

Monica started giggling and continued until Emma joined in. It was her first giggle since being abducted. It felt good to laugh. Emma found the doll down right funny. She began to guffaw. Monica laughed at her and with her. Soon everything made Emma laugh. Her lumpy mattress, the stupid video, their masked captors, the mechanical voice, the whole situation was suddenly hilarious. It was all just so surreal. The dam had burst. The girls laughed until their stomachs ached. Then they cried.

.   .   .

Juan Carlos smiled. He sat in front of the cell monitors watching for Emma's reaction to his gift. At first he couldn't tell if she liked it. But now after witnessing her fight over the doll and take it back, he knew she loved it. He'd been right about her, after all. She was the one for him.

He got up from the monitors and headed out to do his evening chores. Rosa cooked and kept up the house. Raul maintained all the farm equipment. The farm animals had to be fed and watered and that was his responsibility. He whistled a jaunty tune as he left the barn. Juan Carlos could imagine his new bride at his side, helping him sell halters and bridles, as they travelled the rodeo circuit across Mexico.

"Juan Carlos," Hector's voice woke him from the daydream. "Go get Raul and set up the knife scene."

"Yes, sir," he replied. He didn't like the idea that Nemo would be anywhere near Emma, but he did what he was ordered.

"We'll shoot it right after lunch," Hector informed him before heading to the ranch house.

That evening Monica woke from a restless nap to the bright light that perpetuated their cell throughout the day. The Arthur girl had no idea what time it was, anymore. She rolled over and glanced at Emma's cot. Her friend typically roamed the cell from corner to corner when she wasn't asleep. Today was the exception. The other girl had crammed herself up against the far wall, with only her back visible. Her shoulder's rocked back and forth rhythmically, her busy hands hidden from view.

The hulking man had been quite a bit rougher with Emma during the video that afternoon, than with her. He was scarier and different from the other two kidnappers. Monica had been very worried when he'd put a huge knife to her friend's throat. Thankfully, Emma had not been seriously hurt. Although Monica could see that a large red welt had appeared on Emma's shoulder where he'd held on to her.

Monica sat up. She missed her own bed. This stupid, thin, lumpy mattress had no blankets or sheets. Her sheets at home were soft and smooth to the touch. She rubbed the crook in her neck. My kingdom for a pillow! She missed her pillow more than just about anything.

"Ems, what are you doing?" Monica finally asked her friend.

"Nothing," Emma answered. She stuffed something under her mattress and rolled over. "Did you have a good nap?"

"Just like Cleopatra floating down the Nile," Monica quipped sarcastically and crossed the six-foot gap between the cots. "I know when you're up to something, Emma."

"Okay," Emma grudgingly gave in, knowing that Monica wouldn't let it go. She couldn't afford to have her friend reach under the mattress and pull her little project out into the open. Emma knew they were being watched, since the captors always came for their plates and utensils immediately after the girls finished eating and had known where to look for the plastic fork that had *accidentally* fallen under Monica's cot. "I'm unwinding the doll and turning it back into a rope," she whispered.

"How very McGyver-like of you," Monica smirked. "What's your plan?"

"Quiet," Emma hushed her friend. "They might be listening." She scooted over beside Monica. "I don't really have a plan, yet. But I have to do something, Monica, because I don't think they're going to let me go."

"I'm not going anywhere without you," Monica declared and gave Emma a big hug. They both knew that it wouldn't be up to her, though.

The sound of the door locks sliding open alerted them to an impending visitor. Emma froze, certain that her kidnappers had heard about the rope.

The younger of the kidnappers, wearing a woolen balaclava over his face, entered carrying two plates of food for dinner. Emma breathed a sigh of relief for two reasons. First, because the kidnappers hadn't overheard and, also it wasn't the creepy old guy. He set the cardboard dishes on the end of the empty cot and backed out. The girls could hear the door locks reset.

Monica picked up the bowls. Another bean and rice mixture. She turned and brought one to Emma. "I'm in," she silently mouthed, "we definitely have to get out of here. After we're home, I'll never eat another bean again. I swear, on my favorite pair of shoes."

Emma smiled, happy to have a coconspirator. Now, coming up with an actual plan would be nice.

She began to eat, her appetite returning. Actually, the food tasted much better than she'd expected.

CHAPTER 14

Fighting Fire with Fire

The present
Puerto Penasco, Mexico

Earlier that morning, Janet and PB readied themselves for another day of surveillance. Today, however, Janet would be watching the Morales family while PB watched Hector at work.

PB set up shop in Janet's spot from the day before. He could see Hector working at his desk. Hector made a few phone calls and shuffled papers for a little over an hour. He got up from his desk and disappeared from view. After a full ten minutes had passed and Hector had not returned to his desk, PB decided to move to the back of the machine shop.

PB was in full tourist attire as he made his way around the block. Big sunglasses, a colorful cotton shirt and shorts, a baseball cap with Rocky Pointe and a palm tree embroidered across the front, along with his light-colored hair and fair skin, sold the disguise. But it was the map of the small city held open in front of him that allowed PB to keep watch in all directions without looking suspicious.

He was half way down the side street when a small truck emerged from the alley almost running into him. The driver honked and swore at him.

"Something, something, Gringo," was all that PB could make out. PB shrugged and feigned being lost as the truck went around him and accelerated away. PB continued down the street for a few steps before stopping. He listened to the exhaust of the truck. It sounded almost identical to his first and, arguably, favorite sports car, a Datsun 280Z. That rusty looking truck shouldn't have had a high performance six cylinder engine under the hood. He turned just in time to see the truck turn the corner. He noted that the wheels and tires looked wider than usual for the small truck.

If the truck wasn't what it seemed, maybe the driver hadn't been either. Upon reflection, the eyes of the angry driver hadn't seemed quite right to PB. He realized that while he couldn't be sure it was Morales behind the wheel, he equally couldn't be certain it wasn't.

PB backtracked and went down the alley. He spotted some fresh rubber tracks on the pavement coming out of an apparently empty building. He walked around the building to confirm that it was not in use. It looked abandoned, but was locked up tight. PB noted that it was basically just across the alley, kitty-corner from Morales Metals. He was suddenly now certain that the old man in the truck had been Hector Morales. To confirm his suspicions, he went in search of a new vantage point that would allow him to watch for the return of the little truck, as well as Hector's office window.

The new location wasn't ideal, but it did afford the view PB needed. Tucked behind some rose bushes, under the open window of a dentist office, he could clearly hear the receptionist welcoming patients and taking appointments over the phone just above him.

In the middle of the afternoon the ex-soldier's cell phone began to buzz. The caller ID revealed that it was Ben Morrison. PB slid a blue tooth receiver and sensitive microphone over his ear and answered the call.

"Hi Ben," he said in a low quiet voice, not wanting to give away his position. "This is PB."

"Can you talk?" Ben asked, noticing the tone of his friend's voice.

"Yes," he confirmed. "Go ahead."

"We just received another video," Ben started. "It was horrible, PB. I'm afraid she's going to get hurt, or worse. I don't think that my son or wife can watch another one of those damn things."

"I'm sorry Ben," PB sympathized. "How are you holding up?"

"I don't know what I'll do if they hurt Emma..." Ben's voice faltered, then he found it again. "I think the Arthurs are about to agree to pay for Monica's release. They're now demanding ten million dollars. We don't have that kind of money!"

"What did the FBI negotiator say about that?" PB asked, to keep his friend talking.

"He says that in the past, the kidnappers have agreed to take less for one of the girls if her family is not rich."

"That's good news," PB assured him.

"Robert was able to get approval for a second mortgage," Ben told him. "Combined with Rita and my savings and pensions we can put together about eight hundred thousand. Agent Novak thinks it might be enough."

"You and Rita would be wiped out financially," PB stated; immediately wishing he hadn't.

"We'll be alright," he said. "Getting Emma home safe is the only thing that matters."

"Yes, of course it is," PB agreed. "Ben, promise me that you won't release any money until you speak with me or Janet first."

"Have you found something there?" Ben asked.

"So far it's just a small lead and a hunch," Reese admitted. "Just promise me, okay."

"I promise," he conceded. "No money until I speak to you first."

"That's good Ben," PB said, feeling both a sense of relief and renewed urgency to find the girls and get them home. "Now tell me about the video."

Ben described the video in detail to PB. It had featured a monstrous man, covered in red leather and wearing a devil mask, leering and pawing at the girls. Then he grabbed Emma and put a knife to her throat. This had been mixed together with footage of two previous kidnapping victims being raped and savagely beaten by that same man. Within minutes of viewing it the Arthurs started making arrangements for a money transfer. They'd had enough. The Morrisons would have paid anything at that moment, also, if they'd had that kind of money.

"I've got to go PB," Ben told him. "I'm meeting with our accountant."

"Remember your promise," PB said.

"I'll call you first," Ben said, though his voice betrayed that he didn't hold out much hope. "No matter what, thank you for trying."

The connection went dead before PB could reply. His fists clenched in frustration. He refused to let Ben and Rita down. Frustration began to set in. He calmed himself and focused on the immediate job at hand. Every detail becomes paramount for the success of a mission. Observe and gather as much intel as possible on the enemy, he reminded himself. Great intelligence is the key to any good plan. He called his wife and told her about the video and ransom.

Just after 5:00 pm, PB spotted the truck as it turned into the alley. He watched the old man get out and swing open the doors to the building. The man drove the truck inside and then came back out with a bucket and long handled brush to scrub away the tire tracks left by the truck on the bleached white concrete. Once satisfied with his work, he took a look around to be sure no one was watching and then disappeared back into the abandoned building, closing the door behind him.

Thirteen minutes later, Hector Morales, once again in business attire, appeared in his office. He spent a few minutes going through the inbox on his desk and then headed out of the building, got into his Porsche and drove away.

With all doubt about Hector Morales' involvement in the kidnapping erased in PB's mind, he again had the overwhelming urge to grab Morales and wring Emma's whereabouts out of him. If the man didn't talk, though, Emma could be lost forever.

Instead, he left his hiding spot and headed for the condo. He hadn't walked more than half a block when PB felt eyes upon him. A few steps later a tough-looking man turned the corner on the sidewalk twenty meters in front of him. PB stopped in his tracks and pretended to consult his street map as he assessed the situation. Two more men came up the sidewalk from behind. Three men were quickly converging on his location. He decided that they meant to rob the foolish tourist that had wandered off the beaten path. He wasn't about to let these goons have his gun or other equipment. He noted that the man in front of him was hiding a small iron pipe behind his right leg as they closed the gap. He looked up from the map with a big smile on his face.

"I'm lost," he said chuckling. He turned to look at each of them. "Do any of you fellas speak English?"

The pipe made its first intentional appearance as the man in front of him slapped it into his left hand, menacingly.

"Your stuff!" the lead man demanded, using a couple of the few English words he knew. The men closed in tightly to intimidate the tourist. This was a tactical error.

Suddenly, the Special Forces soldier shoved the map into the face of the man with the pipe. At the same time he shifted to his left and grabbed the man behind him, pulling him forward. The blinded man swung the pipe aggressively, connecting solidly with jaw of his younger brother. Barely a moment later, the third man found himself writhing on the ground holding a shattered knee cap. PB twisted around and was now behind the man with the pipe. Finally shoving the map out of his face, the remaining goon was shocked to see his brothers on the ground in front of him. As he spun around, his nose met PB's hard left jab. There was a loud snapping noise inside his head, followed by a kaleidoscope of light dancing before his eyes. The pipe dropped from his hand as he fell into a heap amongst his brothers.

"I don't like bullies!" PB informed the moaning group in perfect Spanish, as he pulled a set of brass knuckles from one of the guy's hands and rifled a knife out of the pocket of another. PB stashed these into his back pack and picked up the pipe. The man holding his injured knee cringed, expecting to be beaten with it. Instead, the pipe sailed over a nearby fence. Their uncle, Police Chief Ramirez, would not be pleased. His nephews wouldn't be turning in any protection money while they healed their broken bones.

"Thanks for the help, gentlemen," PB called out in English, as he retrieved his map from the sidewalk, once again heading to the condo. "I can find my way back from here."

.   .   .

That morning at 8:40, Janet had followed as Maria and a driver took Ali to school and then Gabriella to pre-school.

Maria went inside with the five-year-old and spoke briefly with her daughter's teacher. Meanwhile, the driver drove ahead to the end of the street and made a u-turn before returning to the front door of the learning center. The driver jumped out and held the rear door open for Maria, as she returned a few minutes later.

Mrs. Morales had been impeccably dressed in a cream-colored skirt and blouse. The blouse had a small splash of color on the left side that matched her tangerine purse and pumps. She did look gorgeous, even though Janet thought the woman's skirt was just a little too tight.

The driver then delivered Maria to an upscale beauty salon. An hour later she came out looking even prettier. After that, she was taken to some trendy clothing boutiques a block in from the main beach. Janet parked and was able to get a little closer as Maria did some shopping.

Janet noticed the air of superiority that surrounded Maria. She treated the clerks that fawned over her as though she owned them. Maria bought a few things from each store, all the while complaining about the lack of good quality merchandise. By the end of the morning Janet had a strong dislike for the bitchy beauty.

At lunch time, Maria and her driver picked up Gabriella from the pre-school and brought her home.

After lunch, Maria got into a white Mercedes SLK and drove herself back down to the same shopping area. The woman seemed to be returning most of the merchandise she had purchased that morning. Janet couldn't follow her inside after having been in many of the boutiques earlier. Janet observed Maria from a coffee shop at the end of the block as she returned to each and every store she'd frequented that morning. After each visit, it seemed to Janet as though Maria's fashionable Louis Vuitton purse was getting thicker.

From there Maria drove to an upscale Spa and fitness facility. The valet parked her car as she went inside. Mrs. Morales was inside from 2:30 until 4:00. As she waited for the Mercedes to be brought around, Janet noted that Maria's purse looked as thin as it had at the beginning of the day. Whatever had been in the purse now remained somewhere in the spa.

Janet followed Maria as she drove from there to Alejandro's school. After picking him up, Maria drove home.

Two hours later, Maria and the children loaded into a family sedan and went out for pizza. The Morales children were thrilled when their father joined them only a few minutes after they sat down.

Janet decided that she had done enough surveillance for the day and headed back to the condo for a debriefing with her husband.

The couple compared notes over a spicy Hawaiian pizza and diet Cokes. After considering the contents of Ben's latest call, they agreed that a more proactive approach was required. Weighing the pros and cons of a few different scenarios and then dismissing them, Janet came up with the idea of fighting fire with fire. The more PB thought about it the more he liked it. The couple hatched a plan and went over logistics. When the tasty pizza was all gone, they went back out to scout locations and firm up the final details of the operation. It was 1:15 am by the time they returned to their condo.

CHAPTER 15

Majestic and Massive

1975
Hermosillo, Mexico

Guadalupe Suarez didn't mind cleaning the Mayor's house. She tolerated his constant advances whenever the two of them were alone in the same room. Guadalupe was used to men and their ways. She'd been born into a dirt-poor family but had been blessed with much better-than-average good looks. When she was younger, her mother had dressed her very conservatively, but there was just no hiding curves like hers. Grandma Gutierrez had been a beautiful woman, too. These things often skipped a generation, her plain mother had told her.

When she was seventeen, the Governor of Chihuahua came to Hermosillo to attend an economic conference. His aide, twenty-year-old Felipe Suarez, accompanied him to the small city.

During a break between sessions, Felipe slipped outside for a cigarette. When Guadalupe walked by, it was love at first sight. Not too bad looking himself and all dressed up in an expensive suit, he made an impression on her, as well. They met for coffee that afternoon and then dinner the next evening.

Over the next year and a half, Felipe made the eight hour drive to Hermosillo once or twice a month. Shortly after turning nineteen, Guadalupe married Felipe and moved to Chihuahua.

Ten years later, they had a five-year-old boy named Nemesio and a three-year-old daughter, Maria. The future looked bright for the Suarez family. City councilman Felipe Suarez had plans to be governor one day and there was little doubt in the minds of any who knew him that he'd get there. A tumor in his lung was the only thing standing in his way.

Guadalupe had nagged him for years to see the doctor. Felipe had a persistent cough just like his father and grandfather. All had smoked since the age of nine or ten. The Suarez men all coughed; it was nothing to worry about, he had assured her. Unfortunately for Felipe, both his father and grandfather attended his funeral. Cancer can be a fickle mistress.

Though Guadalupe wouldn't remember much about that day, she'd been told that Felipe's funeral was a magnificent affair. It was held at the majestic and massive Metropolitan Cathedral of the Holy Cross, Our Lady of Regla and St. Francis of Assisi.

The tragic loss of the popular councilman was the talk of the region. It was widely believed that he'd have been mayor after the next election. Felipe Suarez had touched many. Few had ever seen the church full, except during lent and at Christmas mass. What Guadalupe did remember was standing in a condolence line that seemed to last for hours and one thing that the priest had said during the Requiem Mass. "A man so well loved will never leave us, as love gives us immortality." These words touched her. She had loved Felipe with all her heart and soul.

Six months after the funeral, Guadalupe had to face a harsh reality. She could no longer afford the big house they'd enjoyed. The savings were running out. She sold the house, took the equity and bought a small home back in her much more affordable home town. Her parents were thrilled to have their grandchildren nearby.

Guadalupe's mother was a house cleaner. A bad back was beginning to hamper her abilities, though. Ready to slow down, she encouraged her daughter to take over her little business. Working hard was good therapy for Guadalupe. She found that she enjoyed it and was quite good at it. She'd had her own mini-mansion and servants and could relate to her employers' needs and expectations. Within three years she was running the households of two of the wealthiest families in town. She was making far more money than her mother ever had, but was working longer hours, too.

Things had been tough on Nemo and Maria. First they lost their father, then their home and now they hardly saw their mother.

Always big for his age, everyone described Nemo as a gentle boy. Losing his father caused a pain in Nemo's soul that just wouldn't go away. For a long time he became withdrawn. He started spending more and more time alone. One day sitting in the backyard of his grandparents' home, the neighbor's cat was curled up in Nemo's lap. He was petting the friendly animal, as he often had before, when his fingers curled around its neck. The cat's claws dug deeply into his thighs as his fingers tightened more and more. For just a minute, the constant ache inside him faded away. The cat went limp and his fingers finally relaxed. He looked at the dead cat and then his hands. It had almost been as if they'd acted on their own. Nemo stood and the furry lump tumbled to the ground.

The boy looked around to see if anyone had been watching. He remembered that Grandma and Maria were at the market. Grandpa was in the house, but he'd be sleeping in his easy chair. His eyes weren't so good anymore, anyhow. Nemo looked down at the white, gray and black cat at his feet. It had been one of his few friends in recent months, yet, he felt no remorse. He walked to the tool shed to get a spade. When he returned the cat was sitting on the fence between the two properties. It hissed at him and then high-tailed it down into the neighbor's yard. From that point on the cat was terrified of him. This gave Nemo a far greater feeling of power than the thought of killing it had. Fear and pain were his new best friends. No one, not even his mother, ever described Nemo as gentle again.

The bully of Hermosillo had been released. Nemo terrorized the school yard for several years. By the time he was fourteen, Nemo was larger than all the teachers. For the safety of everyone at the school, they kicked him out.

Nemo had never brought his bullying home before, but when he threatened to hit his grandfather, his grandmother banished him from their home. The sweet little boy they, and his mother, once knew had been gone for a long time.

His only friend, a small but tough kid named Hector, dropped out of school and joined him on the streets. Hector was smart and an excellent thief. Together, the two of them survived and eventually even thrived.

Maria was a mama's girl. From the time she could walk, she followed her mother everywhere. Guadalupe loved having a little shadow and until Felipe got sick, the two of them were inseparable. After Maria's father died, her mother stayed in bed for days. When she did come out of the room, she sat on the back porch and stared. Though not yet five years old, Maria assumed her mother's duties around the house.

The staff thought it was cute, at first, when she roamed around the house giving instructions like her mother had. After a few weeks the demanding little girl wasn't so cute anymore. When one of the staff finally complained, Guadalupe shrugged and said to do whatever Maria wanted. For the next few months the staff stopped calling Maria a princess and referred to her instead as the little tyrant.

After the family moved from the mansion, Maria was devastated when she discovered she no longer had a staff to order around at the tiny new house. Things quickly went from bad to worse when her grandma would not tolerate her bossy attitude. She eventually learned to hide it, but her sense of entitlement never went away. The prized possessions of the other girls in the neighborhood began to disappear. Maria didn't keep any of the things she stole. She just couldn't stand anyone having nicer things than she. Maria discovered what a convincing liar she could be when she reported that the precious doll her dear grandma had given her for her birthday was missing, too. The clever girl had never liked that doll and the neighborhood thief was never caught, either.

At school, Maria organized and ruled over the popular girls in her class. Beauty had not skipped a generation in Maria's case. As she got older and the baby fat melted away, her face morphed into a version of her mother's. Her looks were striking. Many commented that she was even more beautiful than her mother. Maria had higher cheek bones and a more chiseled chin than Guadalupe, though her pretty eyes were piercing and harsh, where her mother's were soft and inviting. Grandma had tried to explain to her that beauty could be a blessing or a curse. Maria used it as a weapon. She learned how to wrap almost any male around her little finger. By high school, even her best friends knew better than to cross her in any way. No one's boyfriend was safe if Maria had a reason to turn her attentions his way.

Maria never forgot her mansion. She dreamt of having the biggest, most beautiful house that anyone had ever seen. Hard work was not the answer. She'd watched her mother and grandmother work very hard; neither of them was rich. No, she needed to find a rich man. Maria decided not to go on to university after graduation. What was the point? Professors made a comfortable living, but they weren't rich.

After some research, Maria determined that Mayor Gomez was the richest man in town. She remembered her mother's stories about him. How hard could it be to steal him away from his wife? Maria surprised her mother when she asked to learn the cleaning business. It didn't take long for the Mayor to notice the new girl. Within weeks, he was smitten. Things were going according to plan for Maria, who was showing a little more leg and cleavage during each visit, when a strange thing happened.

Maria had kept in touch with Nemo. She loved her brother and understood him in a way no one else did. Lately, he was flashing lots of money around. Money always caught Maria's attention. She knew his friend Hector, but had only met him a couple of times. She'd barely noticed him before. This time he was driving a brand new Mercedes sports car and wearing the fanciest cowboy boots ever seen in Hermosillo. She noticed him now! When he offered to take her for a drive in his new car, she accepted.

Hector found it easy to talk to Maria. They parked and talked for over an hour, a first for Hector with any female. Hector was captivated by her looks, as most men were, but there was something else. They shared common goals. Both had a pathological need to be rich and prove something to the world. She felt the connection, too.

The next day Hector did something he'd never done before. He took her with him up north and showed off his operation to an outsider. Maria was fascinated. Hector was taking a chance, but for some reason it didn't feel like much of risk to him. Maria hadn't flinched when she found out that he and Nemo were in the drug trade. Instead, she was fascinated with the incredible profits. Nemo's sister was a kindred spirit.

He showed her an old warehouse on the edge of Magdalena, a town between Hermosillo and Nogales. A sign on the side of it read: Magdalena Appliance Repair. Inside, on the main floor, there were half a dozen repair trucks and two well-armed men. Each truck had at least one appliance sitting in the back ready for delivery. Hector explained that one of his men actually did repair appliances. It was a great cover that allowed them to move freely around the area in the light of day.

He took her through a doorway in the back, past another guard. In the product room were hundreds of small bales of marijuana stacked in separate piles. Written on the wall behind each were strange names like Blueberry Sundae, Champagne Kick, Donkey Piss and Smoky Volcano. She laughed as she moved from one stack to the next. Hector pointed out that most of it was harvested in the surrounding mountains, nearby. Maria asked what it was worth and Hector explained to her that it wasn't worth much here in Mexico, but once it crossed the border it became quite valuable.

When Maria saw the stacks of cash in the money room her knees almost buckled. She wanted in on this money-making machine. And why not start at the top? The next room was Hector's living quarters. Nemo and a couple of Hector's other men also lived right in the building.

Maria played hard to get for the rest of the day. The next day she let Hector take her to bed. As her fingers traced over and squeezed his impressively hard, muscled body she tried to forget how close she had come to giving herself to the saggy old mayor. Hector had saved her.

The next day she quit her stupid job and moved in with her brother's best and only friend. A few weeks later she was in the Spanish Riviera. While she hadn't had the fairy tale wedding of her dreams, Hector had given her a honeymoon beyond her fantasies. Nothing was too good for his Maria, he kept telling her.

Immediately upon their return home, Maria got involved in the business. Hector welcomed her input. First, she convinced him that there needed to be some separation between them and the business operations. While Hector had been great at staying one step in front of the police, to that point, some of his business practices needed improvement. They needed deniability. The couple moved into a temporary place until they could find a suitable property. She also convinced Hector to buy a legitimate business and put his name on it. She made a strict rule that there could never be any evidence that would tie them to the drug business at home or the office. Maria then pointed out that all of their eggs were in one basket. A raid could take everything. They left the inventory at the warehouse and moved the money to a separate and secret location. Maria was less trusting of the men than Hector. Only the two of them and her brother Nemo knew the money's location.

They even added a computer to the operation. Together they learned how to track inventory and monitor the flow of money. The operation grew and so did the margins. Hector soon learned that Maria had a tough side. She started monitoring everything. Those she felt were not performing to her standards or she suspected of sampling the products were soon gone. Mrs. Morales usually had her brother remove them from the operation. Most were never heard from again. No one dared cross Maria. Profits soared and los Diablos Rojos grew in size and power with a new devil managing the business side of the gang.

When Maria wasn't streamlining the business, she was hunting for a new home. She wanted stability and stature, as well as riches. After a couple of months she realized there was nothing in the region for sale or that fit her vision of the lifestyle she deserved. She did find a property in Puerto Penasco that she deemed suitable. A small beach-front hotel was for sale. The ocean view was spectacular. The town was vibrant with an interesting night life for the young couple. Puerto Penasco also happened to be where Hector's new legitimate business, Morales Metals, was located.

Maria spent the next few months designing the home of her dreams. With the help of a local architect, she drew plans for a house that rivaled any on the entire North American west coast. Like the Metropolitan Cathedral in Chihuahua, the Spanish Colonial design was both majestic and massive. The demolition of the hotel had already begun. It would take more than a year to bring Maria's dream to a reality. It was to be a year of many changes for Hector and Maria.

CHAPTER 16

Catching a Heel

The present
Puerto Penasco, Mexico

Hector went to work early Friday morning. However, he couldn't concentrate on the steel business. Excitement and dread grew equally as the biggest payday yet drew closer. They were not going to get fifteen million dollars for each girl. But ten million for the Arthur girl was not out of the question.

It had been Maria's idea to specifically target the families of those who made the Forbes Five Hundred list. In 2006 and 07, Walter Arthur had appeared on the list with assets that totaled just north of three quarters of a billion dollars. By 2008, the economy and collapsed housing market hit the home building magnate hard and he was no longer a consideration for the list. Rosa had dug deeply into the Arthur's finances. Castle Homes was building again. A few of his competitors hadn't weathered the storm as well as he had and Castle Homes was poised to become America's number one new home builder. It looked, for all the world, like Arthur would be back on the Forbes listing in no time.

Maria would be very pleased. Maybe he could talk her into that cruise up the Nile he had always wanted to take. The pyramids fascinated Hector. He'd been awed by the massive Pyramid of the Sun near Mexico City, however, the Great Pyramid of Giza was almost twice the size of it. Most likely though, they would take another trip to the Spanish Riviera. Maria loved it there and Hector loved making her happy.

During the last round of negotiations, Hector had dropped the ransom demands to ten million each. Rosa's research had confirmed that the Arthurs were good for that much. From the body language and facial reactions of FBI Agent Novak, Morales could tell that one more good push should get the job done. Since she'd seen the faces of his men, the Morrison girl would be of little ransom value other than as an extra incentive for the Arthurs.

He'd string the other gringo family along for a while, but the cute little blonde wasn't going home. It was time to start playing rough. He'd eventually sell the girl to the sex trade, but not before she had been of service to him and some of his friends. The Mayor had certainly earned a bonus with his help on the pier contract. You couldn't have too much good will built up with local law enforcement either. Chief of Police Ramirez enjoyed himself with the last girl and Hector had the DVD to prove it. More than a year had passed since they'd kept and sold a showgirl. Some of the natives were sure to be getting restless.

Hector's secure cell phone rang. The news wasn't good. Rosa had been routinely monitoring the American news channels, when suddenly her husband's picture splashed across one of the monitors. NBC had obtained exclusive information about one of the suspected kidnappers. Within minutes, several other stations were running their own versions of the now nationally prominent story. Pictures and video clips of the girls and the Arthurs were soon added to the story.

NBC stayed ahead of the pack by releasing Raul's name. Now that Raul had been identified, he would have to lay low and stay south of the border indefinitely. Fortunately, a large cowboy hat and dumb luck had prevented any clear images of Juan Carlos from being captured by the mall cameras. Photo enhancements hadn't given the locals much more than a very general description of the old cowboy.

Maybe it was a sign, Hector thought. First Juan Carlos had been seen by the Morrison girl and now this with Raul... He had worried that something like this might happen. These days there were cameras everywhere. Modern technology was making it harder to operate anonymously.

Now might be the perfect time for Morales Metals to expand. The large ransom could be used to open another branch, the first of many Hector imagined nationwide. Raul and Rosa could run a branch in Mexico City or possibly Merida on the east coast. He could go completely legitimate.

Of course, he'd have to run these ideas by Maria. It could take five or six years just to recover the costs of a new branch. He didn't think she'd be persuaded. Unless... Maybe he could think of a way to get her brother Nemo involved. What if the big man ran the warehouse? No, that wouldn't be good enough for Maria. He might be able to convince her if Nemo was to be the branch manager. Hector had a hard time imagining his old friend Nemo in a suit, but maybe, just maybe, Maria could.

First things first, he left his office. It was time to make the final push with the girls.

.   .   .

Uni Niño's Excelencia Academia was still dark and quiet when PB and Janet arrived at the combination daycare and pre-school earlier that morning. The timing for this part of the plan was critical. The highly-rated preschool was one of the few locations that the couple believed, with some certainty, their target would appear. One day of observation was not enough to know whether Maria Morales would do more shopping, spend another morning at the beauty salon, head directly to the spa for a massage or do any other of a myriad of possible activities that day. Taking the kids to school five days a week was a necessity, though.

Abducting Maria, at this point, had the added bonus of removing the children from the equation. After all, they were innocent. Janet and her husband had discussed this at length the night before and decided to spare them the trauma of being kidnapped, even though they would be additional leverage. There would have been far less public risk to take Hector's entire family in the privacy of their home, once he left for work that morning.

Another option would have been to wait for the woman of the house to return home, but time was of the essence. Maria might not return until the afternoon or later, for all they knew. They couldn't risk losing another day.

The Morrison family would be financially devastated if they paid out the ransom, and Emma was at serious risk of physical harm should the video demonstrations escalate. Janet and PB needed to step up their actions, for all of the Morrisons' sakes.

The plan was straight forward, but the execution quite tricky. All the couple had to do was subdue the driver of the car, replace him with PB and drive off with Maria. It also had to be done without the dozens of people dropping off their children witnessing the whole event. They also had to accomplish all this with the materials they had at hand, since there was no time to go shopping for props before the abduction.

At 8:38 am, the Morales' Town Car arrived at the school. Maria and Gabriella got out of the car and went inside. The

Town Car pulled away. As soon as it passed, Janet, dressed as a sales representative, walked across the street in front of the next car in the drop-off queue. She was carrying a stack of books and an easel loaded with large sheets of paper that they had borrowed from their condo's supply room. As she stepped onto the sidewalk in front of the Academia she caught her heel. The easel flew into the air releasing the large colorful sheets of paper everywhere. The would-be school supply sales representative made a big production of maintaining her balance while juggling the books. Soon they were flying through the air as well.

All eyes were on Janet as PB forced the Town Car, now at the end of the block, to pull over at gun point. He quickly zip tied hands and feet and then taped the driver's mouth, before forcing the man onto the floor of the passenger side of the front seat. Already dressed in black, as the driver had been in previous days, PB borrowed the man's hat and sunglasses. He took the driver's place and resumed the return route to pick up Mrs. Morales.

By the time Gabriela's mother came out of the school, several people were helping Janet recover the books and scattered papers. No one, including Maria, paid the driver any attention. Anyone looking closely may have noticed him shielding his face from view, or that he was wearing a shear stocking under the hat and sunglasses. Thanks to Janet, he remained unnoticed as he closed the rear door of the car, got quickly into the driver's seat and drove off.

Thanks to all the kind helping hands, Janet had her supplies back under control. Feigning embarrassment, she hauled them quickly back to her car. Soon she was on the road, barely a minute behind the hi-jacked vehicle. A couple of turns later, the Town Car sat right where it was supposed to be. Janet pulled up to the curb behind it. The rest of the street was empty. She removed the light-colored suit jacket revealing a black pullover. Her pants and shoes were also black. Taking one last look around to be sure they were still alone, she added a shear stocking and a gun to complete her transformation from school-supply saleswoman into kidnapping accomplice.

Mrs. Reese joined Mrs. Morales, who was already staring up the barrel of a gun, in the back seat of the luxury automobile.

With his wife in place PB resumed driving duties. The Town Car soon rolled to a stop at the side door of the Morales mansion. Janet kept her gun trained on Maria while PB found a suitable holding location for the driver. He then entered the house and rounded up the staff. The upstairs maid, the downstairs maid and the cook were herded into the garage to keep the driver company. Once they were secured and properly gagged, PB helped escort Maria into her home.

Part two of the plan was about to begin. They worked quickly. Using smart phone cameras, the couple set about making a ransom video of their own.

CHAPTER 17

Back at the Ranch

Early Friday morning
The Morales ranch, Mexico

Most of the doll's twine was bright red. That wasn't ideal. However the legs, arms and head had all been woven with white twine. Emma had tied together a long enough rope to reach all the way across the room from corner to corner. She used the red twine at the ends of her rope and the white made up the middle.

Earlier that morning, she had coiled up the rope and tucked it under her shirt. She walked across the room and sat down on the commode. Emma looped one of the red ends around the base of the porcelain toilet. Trying hard not to be too overt about it, she tied a secure knot. She trudged slowly back to her cot, allowing coils to drop as she went.

Emma lay down on her cot, rolled against the wall and started to pull the rope taught. The cot, bolted to the floor, made an excellent anchor. Keeping the rope tight and tying it with one hand had been challenging. However, after ten nerve-racking minutes, she finally managed the feat.

She looked over her handy work. A foot and a half of the red rope peaked past the low concrete privacy wall. There was nothing she could do about that now, except hope that it wouldn't be noticed. She'd just had enough rope to tie a solid knot to the far inside leg of the cot. The cot itself completely hid the red twine at this end of the rope. As Emma had hoped, hanging six inches above the white concrete floor, her trip line was barely visible.

One of the men would arrive with breakfast soon. Emma needed to wake Monica and share her escape plan. Emma left her cot and sat down on Monica's. She put her hand on the other girl's hip and rocked it gently. Groggy brown eyes slowly opened.

"Wake up, Monica," Emma whispered. "We're getting out of here this morning."

Monica sat right up at the news. She looked over at the door, which she discovered to be tightly shut. Her disappointed eyes turned to the other girl.

"What are you talking about?"

"The plan," Emma explained quietly. "I came up with a plan."

Monica looked skeptical but didn't say anything. Emma leaned close and continued.

"When one of the men, it doesn't matter which, brings in our breakfast..."

"If I see another bean, I'm going to explode!" Monica interrupted.

"He'll trip on the rope," Emma ignored Monica's comment and continued laying out the plan. She nodded subtly towards the floor. It took Monica a few seconds to spot the braided twine.

"Poor Mini Emma," Monica stated, and then asked. "You got all that from the doll?"

Emma nodded, "Then we jump him, tie him up and run away."

"You've got even more rope?"

"No," Emma responded proudly. "But I used quick release knots on the trip rope."

"Let me guess, Girl Scout?" Monica asked.

"Campfire Girl," her friend shrugged, "for five years."

"I don't know about this, Emma," Monica told her. "If it doesn't work, they might get pretty angry."

"It will work!" Emma exclaimed her voice louder than she wanted. Then she whispered, "It has to work."

Before they could discuss the plan any further, they heard the door locks slide open. Emma jumped over to her cot, sat on the end of it and readied herself. Monica took a deep breath and mirrored her friend's position.

The door opened. The clothes and slight body told Emma immediately that it was the older man; the creepy one that was crushing on her. Come on, come on, she thought to herself, willing him to fall. She tried her best to smile innocently as he entered the room. He was carrying two paper plates.

He took one step towards the girls. Time seemed to slow to a crawl. Then he took another.

This is it, Emma thought, as his foot neared the rope. Then time jumped to hyper speed. The plates of food flew from his hands as the old man took a nose dive forward. Before he hit the floor both girls pounced. A loud grunt escaped his lips as they landed on him. Emma had hold of his legs, while Monica had one knee on the man's neck and the other jammed into his lower back.

"Get the rope!" Monica shouted as she got control of an arm and twisted it back.

Emma rolled off him and quickly snaked her way to the base of the toilet. She tugged the red end of the rope. It released just as it was supposed to. A second later she began hog-tying her tormentor. Fifteen seconds from trip to tied. It reminded Emma of the calf roping event she'd watched at the

Calgary Stampede the year before. She had always hoped the calf would get away. But not this time.

Monica wiped some breakfast beans from her pants. "I knew it!"

"Que pasa?" a loud angry voice filled the room.

The girls looked up in unison to see the younger kidnapper pointing a gun at them. The jig was up. He waved the gun at them and they moved away from their prisoner to the back of the cell. Victory had been short lived.

"Esta herido?" Raul leaned over Juan Carlos and asked if he was hurt.

"Estoy bien," Juan Carlos nodded, as he replied in a shaky voice.

Raul looked at the rat's nest of twine around his friend's hands and feet. He couldn't untangle that mess with one hand. He stepped back and pointed the gun directly at Emma.

"Remove the rope," he spoke in heavily accented English.

Emma did as she was told. Once the older man's hands and feet were free, he slowly stood. He turned around. Emma could see the hurt in his eyes through the balaclava. He had given her a gift and she betrayed him. She backed away as he gathered up the unraveled twine. He tugged at the end still tied to the bedpost. Emma climbed onto the cot and reached under to untie it. Carrying a jumbled bundle of twine, the old man shuffled out of the cell. His partner backed out behind him. The cell door closed and locked. Angry Spanish words filtered through the thick walls of the cell, as the younger man shouted at the other.

Monica stood still as a ghost, staring through glazed eyes at the closed door. The blood had drained from her face. Emma could see that her friend's unshakeable belief that they'd somehow be okay had died.

"Oh, my God," Emma whispered, "I've killed us both."

"We're not going home," tears spilled from Monica's eyes, finally turning to her cellmate, "are we?"

"I'm so sorry," Emma said, as they fell against each other for support.

The girls clung together for a long time, fearing that the wrath beyond the wall would be turned against them at any moment.

CHAPTER 18

Money Talks

November 18, 1982
London, England

Darby Penrod had hung around with the wrong crowd in high school. The rebellious teen added tattoos, piercings and bleached white hair to enhance the dark gothic style she'd adopted. Relatives and former friends barely recognized her anymore. Her frustrated parents had no idea what happened to their quiet little girl. Shortly after Darby turned seventeen, she left her parents' middle class home in Birmingham and moved to a seedy part of Soho with her new twenty-year-old boyfriend, Teddy.

Drugs and theft became a part of her life. The day before her eighteenth birthday, Darby and Teddy were arrested on a breaking and entering charge. Teddy had several priors.

Good fortune shone on Miss Penrod. The charges would be dropped provided that the young woman join Alcoholics Anonymous and clean up her act. Seeing glimpses of their former daughter emerge, Darby's parents welcomed her home and she took advantage of the opportunity. Eight years and a lot of hard work later, Police Officer Darby Penrod was now working in the Vice Division, for the very group that had once arrested her.

A few months earlier, she'd reconnected with a former neighbor and school chum. Both shared a common interest in law enforcement.

"Most of the Johns that I arrest," Darby paused to take a drink from the orange juice she'd brought with her, "believe that what they are doing is a victimless crime."

"I can see how they could think that," Janet Porter replied, then took a sip from her steaming coffee. The two women had been meeting a couple mornings a week since they'd bumped into each other while visiting their parents, who lived just two doors apart.

They met at Piccadilly Square, near a coffee vender, Tuesday and Thursday mornings at seven o'clock. Janet was on her way into work, while Darby had just finished a shift. It was quiet this time of day, before the shops opened and the droves of tourists were still in bed.

"It never occurs to any of these blokes," Darby continued, "to find out if the girl is there of her own free will."

"Don't ask, don't tell," Janet added. "They don't want to know."

"All they really worry about," Darby agreed, "is that the little woman at home doesn't find out."

Janet checked her watch. It was 7:40 am. "Well, I guess I'd better get to my desk." There was annoyance in her voice when she added, "reports don't file themselves, you know." She envied Darby who was out on the streets making a difference.

"Hey, do you think you can get away later?" Darby finished her orange juice and stood. "After lunch they're deposing Madam Woo at the station." The legendary London Madam had run a successful call girl business for twenty years before being shut down. In exchange for immunity she would tell all.

"Won't you still be asleep?" Janet asked.

"I wouldn't miss that interview for the world," reported Darby. "Full disclosure, Sweetheart. Names will be named!"

"I'd bet that a few gentlemen around town didn't get much sleep last night," Janet smiled.

"A safe bet, to be sure." Officer Penrod stifled a yawn. "See you at one o'clock, if you can make it."

"I'll try," Janet said as they exchanged a light hug and then hurried off in separate directions.

By the time the Interpol desk jockey managed to make it to the deposition, the crowd had begun to thin out. Judges, Senators, a few footballers, a former Police Chief, two well-known movie stars and several other local celebrities had already been named as clients by the diminutive madam. Janet was able to slide in next to Darby, three rows from the front.

She'd seen Madam Woo's face plastered all over the front pages of several newspapers, but only the back of the woman's head was visible from where they sat. She could see the faces of the three magistrates that were deposing Woo. They sat, in robes and wigs, behind a huge walnut desk on a slightly-raised platform. This made the small woman sitting, on a single wooden chair with a small side table, in front of them look very tiny and frail by comparison.

"You missed all the juicy stuff," Darby whispered. "They're down to the nuts and bolts of the operation now." Janet nodded, happy to have not missed the entire thing.

"Have you ever owned or kept any women against their will for the purpose of prostitution?" The youngest of the magistrates posed a question that seemed to stun the older woman for a moment.

"Yes," she answered, after a number of seconds slid slowly by. "In the late seventies demand was exceeding my normal resources. I purchased a dozen young women. I've always regretted that decision. After I recouped my investment, I set the girls free." Her voice turned soft and seductive, with a cultured London accent, as she added with some pride, "Two of these girls stayed on with me for a few more years."

"Just how much is the life of a young woman worth?" the magistrate asked.

"I won't answer that question, young man."

"I'm sorry if I offended you," he had a syrupy voice of his own. "Let me rephrase the question. From strictly a business point of view, what is the going rate for a new girl, just off the boat?"

"I paid three hundred thousand pounds each," she answered with no hesitation, "give or take, depending on the face and body."

"That seems like a pretty big investment," he responded. "How long does it take to get that money back?"

"Two and a half years," she told him, "when you factor in expenses."

"You seem to have a very good understanding of this whole business," the young magistrate pointed out.

"I recently had an organization pitch the merits of ownership," she clarified. "They were very professional and had run the numbers. They even brought along samples," Woo said. "But as I told you earlier, that part of the business is not for me, any longer."

"You said that they ran the numbers for you," the oldest of the magistrates, seated in the center of the group spoke up. "Could you tell us what you remember of their presentation?"

"I'll do my best, Your Honor." Madam Woo answered. "First, they spoke about product shelf life. Their merchandise was of the highest quality in the industry and would last seven to ten years, which according to them was at least two years longer than average." The woman paused to take a sip of ice water from a glass that rested on the small table beside her.

"One could expect a return of one hundred thirty thousand pounds, after expenses, in the first year," she recounted. "They factored in diminishing revenues of fifteen percent per year, thereafter."

"Could you elaborate on the expenses involved?" the center magistrate asked. Of the panel, he appeared to be the most engaged by this line of questioning.

"I don't remember the numbers that they used," she began, "however, in addition to the security and transportation normally supplied to an employee, these girls would also require clothing, food, drugs, housing and around-the-clock supervision."

Darby leaned toward Janet and whispered, "That appears to be it for juicy details. I'm going back to my flat to try and catch a few more winks before my shift starts."

"Thanks for the invite, Darby," Janet whispered back, "I'm going to stay for a few more minutes."

"See you Thursday morning," Darby told her and quietly left.

Janet ended up staying another hour. She'd have stayed longer but the inquiry recessed for the day. Janet was much more interested in the workings of these organizations than who got caught with their pants down.

Madam Woo's testimony etched itself into the young Interpol employee's brain. One of the more interesting pieces of information came out during the last few minutes of testimony. There was a trade-in program offered by this mysterious human trafficking organization. After three years, the girls could be traded in towards new merchandise. Even Madam Woo had never heard of such a thing. A one hundred thousand pound credit towards the purchase of a new girl was offered, as a sort of performance guarantee. Which, of course, meant that refurbished products were also available.

WAYNE A D KERR

Janet couldn't help but wonder what the refurbishing involved. Madam Woo hadn't yet elaborated. Perhaps new tires, an engine tune-up and detail the chassis? 'Hey Boss, I sold the thirty-seven blonde and that brunette clunker from the back corner of the lot today. Yeah, I had to put new headlights on that one'. What was next, a lease program? These monsters had completely dehumanized the business they were engaged in. Someone needed to stop them. She knew that Interpol and many other organizations around the world were trying.

When asked about how Woo contacted this group, she told the panel that the organization had contacted her. After their presentation, they gave her a local phone number that would only be valid for forty-eight hours. She'd thrown it away a few days later, unused. The madam did not know who ran the organization, where they were based or how to contact them.

Janet returned to her desk, more determined than ever to get into the field and join the fight against human trafficking. People were not meant to be merchandise or livestock to be bought, sold or traded. Lives were being stolen and ruined every day and she was determined to try and stop this horrible business. Within a year, she got her chance and she made the best of it.

Even as successes against small players in the business began to pile up, the Interpol agent never forgot about the slick organization described by the London Madam. It took more than a year, but she finally dug up some intelligence on the group and learned that it was headed by an ethereal man known only as *the Austrian*. She set her sights firmly on him.

CHAPTER 19

Turnabout is Fair Play

The present
Puerto Penasco, Mexico

Later Friday morning, using one of the six burner phones purchased at a local pharmacy, PB called a friend of his in Montreal. "Luke, I need an untraceable call put through to the FBI."

"But of course, Mon ami," Luke, a former communications specialist with the Patricia's Light Infantry, responded. "Are you and Janet planning to visit Mary and me this summer?"

"The last week in June," PB told him.

"Excellent," Luke responded. "Ah, here we go. I'm connecting you now."

"Thank you, Luke."

"See you in June, PB." Luke's voice was replaced by ringing.

After answering quite a few questions and several transfers, PB was finally put through to Supervisory Special Agent Novak.

"Special Agent Novak I have some information that may help with the kidnapping case you are currently working on."

"Who am I speaking with?" Novak questioned the caller.

"You can call me John."

"Well, John, the case is progressing in the right direction, at this point, so I don't think your help will be necessary."

"I have the kidnapper's wife."

"What did you say?"

"You heard me correctly. I have the kidnapper's wife," PB repeated, careful not to use any names. "And if he would like to see her again, both girls need to be released unharmed within the next twenty-four hours."

"What the hell have you done?" Novak was incredulous. He got up from his desk in the mobile command center and checked to see who was watching him. His tech guys were busy and the families were back in the lounge area talking. He nonchalantly left the trailer.

"You have seriously jeopardized this whole operation, my friend!" he said angrily. "I had the situation under control. Now those girls are as good as dead!"

"I don't think so," PB calmly replied.

"Release the woman immediately and I might be able salvage this thing."

"Listen to me carefully Agent Novak," PB instructed, "I want you to get in touch with the kidnapper right now. There is a proof of life video, attached to an email in your inbox. You will pass it on to the kidnapper. I mean business!"

.   .   .

The line went dead in Novak's phone. The FBI agent poked the screen a few times.

"Caller identification unknown," a computerized voice spoke. After Novak pressed a couple more buttons, it added, "origin of call unknown."

"Damn it!" Novak said, as he killed the link to the FBI's automated telephone tracking system.

He rushed back inside and sat in front of his computer. Roger opened up his email inbox and was shocked to find an email from Interpol. He opened it.

It read, "Supervisory Special Agent Novak, I received this video from an anonymous source. We tried to trace its origin but had no success on that front. The content appears to be legitimate. I understand you are running the kidnapping case connected to it. If you have any trouble opening or viewing the attachment please contact me right away. I wish you good fortune in this matter. Best regards, Sarah Woodrow, Interpol Intelligence Officer."

In reality, Sarah had used Interpol's resources to scrub the video clean, rendering it untraceable by the American Federal Bureau of Investigation or any other agency.

After watching the attachment and recognizing Maria, the supervisory special agent rushed outside again for some fresh air. He paced for ten minutes, trying to decide how to proceed. This, on top of Raul's identification, was more than an omen. It might just be time to cut and run. Perhaps he should insist on delivering the ransom personally again. He considered the positives and negatives of ignoring the crazy man and the video. On the plus side, he'd have ten million dollars to add to his retirement fund. On the minus side, though, he'd be on the run from both the FBI and Hector Morales. Roger noted that his reputation was still intact, his children and mother were still proud of him and his career. That would change, forever, if he disappeared with the money.

For a few seconds he mulled over the idea of taking the kids with him. However, like every other time the thought had occurred to him, reality set in. As much as he would miss them, they were better off with their mother. He knew it and the kids knew it. Besides they would cramp his style. Bikinis and beaches were his consolation prize. *Poor me.*

Then the image of Nemesio Suarez appearing at his doorstep late one night came to him. It sent a shiver down his spine. He knew what he had to do.

.   .   .

Hector arrived at the ranch anxious to finish the negotiations. He was a little disappointed that there had been no takers for the Morrison girl after posting her online the day before. At four hundred and fifty thousand American dollars she was a bargain, undoubtedly the pick of the litter available right now. The economy was tight all over these days, though. Novak seemed to think they could have gotten close to a million out of the Morrison family. The FBI man didn't yet know about Juan Carlos' little screw up. The girl would not be going home at any price.

Hector couldn't afford to lose his whole crew at once, now that Raul had shown his face all over the mall security videos. Juan Carlos would have to be the point man on the northern side of the border, at least, for the time being. It had taken an hour for Hector to convince Maria that Raul still had some value. It was a good thing his wife didn't know that one of the girls had seen Juan Carlos' face, since she barely tolerated the quiet old cowboy as it was. Both Raul and Juan Carlos had worked for him since he started the Red Devils gang more than twenty years earlier. Hector missed the early days sometimes. Damn cartels...

Rosa emerged from the house as he got out of the truck. She looked unusually stressed.

"Mister Morales, Agent Novak wants you to make contact as soon as possible."

"We haven't even made today's video."

"He was very adamant," Rosa pointed out.

"Put together some footage of the girls crying in their cell after you connect me," Hector told her, then shook his head.

"I'll have some ready and cued up in about ten minutes." Rosa rushed back into the house.

Hector wasn't too worried. Novak had a tendency to get worked up about small details. Maybe the Morrisons hadn't put together the cash after all. An image of Emma in her pink lacy underwear popped into his head. Novak was still in the dark about her not returning. This might even be good news. The Morrisons could take the blame for losing their girl. No one would ever have to find out the real reason she did not come home.

Morales decided to keep the young blond around for a while. He'd have Rosa pull the girl off the market. The economy could only get better. Miss Morrison could be quite valuable in the meantime. There were a couple of city councilors he didn't have hooks into yet. Another judge wouldn't be a bad idea, either. He'd ask the Sheriff which to approach. He might even partake himself, although if Maria ever found out... He'd have to be careful. Make lemonade, he smiled to himself on the walk down to the barn.

Juan Carlos was inside braiding another halter. He stopped when Hector entered the barn. The old cowboy expected a tongue lashing.

"Good morning, Juan Carlos," Hector called to the older man. "Finish what you are doing there. We won't need the set dressed this morning."

Juan Carlos nodded, surprised at the boss man's good mood towards him. Raul must not have told him about the incident. Maybe Raul would not tell him at all. Juan Carlos had felt so embarrassed after explaining where the rope had come from. Raul had been right to yell at him. 'What was I thinking? I will do what Raul tells me to do. I'll forget about the pretty

American girl and find myself a good Mexican woman. She'll have to have all her teeth though, I insist upon that much'. He picked up the half-done halter. He was weaving a shiny black plastic twine into this braid and the new design was looking very sharp.

By the time that Hector got settled at the studio desk, Rosa had cued up video of the day the girls had arrived. Rosa was visible in a small frame in the upper corner of his monitor, just as he was in hers. Hector signaled that he was ready to begin. Rosa faded away and was replaced by Novak in the mobile command bus.

"Have you got my money?" Hector began, his own voice and image distorted by the built-in modulators.

"I have a video that you need to see before we proceed any further."

"You have a video for me," Hector laughed at the irony. "That's a new one."

Special Agent Novak pressed some buttons and was replaced on the monitor by a slender female figure. The hand-held camera jiggled as it moved closer to the subject: a blindfolded and gagged woman dressed only in black lacy underwear. The shivering woman looked familiar, but it couldn't be. Hector's heart sank as he swapped the image to a larger monitor. The woman was unmistakably his wife.

Hector was unable to move or speak. Anger flooded his mind. Whoever was responsible for this would pay dearly. Maria looked terrified. Slowly his rage gave way to helplessness as he recognized the absolute fear he had witnessed in the body language of many of his own victims. A horrifying thought chilled him to his marrow.

Where are my children? Are they safe? A fear, unlike he had ever before felt, stabbed at his heart. Immediately, he realized what he had been putting every parent through all these years as an agonizing helplessness began to overwhelm him. In the space of a few moments, Hector was ashamed of what he had become. He had previously justified his actions as just business. Hector suddenly regretted the power he had felt over all those people. In reality, he had been nothing more than a fear-monger, a terrorist. Just like all his victims' parents, Hector realized he would do whatever it took to make his family safe again.

Morales didn't know whether a few seconds or a few hours had passed when a voice came through the monitor.

"You will release Monica and Emma unharmed if you want to see your wife again."

Hector still couldn't speak. Instead, he cut off the transmission. He pulled his cell phone out of his pocket. Maybe this was some sort of trick. Maria and the children had been fine when he left the house only a few hours earlier. He hit speed dial one. The phone rang four times before going to voicemail. There he heard the same voice as on the monitor. "Don't bother leaving a message for Maria, she's tied up at the moment."

Hector screamed and threw the cell phone as hard as he could into the far wall.

Rosa's scared face filled the monitor. "Mister Morales, I think they might be in your house."

"What?"

"Look," Rosa said as her face was replaced with a still shot from the video.

At first, Hector saw nothing. Then Rosa zoomed in on the wall above Maria's head, until an ornate white marble light switch plate filled the screen. Hector recognized it immediately. His home was the only one in Mexico, possibly all of North America, with this type of switch plate. Maria had this one and the rest of the custom electrical covers throughout the house flown in from Italy.

"Get the police to my house right away!" he yelled at her, as he scrambled to his feet. "Wait!" He changed his mind. "First call Ali's school. I'll call Gaby's."

News of the children's safety was a great relief, but he could not shut out the haunting images of his shivering, terrified wife.

CHAPTER 20

Gringos

The present
Puerto Penasco, Mexico

Hector drove madly back to town and straight to the mansion, using every available horse power he could wring out of the performance engine. Police were all over the grounds. Morales spotted Chief of Police, Jesus Ramirez in one of the cars, and ran over to him.

"Is there any sign of Maria?"

Ramirez looked at him strangely. Hector realized he was still in his old man disguise.

"It's me," Hector exclaimed as he ripped off the gray wig and mustache.

"Hector, my friend," the Police Chief responded after quickly getting over his confusion at the disguise, "I am so sorry. We found only your driver and two of your housekeepers. They were tied up and locked in the garage."

"No sign of..." Hector choked as he tried to say his wife's name.

"No," Ramirez shook his head. "I have forensics combing the property." Police Chief Ramirez, wearing a very expensive watch and shoes, pulled Hector off to the side and removed a Polaroid photo from his pocket. "This was taped to the inside of the front door," he explained as he held it out to Hector.

An eye for an eye was written in red crayon across it. Morales angrily snatched the photo of Maria in her underwear from Ramirez and crumpled it.

"How could this have happened?" Hector asked, as much to himself as to the man beside him.

"According to your driver," Ramirez explained, "it was two gringos, an American man and woman wearing masks, who took your family."

"I want this city torn apart!"

"We'll do everything we can. But it is the tourist season."

"I don't care!" Hector demanded. "Have your men turn over every grain of sand if need be. I want my wife found!"

Hector made a show of storming back to the truck. Deep down inside, however, he felt sick and weak. He needed his wife back. His life had been so empty before Maria. He'd give everything up for her. He stared through the windshield at the house he'd built, wanting nothing more than another meal, movie or board game together with Maria and the kids. He knew, deep down, that he was done with the kidnapping business.

"Dear God," el Pequeño Diablo prayed for the first time since he was a child, as he drove off to pick up his own precious children, "I promise to never harm another person, as long as I live, if you'll just bring my children's mother back to me."

PB had removed the batteries before throwing the burner phone away. He drove back and found a good vantage point near the Morales mansion. He wanted to see Hector's return. An hour later, the police swarmed the place. PB was certain that every available cop in the city was there.

Three quarters of an hour after that, he was rewarded with the arrival of the Datsun. An old man jumped out of the truck and ran directly to the closest police car. PB watched as Hector stripped off his disguise and spoke with the chief of police. A few minutes later, Hector ran back to the Datsun, sat in it for a few minutes and then sped away.

PB followed Hector long enough to be sure that he didn't return to the building behind Morales Metals, where Janet held their hostage.

PB parked the rental car back at the Condo and carefully made his way to the abandoned metal shop. Once inside, he pulled on the stocking and entered the office where Janet was guarding Maria Morales.

Their hostage was now fully clothed. Her hands and feet were bound with zip ties. The blindfold and tape over her mouth had been removed. A bottle of water sat unopened on a flimsy card table in front of her. Now confident that she wasn't about to die, Maria sat rigidly on a dusty crate, with a smug look of defiance on her face.

"Is everything going okay?" PB asked in English.

"Fine," Janet answered and nodded towards Maria, "but this one is a real piece of work."

As if on cue, Maria spoke at PB in Spanish. "You have made a terrible mistake, Gringo. If you don't let me go immediately you will die a slow and horrible death at the hands of my husband."

"I'm sorry that it had to come to this, but your husband is a murderer who kidnaps and tortures young women for profit," PB answered in Spanish.

"Spoiled little bitches that live in a decadent world," Maria spat back.

"How ironic of you, Mrs. Morales," PB shook his head. "Don't forget, we've seen the poor, humble dwelling you call home."

"I'll be back in my beautiful house soon enough and you both will be in the cold ground."

PB grabbed the roll of tape and re-covered the woman's mouth. He had heard enough from Maria Morales. She knew exactly what her husband did and was. The woman was certainly no innocent bystander.

"An entire family of psychopaths," Janet commented. "Mother, father and uncle; their poor children don't have a chance."

"There is always hope," PB shook his head, "but right now, we have to worry about saving Emma and Monica."

"How did things go on your end?"

"Every policeman in town swarmed the mansion," PB reported. "Then Morales showed up. He was driving the pickup and still in disguise."

"Good," Janet said relieved. "I was afraid that he might be happy to be rid of her."

"There is no accounting for taste," PB said, glancing at the muffled woman. "Morales appeared to be genuinely upset."

"Let's hope so," Janet replied.

"In an hour, I'll call with the exchange details," PB told her. "Then we'll know for sure."

CHAPTER 21

The First Cut is the Deepest

October 20, 1985
Northern Iraqi Border

The Kurdish region of Iraq borders Turkey to the north, Iran to the east, Syria to the west and of course it had never really gotten along with the rest of Iraq to the south. Skirmishes, battles, wars and genocide have been a way of life since prehistoric times. Neanderthal skeletons, dating back seventy thousand years give or take about ten thousand, had been discovered in the nearby Zagros Mountains. Survival had not been easy for anyone living in this area, ever.

The Princess Patricia's Special Forces unit was stationed at a temporary medical facility outside a small village located forty kilometers west of the city of Zakho. "Roughly a Terry Bradshaw Hail Mary pass from the Turkish border," Sergeant St Jean had joked shortly after they arrived. The village was also just five kilometers from Syria.

An outbreak of tuberculosis in the region brought assistance from the Red Cross. This had not gone over well with a few of the fundamental religious groups. They were opposed to outside help and definitely against the use of Western medicine.

Having already warded off two attacks on the facility, the Pats were on high alert. PB and Bobby patrolled the perimeter. The ambient light of the impending dawn worked at chasing away the darkness. The chill from the previous night wouldn't disappear from the air until the sun had fully risen. Bobby kept an eye on the village side of the facility, while PB swept through the rugged hills on the Turkish side.

Some movement caught PB's attention near some boulders about fifty meters to his left. He spoke softly into his mike.

"I've got some movement on the northwest corner. I'm going to check it out."

"Keep me posted," Bobby replied.

The team carried Canadian-made versions of the British-designed Sterling Mark Five machine guns while on patrol. The suppressed guns were light, quiet and quite accurate. Recently promoted, Master Corporal Reese readied his as he approached the boulders. He slipped silently around the largest of them. On the other side PB found three black and white goats and an old man watching over them. He relaxed and lowered his weapon.

"All clear," he reported to Bobby. "It's just a few goats getting an early breakfast."

"Breakfast sounds pretty good to me," Bobby, the unit's unofficial cook, replied. "One more sweep and I'll head in and get it started."

"Roger that." PB nodded at the old shepherd and then headed back to resume patrolling.

.   .   .

Jalal Ali Qarif shook his head. If you wanted something done right you had to do it yourself. He'd sent his son and nephew to steal supplies and scare off the infidels twice. Both times, they had returned empty-handed and unsuccessful. Not only that, both his protégés returned with injuries the second time.

A rebel fighter his whole life, Jalal had more recently been teaching hand-to-hand combat in the rebel and terrorist camps as far away as Afghanistan. His prowess with a knife was something of legend. However, disagreements with most of the methods used by those he worked with, had driven Qarif to go out on his own. Now he could battle injustice as he saw fit. His two sons and a nephew were the extent of his organization. He'd left his youngest son at home to tend to the injured boys. Perhaps Houari, his eldest, was not yet ready to receive the prized knife that had been passed down by Jalal's own father, and by several generations before that.

The Red Cross encampment was guarded by only five soldiers. They had to eat and sleep, and therefore could not watch the entire complex all the time. Jalal would prove to the boys that this was a relatively simple task he had asked of them. Jalal's weathered and sun-beaten face, like many others in the harsh local climate, looked aged beyond his sixty-three years. His dark eyes, though, were clear and sharp. Beneath his clothes was the ageless lean, wiry body of a man who chose principles over comfort. He lived his life prepared at any moment to meet Allah face-to-face with no regrets and no excuses.

Several hours before sunrise Jalal rose from the simple cot he'd been sleeping in. He ate some goat cheese and flat bread, both made by a local woman from the village below the hills. The old shack he and his sons lived in had no adornments on the walls. There was no television or radio. The only modern conveniences in the home were a two-burner gas stove and a small Soviet-made ice chest, also powered by propane. A collection of handguns, rifles and knives were laid out neatly on the wooden kitchen table. The comforting smell of gun oil and wax told him that the boys had cleaned the weapons by candle light the night before. His fingers traced across them, in the dark room, taking inventory. He removed only his knife from the arsenal. Jalal had not lit a candle, or made the slightest sound, while he dressed. The fundamentalist chose to wear the loose cotton clothes and sandals of a goat herder rather than the combat attire he usually wore. His sons still slept as he rounded up their three goats and herded them down towards the village.

A couple of hours later Jalal was observing the large Red Cross tents from the top of a boulder that overlooked them and the village behind. Every few minutes, he tossed some grain from the small feed bag he had with him, down to the goats to keep them from wandering off. He was impressed by the vigilance of the two sentries below. Neither soldier had stopped during his rounds to smoke a cigarette or consume alcohol as many infidels were prone to do. These men were disciplined. Still, he was confident that he could get past and accomplish his goal of destroying the medical supplies. The soldier patrolling on this side of the tents began walking his way. He slid down the boulder and perched himself on a smaller rock just above the goats. He tossed out some more grain, laid the herding staff across his lap and assumed the role of goat herder. A few minutes later the soldier appeared in the clearing.

The young soldier saw what Jalal wanted him to see: an old man herding goats. The soldier relaxed, lowered his weapon, spoke into a small radio and nodded at him before leaving to continue his rounds. Jalal smiled. He would use this deception to his advantage. He was already planning to move the goats nearer the large tents, when he heard the faint scrape of a boot returning. He now had to assume that his ruse hadn't been successful. He flattened himself against the boulder at the entrance to the clearing.

PB had gone perhaps ten or twelve steps beyond the huge outcropping of rocks when it occurred to him that there was no vegetation growing behind those boulders. He had been through there several times previously; it was quite barren. Yet the goats had been busy nibbling at something on the ground. The old man must have tossed some grain out for them to feed on. There was no logical reason to be feeding the livestock grain back there on the cold hard rocks, the former farm boy realized. You would either move the animals to an area where they could graze on grass or feed them by hand at home. He went back for another look.

As he came into the clearing, the herder was no longer in sight. Before he could take another step something smashed into the machine gun, knocking it and his radio from his hands. He barely ducked away from what he now recognized as a wooden staff, this time aimed at his head. PB had to jump as it quickly came around again, this time low to sweep his feet out from under him. He leapt and contorted avoiding several jabs and strikes, in a matter of seconds. The old herder clearly knew how to use the simple weapon.

Finally, PB saw a chance to even the odds. This time instead of moving back out of the reach, he jumped forward using the leverage of the six foot staff to his favor. He absorbed the blunted power of the staff, as two-thirds of it swept past, at the same time he hammered down on the hands holding it. The clattering staff echoed loudly on the stone floor of the clearing as it bounced and cartwheeled away, just missing an unconcerned goat. PB grabbed for the old man, but he slid smoothly out of reach.

The soldier reached down and removed the combat knife from the sheath on his belt. The herder, PB realized, had been expressionless the whole time and certainly did not move like an old man. He also produced a long knife of his own from somewhere in his loose clothing. Then the herder smiled and ceremoniously bowed toward him. He did not appear to be at all concerned that they were now evenly matched weapon to weapon. The knife swung smoothly back and forth in front of the herder. His weight balanced evenly on the balls of his feet.

This time it was PB on the offensive. He attacked fast and furiously. Steel clashed, fists and feet were met by blocks and parries. A minute later both men circled each other watching for weaknesses and openings.

The herder lunged, his knife leading the way. PB saw that another move would follow it closely. He avoided the snap kick and launched a fist that glanced off the face of his opponent. The fight continued on like this for several minutes, one man's offense against the other's defense, then defense transitioning into offense and vice versa. PB had a slight advantage in speed and strength, but the anticipation and experience of the older man more than cancelled these.

The sun spilled over the horizon east of the village. The bright rays bounced in all directions off the light-colored rocks, providing good vision for the combatants. The goats had wisely moved out of the enclosed area providing the fighters with plenty of room to move.

When equals compete, they have no choice but to respect each other's abilities. Many times pushed by their rival to reach higher levels, like basketball greats, Magic Johnson and Larry Bird or Borg and McEnroe, of tennis fame. PB marveled at the grace of his opponent. The old man seemed to bend and slide out of the way of each attack. He was incredibly flexible and light on his feet. The bruises forming on PB's shins and forearms were testimony to the hidden power in the herder's smooth strikes.

It had become a game of chess. Attacks, counterattacks and traps were laid for each other. PB realized that his speed advantage was being thwarted by the superior anticipation of the herder. The herder was not tiring and PB could feel the heat of the day approaching. He knew that his heavier clothes and boots would eventually be a factor. The old man likely knew it, too. Perhaps he could use this to his advantage.

The younger man began to breathe heavier. He attacked less frequently, barely avoiding Jalal's recent knife thrusts.

This had been the lengthiest knife fight of Jalal's long life. He believed the impressive quickness would not save the younger man forever. He was proud of how well his old body was holding up. As they circled each other the soldier unclipped and tossed his helmet away. His hair was wet with sweat. The man was definitely getting tired. He now moved like his boots were getting heavy. However, Jalal had enough experience to know the fight was not over until only one man stood. He was reminded of an old saying his grandfather had told him as a child. "Even a sleeping bear could kill you if you got too close."

The master knife fighter was truly enjoying the spirited contest. It had been many years since he'd faced anyone, including his own sons, with such potential. Throughout the fight, he noticed the soldier's technique adapting and improving. This one learned fast. The young man was impressive. Given the proper instruction and training his worthy opponent could possibly even rival Jalal, one day. That, however, was not an option. It was a pity that Allah would be their only witness today. The boys, especially Houari, could have learned a great deal from watching a fight such as this.

Jalal could sense that the fight would end soon, though. He launched another attack. He faked a kick at the shin, closely followed by a knee aimed at the groin. He then sent a convincing fist towards the soldier's gut. All of his opponent's slowing defenses were now committed to his lower body. Jalal thrust his treasured knife directly at the unprotected left eye of the soldier. What a glorious ending for this dance with death. Praise be to Allah, he thought.

"No, this was not possible!" Jalal's mind screamed.

The soldier had tipped his head back, the knife blade barely missing his cornea. The finely-honed edge sliced through the young man's eyebrow and across his forehead, instead of plowing into his brain. Jalal knew in that instant that the young soldier had seen through all the fakes and left a trap for him. He felt the point of the soldier's blade drive home. It pierced his heart. The student had become the master. Most impressive!

PB staggered back. Blood gushed from the herder's chest. The old man sank to his knees. He looked up at PB. A slight mystical smile crossed his lips. Jalal held out his knife handle first, as if offering it to the younger man, and then toppled forward, dead.

PB was at once filled with mixed emotions -- elation for surviving the fight, yet guilt from killing the old man. He knew it had been a kill or be killed situation, but he felt the guilt just the same. It was the first time he had taken a life this way. The Master Corporal bent over and picked up the knife that had fallen at his feet.

The twenty-five centimeter long double edged blade was as sharp as a razor. Though obviously old, it was perfectly preserved. There was a small polished black onyx hilt between the handle and the blade. PB noted the perfect balance of the weapon. It reminded him of a throwing knife. The ivory handle had Cyrillic letters carved ornately into it on both sides. PB would later have the writing translated. He'd discover that it read, "The truth of a man shall only be revealed during the dance with death."

PB didn't get much time to contemplate all that had transpired in the last twenty minutes. His best friend and teammate, Sergeant Bobby St. Jean, came around the boulders into the clearing.

"I've been trying to get hold of you," his voice cut out as he spotted the large pool of blood and motionless body in the middle of the clearing. He looked over at PB, blood flowing freely from the long wound across his brow. Bobby rushed over to check his friend's injuries. "Are you all right?" he asked. "This looks pretty bad. You'll need stitches."

PB shrugged. He hadn't noticed any pain from the gash across his forehead.

There were no more attacks on the Red Cross medical facility after the death of Jalal Ali Qarif. Once locals identified the body, word quickly spread of him being bested in a knife fight. The Canadian soldiers were thereafter afforded a great deal of respect in this region where fighting was a way of life.

CHAPTER 22

Dig Two Graves

The present
Puerto Panasca, Mexico

Rage seethed and boiled inside Maria, occasionally bubbling over. Ten days had passed since her abduction. Hiring a new driver was just one of the many things proving to be difficult. There had been three hires and three firings already. That morning after dropping the kids off at school, she'd finally gone out to do some shopping. Even that had been ruined. Maria drove herself to Ali's school for the second time that morning. She'd been called in by the principal. Alejandro had gotten into a fight at recess with another third grader. After a humiliating meeting with the other boy's mother in the principal's office, Maria drove her suspended son home. She sent him to his room immediately after they arrived.

Mrs. Morales felt like her world was falling apart. Rumors regarding her abduction swirled all over the small city. Now, even the children at her kid's school were talking about her. Maria did not want to leave the mansion. It seemed like weeks since she'd been to the club for a massage. She could feel everyone staring at her wherever she went.

To add insult to injury, Hector was acting as if nothing had happened. He kept spouting some nonsense about this being an opportunity for them to go legitimate. He would not even talk about her abduction. Maria needed information. This could not stand. Half the policemen in town had seen that horrid picture of Maria tied up in her underwear. This morning with Ali was the last straw.

"Lorena," she called to the new downstairs housekeeper, "I'm going out. Take a sandwich up to Ali at lunch time."

"Yes, Mrs. Morales," Lorena answered, just before the front door slammed.

Maria climbed into her SLK and drove off the property again. This time she was headed out of town.

Hector had only just returned from a long lunch. He was in his office going over plans to open the new branch in Merida when Maria burst in.

"You weren't going to tell me, were you?"

Hector got up from his desk nervously and didn't say anything. Maria looked furious. He wondered what she was upset about, but did not want to speculate.

"I made a trip out to the ranch this morning and spoke with Rosa."

Two days earlier, Novak had called the ranch and revealed his discovery about the couple that had taken Maria. Hector had decided not to do anything with the information. Since her kidnapping, he had lost his stomach for violence. Getting his wife back safely was all that had mattered to him. Though he hadn't yet shared his new plans with anyone, he had decided to give the ranch to Juan Carlos and send Rosa and Raul to the east coast to run a new branch.

"You know who did this to me," she glared at her husband, "and yet you have done nothing!"

She stared at him, waiting for an explanation. Several seconds passed without a response.

"You used to be feared far and wide. No one messed with El Diablo," Maria said.

"I just want to put this all behind us," he finally spoke. He walked to her and put his hand on her shoulder. "As I've told you, this can be a second chance for us. A whole new life can begin for our family."

"The entire town is whispering and laughing behind our backs," she said, as she stepped away.

"No one is laughing at us, my love." He stepped closer again, trying to comfort her.

"What has happened to you?" She looked at him with disdain. "Even your eight-year-old son is more of a man than you!"

"Is Ali all right?"

"He's fine," she told him. "There was a minor scuffle at school today. Ali defended my honor -- something you refuse to do."

"Maria," Hector tried to reason with her, "Revenge is not the answer."

"We must make an example of these people, Hector," she demanded. "Without respect we have nothing!"

"We can get respect in many different ways," he tried to explain. "We can go legit."

"If you are too much of a coward to make things right," her coal black eyes flashed, "I will show everyone that there is still a devil in this family to fear!" Maria stomped out of his office.

"Maria, Maria, revenge is not the answer," Hector called after her, but knew she wouldn't stop. He swept the Merida plans off his desk in frustration. He hated the fact that he had developed a conscience but it was there now and it wouldn't leave. He truly did not want to hurt anyone ever again. Hector also realized that Maria would never let this go. He also knew, in his recently enlarged heart, that this could end badly. Revenge is a dangerous game, especially if you rush into it. Maria needed his help. He would do this, if need be, for his wife. Then he would get back to his new business plan.

"Before you embark on a journey of revenge, first dig two graves," Hector recited to himself, as he ran down the office hallway. A shudder ran through him, as he remembered that fateful day when he last set out on a quest for revenge. He'd almost lost everything he'd cared about, including Maria. Only dumb luck had saved them that day all those years ago. Hector remembered it as though it had happened yesterday...

News of his mother's death somehow found its way from the east coast to the west coast of Mexico. Though television broadcasts had yet to release any names, reporting that it appeared to be a drug-related homicide, Hector already had confirmation. Street sources confirmed that she was dead and the man she'd been living with was missing. The police didn't have any evidence that he'd been involved, other than someone matching his description had been seen fleeing from the scene.

Though Morales had hated the bitch since she left, and refused any contact from her, revenge was a matter of principle. Hector needed to get his hands on Ramon Sanchez before the police. The miserable bastard had stolen his mother from him and now he'd killed her. Hector wanted the man's head on a stick. If anyone could find Sanchez it was Buscador.

Fernanda Maria Diaz awoke as the plane touched down in Chetumal. She hadn't been able to get a direct flight to Villahermosa on such short notice, but Chetumal was just over an hour away by car. Fernanda had vague memories of her Aunt Sofia. She'd been only four years old when Hector's mother left the family. Fernanda had very little to go on, since she hadn't seen her aunt since and she had never met Ramon Sanchez. This didn't concern her. She was confident something would lead her to him.

Hector's cousin, Fernanda, was the family seeker. Her father, Dante Diaz, had been one of Hector's top lieutenants until he was killed during a drug trade that had gone south. Her boyfriend also worked for Hector, in product acquisitions. Rodrigo knew more about pot than anyone she'd ever met. Though Fernanda didn't smoke anything, they got along amazingly well.

Cute, but not beautiful, average height and weight, though somewhat less curvy than most latinas, she hadn't been noticed by many men. Unremarkable in almost every other way, Fernanda's nickname within the gang was Buscador because of her amazing tracking ability. She could find anyone, anywhere. Like an FBI profiler she seemed able to get into the mind of her quarry. On a couple of occasions she'd gotten to where they were going before they had. She would ferret out clues from the people and things left behind by runners, which others didn't notice. In the cash-laden drug business, it seemed like someone was always trying to disappear with some of it. After several unsuccessful attempts over the years, most of Hector's employees knew better.

A postcard in the back of a drawer at the abandoned crime scene, sent Buscador north along the east coast. Two days later, she spotted Ramon.

Buscador had gotten a room at the Progreso Hotel. It was right on the beach and had a wonderful view of the pier that had been displayed on the postcard.

After watching him toss a bouquet of colorful flowers, one by one into the ocean, Buscador followed her target to a fleabag motel several blocks in from the shore. Ramon wasn't behaving like any of the previous runners she'd tracked down.

He looked like a man in mourning. Fernanda might have left him to grieve, but Buscador couldn't. She found a telephone outside a nearby pharmacy.

"I've found him," she reported to her cousin, without preamble. Though, they were the same age and went to the same schools, Fernanda hadn't had much contact with Hector growing up. Then, like now, she'd kept her distance from el Pequeño Diablo whenever possible.

"Excellent," Hector responded. "Where are you?"

She gave him the details.

"I'll be there in the morning," he told her. "Don't let him slip away!"

She started to answer but he'd already hung up. Her cousin had always sent one of his men, often Nemo, when she'd found a runner before. Hector coming himself worried her more than if crazy Nemo were on his way. She decided not to go back to her room. She would watch the hotel entrance and the shiny, green Mazda MX-6 that looked out of place in the parking lot, until Hector arrived. Hector's temper was legendary and she didn't wish to be on the wrong side of it. Buscador grabbed a heavy sweatshirt, three diet colas and a few chocolate bars from the pharmacy. It would be a long night.

At 7:00 am a Jeep drove up to the hotel. Buscador was very surprised to see Hector alone inside. She thought he'd have brought some muscle with him. The tracker jumped out of the shadowed nook she'd tucked herself into, and ran to the Jeep. The driver's door opened and Hector slid across the bench seat to the passenger side. Buscador climbed in.

"I'm pretty certain that's his car there." She pointed her cold finger at the Mazda.

"Okay, pull in behind it," he instructed.

"He's staying in room 107," she said, nodding toward the motel.

"We'll take him when he comes out," Hector told her.

Buscador circled the small lot and drove in behind the green car.

They sat in silence for a long time. Finally, the head of the Morales gang spoke.

"Do you have a gun?" he asked.

"Yes," she simply answered.

"I'll need it," he told her.

"Of course," Buscador said and removed it and the holster from the small of her back.

"Thank you," he said, sliding the gun from the holster, flipping it open and spinning the cylinders to be sure it was fully loaded.

"Boss," Buscador began, not sure it was her place to give an opinion. "I don't think he did it."

"You don't think he did what?" Hector asked, as he rested the gun in his lap, the barrel pointed towards her.

"It's just that I've been to their house," she explained, very aware of the gun's position, "and I've observed Sanchez. It's just that he doesn't..."

"Stay in the car!" Hector interrupted, and got out of the jeep.

Sanchez had emerged from his hotel room. He was carrying his suitcase.

Ramon carefully watched the man coming across the street towards him. The well-tailored suit did not fit the profile of a cartel assassin or a policeman. The man was looking past him as if he wasn't even there almost as if he might be late for a meeting. Ramon continued toward his car. They crossed paths in the middle of the street. Ramon breathed a sigh of relief when the businessman continued past. One more flight from Cancun to Miami and then he could get lost forever in the United States. He set his bag down and reached into his pocket for the car keys. He felt a rough jab in his lower back. He knew immediately that it was a gun. He stiffened.

"Are you packing?" A gruff voice asked. Sanchez shook his head. "Forgive me if I don't trust you." A hand patted him down carefully, then grabbed his shirt collar and shoved him towards the black vehicle. "Open the back door and slide in." Sanchez did as he was told. The man in the suit slid in beside him, the gun now jammed into Sanchez's side.

"Buscador, get the suitcase and throw it in the back," Hector instructed.

When she got back in the car Ramon was begging for his life.

"You don't have to do this," he pleaded. "I was bringing the product back."

"You have the product with you?" Hector prodded, jamming the gun deeper into the man's ribs.

"Yes, it is all there, in the suitcase," Ramon admitted. "Please just call Diego so we can straighten this whole mess out."

There was a lot more going on here than just a domestic dispute, Morales realized. "Take us somewhere quiet," he instructed Buscador.

"No please," Sanchez begged, "this is all just a big mistake. I told her we couldn't do it. This wasn't my fault."

"Quiet," Hector commanded, "I need to think."

Buscador pulled away from the curb. She knew just where to go. She and Nemo had dealt with a pair of runners here, a couple of years earlier, the only other time she'd visited Progreso. A half an hour east of town, beyond the main roads and behind a small but rugged set of hills was a depleted and abandoned gravel pit. As they bounced along the unmaintained trail, Buscador was glad Hector had rented the Jeep. The drive out was done in silence. Twice she'd almost reached for the radio, twice she'd thought better of it. When they arrived, she guided the truck down the steep decline to the bottom of the man-made valley.

"I put a shovel in the back," Hector told Buscador, without taking his eyes off Ramon. "Get out, Sanchez."

The only noise in the desolate little valley was the crunching of their feet on the soft gravel surface as they stepped away from the vehicle. There was no shade available. Not yet eight in the morning, the heat was already rising. Ramon Sanchez's last day on the planet was going to be a hot one. Later in the day, twenty miles to the south, the northern tourists would almost melt during their must-see visit to the pyramids of Chichen Itza.

"That's far enough," Hector ordered. A glance from him, told Buscador to hand the shovel to Sanchez.

"Please, we just missed our flight," Sanchez pleaded. "That's all."

"Start digging!"

"Please," Ramon started to cry as he shoved the point of the spade into the ground. "This wasn't my fault." There was no sympathy in the eyes of the man with the gun. He glanced at the woman behind him. She believed him, he could tell.

"Dig!" Hector screamed. His angry voice echoed in the deep pit.

Hope faded and Ramon dug in silence for nearly ten minutes. Unfortunately, the digging went along easily and he was standing in a two-foot-deep oblong hole. Time was quickly running out.

"This is all just a big misunderstanding," Ramon said, dropping the shovel and standing up straight.

"Then why did you kill your wife?" Hector asked.

"I didn't kill her," Ramon answered, confusion evident in his voice. "I thought you did."

"Explain to me what happened that day," Hector told him, pointing the gun at Ramon's eyes to remind him to be truthful.

"Okay." The dig had given Ramon some time to collect his thoughts. "As you probably already know, my wife and I made monthly trips to Miami."

"You were mules?" Buscador interrupted from behind, trying to figure out what was going on. Hector gave her a withering look and she clamped her mouth shut.

"Do I know you?" Ramon asked. Something about the assassin's face seemed familiar.

"Get back to your explaining," Hector angrily waved the gun at him.

"Diego brought the drugs and airline tickets to the house, as usual," he continued. "But, then he asked us if we were interested in moving up north to Nogales. The cartel was about to take over an operation up there and they wanted some people who knew the area. I guess I must have mentioned that I used to be a salesman up that way. We told him we'd think about it. Anyway, as soon as he left, Sofia went crazy with worry. She told me that her son ran the drug trade in the Nogales area and that she needed to warn him. She tried to call him and when that didn't work she insisted that we go there in person. I tried to talk her out of it, but she was stubborn. I told her that her gangster son wasn't worth risking our lives for. We argued through the night. I finally relented. We'd missed our Miami flight by that time, so I went to a travel agent and got flights to Nogales and, from there, on to Miami. When I got back with the tickets..."

Ramon stopped talking and closed his eyes. The memory of his wife lying there covered in blood with her stomach split open buckled his knees. When he opened his eyes and looked up at the face above the gun, a revelation hit him.

He didn't recognize the man, but the eyes and chin looked very familiar. Like the eyes and chin of his dead wife.

"Oh my God," he cried out, "you're not with the cartel!"

"No, I'm not," Hector shook his head.

"You're Hector Morales." Ramon's face reddened. "This whole thing is your fault!" He scrambled to his feet. "You broke your mother's heart and then you got her killed!" Enraged, he leapt at his wife's ungrateful bastard of a son.

Already stunned by the rapid change in his prisoner and the accusation that he'd been responsible for his mother's death, Hector responded to the startling attack by pulling the trigger over and over until the revolver was empty.

Ramon crumpled in front of him. Hector flipped him over with his toe. One of the shots had killed the man instantly. He spit on the man that he believed had ruined his family, then rifled his pockets grabbing the wallet and car keys.

"Burying is too good for him. We'll leave him for the buzzards and coyotes," Hector told Buscador. He looked over at her just as some blood bubbled from her mouth and she dropped to her knees. One of Hector's bullets missed its original target, but had been fatal just the same, piercing Fernanda's lung. He rushed over to his cousin's side and gently lowered her to the ground.

Her lungs were rapidly filling with blood. She couldn't breathe, but managed to gasp out a last request, "Please bury us, Hector."

"Yes, of course," Hector assured her, nodding and caressing her hair until her pleading eyes closed for the last time. Fernanda spasmed twice and was gone. He laid her carefully into the existing grave and filled it in. He was going to leave Sanchez right there where he was, but remembered his promise to his dying cousin. Besides, if coyotes found Sanchez they'd certainly dig up Buscador. She didn't deserve that. He rolled up his sleeves and started digging.

Maybe he'd come back someday and give Fernanda a proper burial, he tried to convince himself, but knew that it was very risky to come back to a crime scene, even one as remote as this. He emptied out Ramon's suitcase. Mixed in with the clothes were two bundles of American money and sixteen cocaine pellets wrapped in rubber. Two ounce pellets that the bitch and the bastard would have swallowed to get past customs. His mother had turned into a God damned drug mule. At least, Hector had to admit, she was going to warn him about the cartel's plans.

Hector's eyes opened wide. She was going to warn him about the cartel! Hector realized he needed to get to a phone and alert everyone at home as soon as possible.

He tossed the suitcase and clothes into the hole and then rolled Sanchez in. Hector carefully wiped down the gun and dropped it into the grave, as well. He quickly filled in and packed down the shallow graves. Hector decided to hide the coke pellets somewhere else, just in case the bodies were somehow discovered.

He couldn't afford to be caught with them, any more than with a dead body. He drove the jeep out of the pit and over to a large rock at the base of a nearby hill. This would be an easy spot to find if he sent one of his men to retrieve the pellets. In his heart he knew that Fernanda was in her final resting spot, unless something did dig her up. A vision of a pack of coyotes tearing her apart flashed through his mind. He shook it away.

"Mother fucker!" Hector yelled at the top of his lungs, "Buscador, you should have stayed in the fuckin' car." He'd already decided that Ramon would get credit for killing her. He had the whole flight home to fill in the details of what had happened. Perhaps Rodrigo could find her body, before the coyotes, when he sent him for the coke.

Hector didn't know it, but Rodrigo was already dead, along with most of his other employees.

Hector stashed the cocaine quickly. He briefly thought about getting the new Mazda and driving it home, but realized that if Buscador could find it, the cartel probably would, too. He headed back toward Progreso, stopping at the first gas station he passed.

He tried calling the main compound, but there was no answer. That was not good. He called his house -- no one picked up there either, not even the housekeeper. El Diablo offered God his life for Maria's safety, as he jumped back into the Jeep and sped to the airport.

When Hector arrived in Nogales, he didn't have to explain Fernanda's disappearance to anyone. So many others were already dead and missing. Her family hoped she had fled, but months later when they still hadn't heard anything from her, they knew that the worst had befallen Fernanda, as well. Hector never told anyone the truth about Fernanda's death, not even to Maria. No one was ever sent to retrieve the drugs or his cousin's body.

Hector found his wife and brother-in-law hiding out at the cute little ranch he and Maria had purchased in the middle of nowhere. It was their secret getaway. They needed a safe place to store the bundles of American money that they accumulated faster than even Maria could spend. It had been her idea to buy the ranch for cash and leave the title in the former owner's name so it couldn't be traced back to Hector. Offering the owner twice the property's value, the farmer had agreed without hesitation.

Once Hector arrived, there was no stopping Nemo. Giving and receiving pain were still his favorite pastimes. His knowledge of the compounds, combined with his fearless attitude, helped him leave a wake of bodies behind. By the end of the day, he had killed seven and severely beaten five other cartel soldiers. Nemo returned that evening with a bullet lodged in his left shoulder, another had glanced off his right hip bone and there was a fresh knife-gash on his cheek. He felt better.

Maria had news for her husband. She found out from the doctor that she was pregnant. Hector had two things to live for now, Maria and the baby. He contacted the cartel. They agreed to let him live if he called off his *dog* and stayed out of the drug business. Two days later, Nemo returned to the ranch with Juan Carlos and Raul, the only other members of the gang that had survived.

Avenging his mother's death had almost cost Hector everything that was dear to him. From that day on, images of scavengers picking at and tearing Fernanda apart haunted his dreams. Hector had learned a valuable lesson that he desperately wanted to prevent Maria from discovering the hard way. As he burst through the front doors of his business in time to see the convertible and his wife speed away, Morales knew there would be no stopping her.

CHAPTER 23

New Girlfriend

Ten Days earlier
Nogales, Arizona

Juan Carlos crossed the border with a load of halters, a pile of old car parts and two unconscious girls well-hidden under it all. He leaned over and glanced into the mirror. He didn't recognize himself. The bushy mustache that had been a permanent resident on his upper lip for the last forty years was gone. Rosa had given him, what she had called a 'makeover'.

Raul had howled with laughter while she plucked his eyebrows and told him that this was the punishment for his foolishness with the doll. That had been humiliating enough, but then she'd taken away his favorite hat, his only hat, as a matter of fact. He'd gotten it at the Chihuahua Rodeo in 1985. A fair bareback rider in his youth, Juan Carlos had earned that hat, a few hundred pesos and a broken hip during his last rodeo as a competitor. Now an achy hip on cold mornings was his only memento left from those days. A store-bought haircut, annoyingly tight clothes and fancy new boots rounded out his new ensemble.

Rosa commented that there had been a handsome man hidden underneath all that grimy hair and old clothes. However, as far as Juan Carlos was concerned, he looked and felt ridiculous.

"New girlfriend," was all he'd told the border crossing guards this morning when they recognized the familiar truck, but not its driver. Rosa had coached him to say that, and she'd been right. The guards had nodded sympathetically and then promptly bent over with laughter as he drove away.

Don Juan Carlos, Rosa's new nickname for him, took a detour past his usual turn on the way to the swap meet on Palo Verde Road. Tucson's traffic was still very light this early in the morning.

Turning onto Contractor's Way, he drove to Illinois Avenue and then to the end of the road past the junk yards and scrap metal businesses. There was no one around yet. He turned the truck around and then pulled into the driveway of a company called Scrap Metal Incorporated. In the event anyone happened by, Juan Carlos removed the old steel fenders, hood and bumpers from the back of the truck and stacked them by the gate.

After one last good look around, to be certain he was alone, he pulled the girls from their hiding place and laid them down behind some old bins. Old habits die hard. Juan Carlos arranged the girls in the Yin and Yang formation. The old cowboy regretted not bringing his camera this morning. He touched Emma on the cheek and silently wished her well.

Working quickly, he cut the braided twine that had been used to tie their hands and feet, then covered them with a couple of old blankets. He got their cell phones from the glove compartment, reinserted the batteries into them and turned them on. Following Rosa's instructions, Juan Carlos punched in the ten digit number, she had made him memorize, on one of the phones and waited until someone answered the call. At that point, he put the phone down and left.

Raul usually handled this side of the job, but since he couldn't cross the border right now, it fell to Juan Carlos. It took him three tries to get the number plugged in while wearing his leather gloves, but he knew better than to remove them. The phone finally connected. On the second ring it was answered.

"Emma, are you alright?" A deep voice speaking English came through the small speaker. The cell phone had already been tossed onto the blanket-covered girls.

"Emma Morrison, are you there?" Supervisory Special Agent Novak asked as he raised his hand to get the attention of the two techs in the truck. He pulled the phone away from his mouth and ordered them to get a trace started. They had the location locked down in just over a minute.

Three and a half miles away, a Tucson Police patrol car, lights flashing and siren blaring, raced toward Illinois Avenue. Police Officer Tommy Mendez found the girls stirring under the blankets, dressed in the clothes they had disappeared in.

"I've got them!" he shouted excitedly into his radio. "They appear to be all right." Officer Mendez removed the tape from their mouths and helped the barely-conscious girls into his car.

Eleven minutes later Juan Carlos pulled into the swap meet parking lot. He was early, but not the first to arrive. A line of vendors was already forming outside the office, hoping to get the prime stalls for that day's meet.

.   .   .

Rosa brought a dish of Tamales and a can of diet Coke out to the barn for Hector. He'd been sitting at the desk staring at the empty monitors for three hours waiting for news about his wife. Juan Carlos had reported in thirty minutes earlier from the swap meet. Things had gone well on his end. All Hector could do now was wait.

"I'm sure we will hear something soon, Mister Morales."

Hector only grunted in response. He pushed the plate of food to the side of the desk. Rosa left him alone. His cell phone rang. The police chief's name showed on the caller ID. Finally...

"Have you found something?" Hector asked with both anticipation and fear in his voice.

"No, but we got an anonymous tip that your wife can be found in your parking spot."

Hector said nothing.

"I sent officers to both your house and business but she was in neither parking area."

"God damn it!" Hector pounded the desk with his fist. The plate of tamales clattered as it settled back on the surface. "Have you found my car?"

"No sir," the chief answered. "Perhaps the call was just a hoax. I just thought you should know about it, though."

Hector suddenly knew where Maria and the car were. He didn't know how it was possible, but he knew the truth. These people had somehow discovered the Bat Cave. "Yes, it is probably just a hoax. Keep looking for them."

"Of course we will, Mister Morales."

"Jesus," Hector added.

"Yes?" the police chief asked.

"I know you are doing everything possible. Thank you." Hector's voice softened just before he shut off the phone and ran out to his truck. The world brightened around him. The possibility of holding Maria, the love of his life, in his arms once again overwhelmed him. It was all he cared about. His life for hers was no contest. The possibility of losing her had changed Hector, forever. He felt it in his bones, in the soul he never knew he had. Hector jammed the gas pedal to the floor and raced back to Puerto Penasco.

CHAPTER 24

SSA Novak

Eight days after the hostage exchange
Tucson, Arizona

The girls had been back for more than a week. The Arthurs were happy. The Morrisons were happy. FBI Deputy Director Clarkson was happy. Supervisory Special Agent Novak was not happy. He would be leaving Tucson more than a million dollars lighter than expected. He could not wrap his head around the events that had turned the operation on its ear. He worried that his role in this and all the other kidnappings might soon be uncovered. He had managed to fight off the initial urge to get into his car and just disappear.

The Mobile Command Center and the techs were gone. Novak stayed behind in Tucson, ostensibly to have a nice visit with his mother. After the successful recovery of the girls, the Supervisory Special Agent had earned some rest and relaxation. He'd persevered all the back-slapping and congratulations on the job well done, now it was time to figure out what in the hell had really happened. The Interpol connection worried him the most. The Morales operation was blown. Someone had figured it out. Whoever that was, might just figure out his involvement, too.

Maybe it really was time to get out of Dodge! He thought about the Caribbean beaches he'd been dreaming of. Could he live the way he wanted on the four and a half million he had stashed in the Bahamas? At forty-five, he'd have to live like a hermit to make the money last. That wasn't the plan. He had a much larger lifestyle in mind. If Morales was done, he'd work with someone else. Or, maybe he should run his own program. He had a successful business model to copy. Why settle for ten percent? First things, first. He needed to know if he'd been compromised.

Who could have done this? A follow up call to Interpol had provided no useful information. Novak turned his attention to Walter Arthur. He had money. Maybe they had underestimated the owner of Castle Homes. A thorough background check had revealed nothing that suggested Walter Arthur had the knowledge or connections to pull off an operation like this. Arthur had dropped out of business school and gotten a job in construction at the age of twenty. Eventually, he became a carpenter's apprentice and later a journeyman carpenter. Over the years, he had gained a reputation for building good homes in Wisconsin and Michigan. He and Castle Homes had ridden the housing boom into national prominence. Novak found little else other than a few minor law suits by disgruntled customers and several speeding tickets interspersed through the years.

That left the Morrison family.

His earlier background and financial check had turned up nothing of particular interest about Ben Morrison. The man had turned a tennis scholarship with the Minnesota Gophers into a Bachelor's degree in Biology. He met his wife, Rita, then a basketball cheerleader and Arts and Science major at the University of Minnesota.

The two married after graduation, Ben got a job with General Mills and Rita stayed home raising the two children.

Ben finished his career as Vice President of Product Development at General Mills.

Robert Morrison had followed in his father's academic footsteps and now, also, worked for General Mills in Product Development. Something of a workaholic, he appeared to be on a fast track to Vice President, like his father, and possibly beyond with the company. His sister Joanne had died in an auto accident her senior year of high school. The whole family appeared to be as harmless as milk-toast. There did not seem to be anything there. He dug deeper. An hour later he'd still not found any leads.

Roger Novak shut down his laptop. He flopped onto the hotel bed and closed his tired eyes. But his mind kept working. There had to be something, somewhere!

.   .   .

The subconscious mind is capable of incredible things. Supervisory Special Agent Novak had finally drifted off to sleep later that night, no closer to a solution to the problem. There was a very minor background player in the game he'd completely forgotten about, until now. Roger had awoken the next morning with the image of Rita Morrison's friend in his mind. Not because she was still pretty hot for a woman in her fifties, but because during the brief time she had been around, she had given him those old familiar feelings of being tested and judged. She reminded him of one of his instructors from Quantico.

Doctor Aimee Friesian taught Human Behavior at the FBI Academy. Roger swore that the woman saw everything and, at the time, he'd almost been certain she could read his mind. He couldn't remember Rita's friend's name but that wouldn't be a problem for long. There had been something not quite typical about the husband, too. CB, VD, or some other stupid-assed name he couldn't quite recall.

Roger did remember being both relieved and also surprised at the absence of Rita's friend during the last few days of the ransom negotiations. Where had she gone? The woman did not seem the type to abandon poor Rita at such a vulnerable time. He decided that a visit to the Morrisons later this morning might shed some light on the subject.

The she-devil herself and her husband were at the Morrison's house when Novak arrived. After exchanging introductions and pleasantries over coffee and an excellent cherry pound cake, the FBI agent excused himself and rushed back to the hotel and his FBI laptop. He was now almost certain that Janet Reese and her husband were the reason his future was in jeopardy.

Hours later, Novak had been surprised to find out that they were both foreign nationals. He had taken them for American. Their accents suggesting that she was from the upper east coast and he from the midwest. Mr. Donavon Reese, where the nickname PB came from he hadn't a clue, served twenty-five years in the Canadian military. "The Canadian military, eh, isn't that kind of an oxymoron?" Roger mused out loud.

It took some digging, but once he'd discovered British-born, Janet Reese, nee Porter's, connection to Interpol, the FBI agent had all the proof he needed. Supervisory Special Agent Novak went out to the navy Ford Fusion he was driving this week, retrieved a burner phone from the trunk and shared the information with Rosa at the Ranch.

Roger could still remember the day four years earlier when he had first made contact with Los Diablos Rojos. It had certainly changed his life and he now realized, quite possibly even saved it.

Special Agent Roger Novak had been with the FBI for twenty-three years then. He'd been recruited right out of law school at Texas A & M University. Born and raised in Bisbee, Arizona, his late father was a mining engineer who had worked at several of the area copper mines while Roger grew up. His mother had been born in Cuba, but escaped to the USA with her parents and brother, a year after the Missile Crisis.

For the past seven years, Special Agent Novak had worked the incredibly stressful position of kidnapping negotiator. He was good at it, but the job was taking a heavy toll. During this time he started drinking heavily and had gone through a bitter divorce, only seeing his son and daughter on the occasional weekend, when he wasn't working. His own children seemingly held for ransom at the whims of his bitter wife, ate at his core. Roger had also watched his once-promising rise through the rankings at the Bureau slow to a halt. Late one night, several months earlier, he had found himself alone in a strange hotel room with a half empty bottle of Jim Beam in one hand and his Browning HP-35 pistol in the other. He managed to survive that long night and vowed to make changes in his life. He rededicated himself to his job.

Novak was called in to negotiate the release of two girls that had been kidnapped from a mall in Scottsdale, Arizona. The unthinkable happened. One of the girls was killed during a live video feed right in front of him and her family. The video abruptly stopped. After the shock and horror wore off, the parents of the other girl were prepared to pay anything for her release. An agonizing two days had passed with no word from the kidnappers. Novak watched the tape over and over while waiting for the call. Though the killer was wearing a mask and covered completely in red paint, there was something oddly familiar about him. Novak poured through his old files looking for a perp that could match the hulking giant in the video. He found no one. This case was not going to help jumpstart his career, at all.

His gut was telling him that he'd seen the man in the tape but he just couldn't figure out where or how. That night in his hotel room, as he got off the phone with his mother, the answer came to him. He was promising to visit, as soon as the case closed, when he remembered a previous visit.

During spring break of his senior year at Texas A & M, the soon-to-be FBI agent had gone home to share the good news of his recruitment. He and some high school buddies had gone down to the border town of Nogales to do some celebrating. At one of the bars, on the American side of town, a fight broke out between a huge Hispanic man and half a dozen biker dudes. The police had arrived quickly, but not before three of the bikers required serious hospital attention. The remaining four brawlers were arrested and hauled away. During the fight Novak remembered seeing a large pitchfork tattoo on the oversized bicep of the Mexican. The powerful fighter had made quite an impression, at the time. He was the same huge man from the ransom video, Roger was almost certain of it.

He rushed back and viewed the video once again. At the start of the video there was a clear view of the killer's arm. The tattoo couldn't be seen through the thick paint. Later though, after the Winger girl had jumped on his back and began fighting and scratching the brute, he thought he had seen something. There it was! He stopped the tape. During the scuffle, some of the paint had been rubbed off. The top of the trident was visible. Now, all he needed was to find the Nogales Police arrest report from more than twenty years earlier...

Unable to get any information on the old case by phone, Special Agent Novak jumped into his rental and made the two and a half hour trip to the southern Arizona town.

Early the next morning, after searching through police archives all night, Roger drove back to Scottsdale armed with enough evidence to possibly mount a cross-border rescue mission and blow apart the kidnapping ring. Besides identifying Nemo Suarez, he'd also uncovered known associates and last known addresses. However, when he arrived back in Scottsdale, FBI Assistant Director Davis was waiting for him and he looked pissed.

"Assistant Director," Roger greeted his boss tentatively.

"You look like crap, Novak," Davis said, shaking his head. Novak's suit was badly wrinkled and there were dark circles under his bloodshot eyes. "Have you been drinking?"

"No Sir!" Roger answered. "I've been up all night, working a lead."

Assistant Director Davis didn't look convinced. "One girl killed right in front of her parents." He shook his head again. "It has been more than forty-eight hours and we've heard nothing more from the kidnappers. We can assume that the other girl is gone, too."

"But Sir," Novak tried to plead his case.

"Both families want you replaced. This whole unfortunate affair is going to be thoroughly reviewed, Special Agent Novak."

"I've found..." Novak tried to explain his findings from Nogales.

"I don't want to hear it," the Assistant Director cut him off. "I thought you had cleaned up your act," he berated his subordinate. "I took a chance putting you on a high profile case, Novak. Clearly, I was wrong about you."

"Sir," it was Novak's turn to shake his head, stunned at the turn of events. He had expected some fallout, but not this. It sounded like his career was in serious jeopardy.

"Leave your case notes inside for Boscoe and then be at Quantico tomorrow morning at 9:00 am for review." Davis turned away, dismissing the bruised agent.

Novak went inside the small trailer that served as the mobile command unit and sat at what had been his desk, soon to be Boscoe's. By-the-book Boscoe, why did it have to be him? Boscoe hadn't had an instinctive thought in his entire life. He would draw into question every move Roger had ever made on this case and probably all the earlier ones. Special Agent Novak sometimes didn't follow the FBI's official playbook, preferring intuition and common sense. If you got results this didn't matter, but when things went wrong, every move would be brought into question. The Winger girl's death hadn't been his fault, but Novak knew he'd be the scapegoat. He glanced around the high-tech trailer. It wasn't much, but it had been his MCU for the past three years. He looked at his watch -- the IT guys would be back soon. Bone tired and dejected, he really needed a drink. So much for sobriety, his career and life in general; they were all about to crash and burn.

Suddenly, one of the video monitors in the trailer lit up. The Turtledove girl's tear-filled face filled the screen. She might still be alive. Novak jumped up and made sure everything was recording. He checked his mike.

"As you can see, Jennifer Turtledove is alive and doing well," the now-familiar electronically modulated voice came through. "We have decided to give you one more chance to save her life."

"I understand," Novak replied.

"Negotiations are over. You will put five million unmarked dollars into a duffle bag and drop it at the east end of the I-10 highway tunnel at midnight tonight. After we inspect the money, we will contact you to let you know where to find the girl."

"No, this is unacceptable," Novak said, thinking quickly. Hoping to save his own bacon, as much as the girl's life, he added, "I'll only make the exchange face to face. I need to make certain the girl is alright."

"If you ever want to see her alive, you will follow my instructions," insisted the kidnapper.

Novak needed some way to stay involved or it was over for him. He had an ace up his sleeve, but he needed a way to play it. "After what you did to the Winger girl, I can no longer trust that you will keep your word. Once you have the money, we'll never see Jennifer again." An idea came to him. "She'll be just as lost to us, as the little fish in that movie, Finding Nemo."

"Nemo?" the mechanical voice sounded startled. Hector knew the Disney/Pixar movie very well. His son watched it over and over and over. He'd been very amused that the tiny fish had the same name as his gigantic brother-in-law. He wasn't laughing now, though. "What are you talking about?"

"You have no morals," the FBI negotiator stressed the second syllable of the word, making it sound like more ales. "I need you to prove your metal." Roger crossed his fingers and hoped that Nemesio (Nemo) Suarez was still connected to Hector Morales of Morales Metal. His gamble paid off.

"I'll get back to you." Hector was stunned. Nemo, morals and metal, the FBI knows who we are, who I am! He glanced at the security monitors. At least they weren't storming the property yet. He needed to call Maria. The Morales family may have to flee the country.

"You've got fifteen minutes, or half the money will be off the table." Novak pushed, sensing that he had gotten the upper hand.

At that moment, Roger realized that if his career was over, he might as well go down with a golden parachute. He began forming a plan. It was filled with personal risk, but at this point in his life, he didn't care. With no career, no money, and no family, Roger had very little to lose. Eight hours later he returned to the Mobile Command Center with Jennifer Turtledove, alive and well, plus five hundred thousand dollars tucked away in the trunk of his rental. Not only had he kept ten percent of the ransom, he had saved his job and earned a promotion.

A week later, still bitter about how close he had come to being jobless, and even worse, penniless, Roger realized that half a million dollars was not going to give him the retirement lifestyle he wanted. The FBI's heroic Supervisory Special Agent took some time off work to visit his mother in Arizona, as he had promised her. It turned out that his mother, who had lived in Arizona her entire life, had never been to Rocky Pointe. She had a great time getting to know the charming coastal town while Roger got better acquainted with his new friends and partners, Hector and Maria Morales.

CHAPTER 25

A Wife for a Wife

The present
Green Valley, Arizona

PB awoke early for the second morning in a row. Something wasn't right. He didn't know what was bothering him, but there was something. He slid out of bed quietly. Janet's rhythmic breathing continued undisturbed. Dawn had not yet broken as he left the house dressed in a dark hoodie and sweat pants. Once the sun peaked over the eastern horizon, the streets would begin to fill with dogs and their walkers. Activity would be brisk in Green Valley for most of the morning, as the active adults exercised and took care of all manner of chores before the heat of the afternoon set in.

PB jogged casually around the neighborhood. Although he looked straight ahead, as he ran in ever-widening circles through the streets, the former Special Forces soldier noticed everything. He wasn't the only one who sensed danger coming his way. A jackrabbit ran out of the desert onto Continental Road, a couple of blocks ahead of him.

Easily the fastest of the animals in the Sonoran desert, the large rabbit had been pursued for several hours by a trio of coyotes that had taken turns in the chase. PB recognized that coming into town had been a desperate move by the tired rabbit. Moments after the rabbit disappeared into a man-made wash, one of the coyotes appeared at the edge of the road. It took off quickly in pursuit. Two more appeared half a minute later. One had its nose to the ground following scents and didn't look up as it crossed the road. The other stopped, looked left and right as if checking for traffic. The alpha coyote spotted PB, now only one block away. The coyote gave the jogging man a second look just before striding confidently across the road and into the wash.

"Good luck, Bugsy," PB said aloud, as he headed for home, satisfied that the neighborhood was at least free of human predators. Janet was in the kitchen when he walked into the house.

"What's for breakfast, Beautiful?" he asked as his hand grazed across the silky running shorts that covered her firm athletic butt.

"Banana blueberry protein shakes," Janet answered. "You saved some energy for our run together, I hope."

"Of course I did," he answered as the hoodie slid over his head. He wouldn't need it for the training run. "I was just loosening up a little."

"I can feel it, too," she told her husband as she handed him the full glass of bluish liquid. "Something wicked this way comes," Janet quoted.

The couple both put a lot of faith in their gut feelings and instincts. Neither said anything while they drank their breakfast.

"Maybe it's just a bad storm headed this way," PB finally offered.

"Maybe," she tried to sound hopeful, but they both knew a storm wasn't the cause of their anxiousness.

An hour later they were running through the pecan groves.

A long way ahead, PB could see a jackrabbit running along the edge of a dry creek bed. There were no signs of pursuers evident. Though he couldn't be certain it was the same rabbit from earlier, PB chose to believe it was. He'd been the underdog on a few occasions himself and took it as a good omen.

"Nice work, Bugsy," he called to the disappearing rabbit. "Take the rest of the day off."

PB's I-pod briefly interrupted *Take it to the Limit* by the Eagles to inform him that he had reached the halfway point of his run and now had five miles remaining. With his spider-senses settling down, PB felt secure for the time being. Just like Bugsy, however, he knew tomorrow was another day.

A half mile west of the peaceful groves, the traffic started to fill in on the Number 19 Highway to and from Nogales. Shoppers from both sides of the border prepared themselves for the bartering battles ahead. Treasures would be found. Deals would be made. Money would change hands.

That afternoon, men would travel this road with no intention to pay for the treasure they were hunting.

.   .   .

After lunch, there was some heat in the air. Summer was definitely just around the corner. The desert was alive with color this time of year. Violet Prickly Pears basked in the bright Arizona sun. The tops of abundant Barrel Cacti were adorned with rings of flowers, some orange, some yellow and others a rusty red. The ocotillos were full and green. They would soon have a bright red bloom at the end of every branch. The ocotillo forest at Elephant Head Rock would be spectacular in a week or two. Janet wanted to face the trail that had gotten the better of her months earlier. She decided to get some trail riding tips from the husband of one her friends.

A yearly ten dollar pass was a great deal for biking on the government land just west of Green Valley and it happened to be located a mere five minutes from the Reese residence. The single and double trails crossed back and forth through several shallow and deep washes. It was a very good training area for mountain biking.

Right now, Janet was concentrating on the trail ahead of her. She let out a whoop as her bike caught a little air diving into a fairly deep wash. She quickly braked and swerved to her left to avoid the Teddy Bear Cholla cactus on the edge of the single trail. As their name suggests, they look soft and cuddly, but anyone who has gotten too close to one quickly finds out differently. The arms of the Cholla fall off easily and are covered with many spines. These spines have small barbs on them that stick to skin and clothes like Krazy Glue.

Once safely past it, Janet down-shifted several gears as quickly as possible. Her bike zigzagged on its way to the bottom of the wash. A birthday gift from hubby, the baby blue twenty-one-speed GT Avalanche fit her perfectly and weighed much less than her old damaged Schwinn. With disc-brakes front and back, the Avalanche was her first serious mountain bike. She focused on the task in front of her now. Twenty-five feet of soft, deep sand lay between her and the other side of the wash. Churning her legs furiously to keep up momentum and fighting to keep the front wheel from drifting off target, she managed to get all the way through. Janet's first attempt hadn't been quite as successful, when she'd failed to get shifted into a low enough gear. This time she peddled proudly up the other side of the wash.

"Good work," Richard Tuttle, one of Green Valley's resident mountain biking experts, congratulated. Tall, dark and lean, Richard also played a mean game of pickle ball. "You did a much better job keeping your front wheel in line this time."

"Thanks Richard," she answered, as she pulled up beside him. Both turned their attention back towards the bottom of the wash as Richard's wife, Roxanne, made her third attempt across. She failed miserably, getting barely halfway this time.

"What gear are you in, Dear?" Richard asked with more than a hint of sarcasm evident in his voice.

"I know, I know," Roxanne snapped back. "I didn't get shifted down far enough. I ran out of time."

Recognizing the potential for another argument to start between the husband and wife, Janet decided to intervene.

"That's enough for me today, guys."

"I second that idea!" Roxanne quickly added as she pushed her new bright red Fuji Outland towards the other two. She would never be capable of pushing this bike to the limits of its considerable abilities.

They followed Richard as he led them back to the main road. The entire valley was displayed below the riders as they turned toward town. The large groves of dark green pecan trees blanketed most of the valley floor. It was obvious where the small city got its name from.

As they rode down Continental Road, the group made plans to meet at the same time the following week. Janet turned left on Portillo Road, while the married couple continued on and turned right on Del Sol. Their bickering resumed moments after that. Two minutes later, Janet pressed the button on the garage door opener that PB had attached to her handlebar. The absence of PB's Kawasaki told Janet that her husband wasn't back from playing tennis in Tucson, yet. She continued into the house, after wiping the dust and grime off her bike with a microfiber cloth.

She kicked off her shoes once she got inside, stepped into her slippers, and headed down the hall into the master bedroom. She had just turned on the shower and was about to disrobe when the doorbell rang. She went quickly across the house to get the front door.

She opened the inside wooden entry door. On the other side of the outer metal security door stood Supervisory Special Agent Roger Novak.

"Agent Novak, this is a surprise."

"Hello Mrs. Reese," he greeted her. "How are you?"

"Just fine," she answered him. "Is there something I can help you with?

"I just stopped in at the Morrison's house," he said explaining his presence. "I'm leaving for Chicago and just thought I'd make sure everyone involved with the case was doing okay before I left. These cases can be very traumatic and I was hoping to discuss some concerns I have about Rita."

"Would you care to come in?" Janet invited, as she unlocked the outer door.

"Yes, thank you," he answered as he stepped inside.

"Can I get you a glass of iced tea?"

"That would be lovely," he replied. There were those eyes again. He could almost feel them probing at his soul.

"Please have a seat, Agent Novak," Janet indicated toward the living room sofa. "I'll be right back with the tea."

"Is Mr. Reese home?"

"He should be home from tennis soon," she replied and started towards the kitchen.

As soon as she turned her back, Novak pulled out his Browning and pointed it at her.

Janet stopped in her tracks when she recognized the sound of the slide being pulled on a semi-automatic pistol.

"Tea won't be necessary, Mrs. Reese."

She turned slowly and faced the man.

"You and your husband cost me a lot of money this week."

"You dirty bastard!" Janet cried out, as she snap kicked at the gun. It flew out of the FBI man's hand and landed on the nearby love seat. Novak reacted quickly, lunging hard at the small woman. He knocked her back off her feet and landed on top of her. His right hand moved back to deliver a punch to her face. Suddenly, a searing pain shot up his left arm, one finger was already broken as she wriggled out from under him. She applied further pressure to the rest of the fingers, keeping him under her control. He grabbed at her in desperation, only to feel another finger snap.

The loud click of a revolver cocking by her ear, stopped Janet from snapping his pinky finger.

"Let go of me, you bitch!" Novak demanded.

Janet let go and stepped back. The older Hispanic man holding the big Colt revolver had cold eyes. She could tell he had pulled that trigger many times in the past and would not hesitate to do so again.

"You might want to get some ice on those," Janet sneered, and then nodded towards the refrigerator.

Novak looked down at his crooked fingers. They were already beginning to swell. He stood in front of Janet. With his good hand he slapped her hard. He was about to slap her again, but Juan Carlos pulled her back and shook his head. Since the Mexican was the only one holding a gun, at the moment, Novak backed down.

Once the FBI agent had his gun trained on the woman, Juan Carlos slipped out to the half-ton and got the supplies. Maria had been very clear how she wanted this handled. He pushed Mrs. Reese onto the nearby chair and carefully followed the instructions he'd been given.

Juan Carlos then produced a hypodermic needle from his pocket and pulled off its protective sleeve with his teeth. He was careful to inject the full amount this time.

"We're not done," Novak promised the former Interpol agent, as her eyes closed. Then he walked over to the kitchen to get some ice for his aching hand.

Forty-five minutes later, Juan Carlos crossed the border at Nogales, with Janet drugged, tied and hidden under the junk in the back of his old half ton truck.

.   .   .

"You've only been playing for four years?" Emma asked incredulously. She'd been playing since the age of three. The runner-up at the previous year's Minnesota High School State Championship took a drink from her water bottle.

"There were no tennis courts near where I grew up," PB smiled. "My first tennis experience was watching a live exhibition match between Carlos Moya and Rafa Nadal in Majorca."

"You're kidding," the mention of Rafa lit up her eyes. Raphael Nadal was her tennis idol. "I love the way Nadal plays. How awesome was that?"

"Pretty awesome," PB agreed as he remembered the athletic display. "The speed and power was phenomenal," he paused for a second. "I knew then there would be some tennis in my future."

"Clay is my favorite surface to play on," the youngest Morrison confided. "I made it to the semi-finals at the Under Eighteen Clay Court Nationals last fall."

"I know," PB said, setting down his water bottle. "It's my favorite surface, too. But there aren't very many clay courts here in the desert, so these will have to do."

"It feels so good to be back on any tennis court," Emma said as she laid her head back and slowly spun in a circle. "I still can't believe it's over. One minute Monica and I are prisoners and the next a policeman is waking us up and we're free." She shook her head, "It's like the whole thing was a dream. Like it didn't really happen, but I know that it did."

"Everyone is just thrilled that you and Monica are safe," PB assured her.

"Mr. Reese," Emma looked him in the eye, "I overheard my grandparents talking and I know that you and Mrs. Reese had a great deal to do with saving us. Please don't deny it."

"Yes," PB admitted, "Janet and I helped."

"I know you did more than help," she stated, as a matter of fact.

"We'd prefer it if our involvement was kept a secret," PB told her.

"Don't worry, your secret is safe with me," she assured him. "I won't tell anyone, not even Monica."

"Thank you."

"No, thank you, and thank Mrs. Reese for me, too." Emma wiped away a tear. "I can never thank you both enough." Emma knew in her heart that without the intervention of the Reeses she would not have come home alive.

"Hitting with the future Minnesota High School State Champion is thanks enough for me." PB gave her shoulder a squeeze.

The setting around the courts was beautiful. Palm trees and the lush green of the golf course fairways, combined with the Santa Catalina Mountains in the background, provided a spectacular atmosphere, especially after being held in a concrete cube for several days.

Emma picked up her racquet. "Have you got twenty more minutes left in you, old man?" she teased and jogged back onto the court.

It had been a good hit up to that point. But the final twenty minutes was great. Both players started hitting out, holding nothing back. The young woman had hard flat shots off both wings. PB used a lot more spin than she. Emma was quite quick around the court and made very few errors. PB's faster foot speed and greater variety of shots made things pretty even. The hand-eye coordination from his hockey days had translated very well to tennis.

He was pleased to note that Emma had a great attitude and applauded the frequent winners that came her way, just as vigorously as he did for hers.

Afterward, Emma thanked him again and promised to beat him on her next visit. PB had no doubts about that, now that her potential was once again limitless. He followed her safely back to the Morrisons. She rode her grandfather's Honda scooter while PB was on his Kawasaki Mean Streak.

During the ride home, the retired soldier began to feel uneasy. The closer he got to his house, the worse it became. As the garage door opened and Janet's mountain bike came into view he breathed a sigh of relief. But the nagging feeling didn't disappear completely. He guided the robust black and red motorcycle onto its rubber mat in the garage and went directly into the house.

He heard the shower running, as soon as he pulled off his full-face helmet. That was a good sign, so what was up with his gut? He set the helmet on the counter in the laundry room just to his right. He dipped his shoulder and slid off the racquet backpack and started down the rear hallway towards the bedroom.

Out of the corner of his eye, he noticed that the easy chair by the fireplace was out of position. PB dropped his racquets and rushed to the master bathroom. The walk-in shower was empty. He shut off the water and listened. The only sounds his sharp ears picked up were the remaining drops falling from the shower head and the gas-jet from the water heater, as it struggled to keep up with the demand. He spun around and silently went back to the laundry room where the couple kept a few firearms in a small safe. He took the top one and racked a bullet into the chamber, before prowling through the house.

Taped to the inside of the front door was a Polaroid of Janet dressed only in her panties and jogging bra, hands and mouth taped, seated in the misplaced easy chair. *A wife for a wife* was written in Spanish across it. The air slid out of his lungs. PB's chin sank to his chest. He'd failed Janet. Reese only allowed himself a few seconds of self-recrimination, then got his emotions in check. He didn't know how yet, but he resolved to save his wife or die trying.

Somehow that bastard Morales had found them out! The fact that Janet wasn't already dead gave him some hope, though not much. The photo was a clear message of why his wife had been taken and by whom. Reese handled the kidnapping of his wife differently than Morales had. He did not panic. PB realized that just getting the girls home safely had not been enough. He should have dealt with the kidnapping crew more permanently. He wouldn't make that mistake twice. If he had any say about it, the el Diablo Rojos gang would not ruin any more lives.

The Special Forces soldier eased himself to the floor. He sat cross legged in front of the picture of Janet, the handgun on the tiles beside him, as he carefully contemplated the situation and his available options. Morales would come for him, too, or send another message. He readied himself for either option.

Two hours had passed when the phone rang. PB stood up and answered it. He listened carefully, then thanked the caller and invited him to come right over.

CHAPTER 26

A Little Black Devil

April 30, 1991
London, England

Billy Mankowski held up his glass of fine whiskey. "I promised a night to remember, boys! To the finest soldier I've ever had the pleasure to serve with!"

The six men were seated around a dark walnut table, in a private dining room, at Boodle's Gentlemen's Club on Pall Mall. The group was composed of the Pat's Special Forces team and Janet's oldest brother, Paul. They had just finished great steaks, a bowl of Boodle's Orange Fool -- a specialty of the club, and were following it up with drinks.

"Here, here!" all joined in.

"Thank you, Gentlemen," PB nodded, before raising his glass again. "Ric-A-Dam-Doo."

"Ric-A-Dam-Doo!" the group repeated, and slammed back another drink.

"How were you able to get us into an exclusive club like this?" Janet's brother, a very successful investment manager with Barclays, asked Billy as the group leaned back into their chairs.

"I know a guy," Mankowski started to explain, but was cut off.

"It's a lot more likely he knows the wife of a guy," Bobby St. Jean offered, bringing a round of laughter at the expense of the team's resident Romeo.

"Very funny," Mankowski answered, then after a few seconds he shrugged, indicating that it might be true. This brought another round of laughter.

"This place is rather fantastic," PB said, winking at Billy. The team sniper had arrived with PB two days before the rest of the group. "Thank you for sharing this night with me, my brothers and soon to be brother," he nodded to Paul Porter and then raised his glass in another toast. "To my brothers."

"Here, here!" they joined and all took a drink. The men were all dressed in suits and jackets for the occasion. The private club wasn't as staunch and stuffy as it once had been. It had a rich décor of dark wood and burgundy leather, as well as a rich history of famous and powerful patrons.

"Did you know that Winston Churchill was a member here?" Paul told the group. A couple of heads shook and a few eyebrows rose. "David Niven, Beau Brummell and Ian Fleming were also members."

"Janet will be jealous," PB pointed out. "She is such a huge James Bond fan."

"She'd drop you in a minute if Sean Connery happened by," Bobby joked. The group bantered for two more hours, while pouring and sipping the exclusive and quite expensive Midleton Very Rare - triple-distilled Irish whiskey.

"I know the wedding isn't for a couple more days, but welcome to the family, PB. The Porter clan couldn't be happier to have you on board." Paul stood and shook PB's hand. "I've had a brilliant time getting to know my new brother and his friends. But, alas, I have to work in the morning, so I must bid you fine gentlemen adieu." After a round of handshakes, he nodded to the group and retreated toward the entry. On the way out Paul gave his business card to the concierge and arranged for the bill to be sent to his office. As it turned out, PB had just become a valued client. Paul's brother-in-law-to-be hadn't done much with his hockey salary and endorsement money since he'd left the game. It basically sat in a savings account in his hometown Credit Union. He needed some proper investment advice. Paul promised to do just that. The oldest Porter sibling was soon managing a seven figure account through his bank's Bahamas branch for Janet and PB.

"What a great guy," Mankowski proclaimed. "It's too bad that Greg couldn't make it tonight."

"You all will like him; he has quite the sense of humor," PB stated and explained who Greg was to the rest of the group, "Greg is Janet's other brother, an actor and a playwright. He had a rehearsal tonight. You'll meet him tomorrow, though."

"He's hilarious, actually," Billy added. "He toured with an improv group for two years. You do not want to get into a verbal match of wits with him, I can tell you from experience."

"I was there and it was more like a match between one wit and one nitwit," PB said, resting his hand sympathetically on Billy's shoulder, causing more laughter around the table.

"We have one more important thing to do tonight," Captain Andrews informed PB, as he tipped the crystal decanter, emptying the final ounce of golden liquid into Reese's glass.

"Come on guys," PB resisted, "I was serious about no strippers tonight."

"We're going to take you to see a hot woman," Bobby said. "But she's no stripper."

"The team talked it over," Andrews told PB, "and we want to make Janet an official member of the Snow Devils."

"Are you serious?" PB asked, sincerely touched by the offer. This was not something done lightly by the small close-knit squad. In fact, PB was certain, it hadn't been done before.

"We're deadly serious, Brother," Johansen replied. "We've known her as long as you have and she's already become a part of the team."

"We all love Janet," St. Jean explained, "She's not just marrying you in a couple of days. The way we see it, she's marrying all of us."

"That's the way you all see it?" PB looked at each man.

"That's the way we see it," they all answered at once, as the group often did.

"Well, then," PB raised his glass, swallowed the last of the whiskey and then continued, "who am I to stand in the way of love?"

"It's going to be a very interesting honeymoon," St. Jean exclaimed, to a chorus of laughter.

"I'm going to have to draw the line on that part of the group marriage," PB laughed along with the guys.

"I think we should let Janet make that decision," Mankowski jumped in, bringing more laughter.

Even though she was seldom there, or even in England for that matter, these days, Janet maintained a flat on Endell Street in Covent Gardens. Still her mother's daughter, she liked to be close to the theater district.

Forty minutes after they left Boodle's the rest of the crew was milling about on the sidewalk outside Janet's flat as PB went and rang the front door.

"What are you doing here?" Janet asked pleasantly, when she opened it. She had thrown on a housecoat over the light t-shirt and soft cotton shorts she often wore to bed. She'd had her bridal shower the night before and had hit the hay early. She got a twinkle in her eye and opened her mouth to invite him in.

"The whole team is here," PB quickly informed her, not giving her a chance to say anything in front of the group that she might regret.

"Oh!" Janet stuck her head out the door, looked over at the group and waved. "Shouldn't you guys be out at a strip club or something?" She was referring to the guys' night out, which she had assumed was code for a bachelor's party.

"I wanted to," Bobby answered.

"That's a given," Janet responded, rolling her eyes and chuckling.

"The guys would like to talk to you," PB told her.

"Come on in," she invited, her British accent more pronounced here in her home country. "Hurry up then, its cold out here," she added as she pulled her robe tighter.

Janet brewed a large pot of tea in the simple galley kitchen. She poured each man a cup, then one for herself and pulled up a chair to the cozy dining table that was really meant for four people, but managed to accommodate six coffee cups and a plate of biscotti just fine.

The clock above the porcelain sink in the clean white kitchen read one thirty. That was zero one thirty in military lingo Janet reminded herself.

She took a sip from her cup and looked from one face to the other. All eyes were on her.

"Okay," she started, "what was so important that it couldn't wait until daylight to talk about?"

"Frankly, Janet, we're concerned about the marriage," Lieutenant Andrews spoke somberly.

"Go on." She glanced over at PB but he looked quickly away, giving her no clue as to what was coming.

"We feel that it will upset the delicate balance that a precision team, like ours, requires to function efficiently in dangerous situations," he continued.

Janet looked around the table. Everyone looked quite serious.

"You've fought with us, flown around the world with us, even jumped out of a perfectly good aircraft with us," the team leader reminded her. "In short, we trust you with our lives as we know you have placed your trust in us."

"What seems to be the problem, then?" she asked. Her voice barely more than a whisper, she was becoming genuinely concerned.

"I'll tell you what the problem is," Andrews spoke a little stronger. "One of us is selfishly trying to keep you all to himself." He turned from her and sent a menacing look toward Sergeant Reese.

Smiles spilled out around the table, breaking the tension that had built up.

"This is an unacceptable situation," Captain Andrews reached across the small table for her hand. Without hesitation she acquiesced and put her hand in his. One by one the rest of the team added a hand on top of hers. "For the sake of the team and world peace, Janet, soon-to-be-Reese, Porter, we would like to make you an official member of the Snow Devils."

"Ric-a-Dam-Doo, Dam-Doo Dam-Doo!" the whole team exclaimed in unison, as they raised her hand up and then slapped it back down onto the table twice.

"I don't know what to say," Janet choked out the words, stunned at the completely unexpected offer. Tears welled in her eyes.

"Say yes, or we'll be forced to cancel the wedding," St. Jean said in a threatening voice, but followed the statement with a snicker.

"Of course, it's yes!" Janet smiled brightly. "I would be greatly honored. I love you guys!"

"I told you she loved us all, PB," St. Jean said proudly, slapping his buddy on the back.

"I never heard you refer to yourselves as the Snow Devils before," Janet pointed out.

"Officially, we're Team Alpha of the Canadian Airborne Regiment. Over the years, Team Alpha has mostly been made up of Princess Patricia's Light Infantry soldiers. In 1948, John's grandfather, John Andrews the first, returned from World War II along with five other men that had served with the Devil's Brigade." PB stopped to make sure she was following. "You've heard of the Devil's Brigade?"

"Sometimes called the Black Devils," she added, nodding.

"John's grandfather and his five comrades, all originally Princess Pats, were the original Team Alpha," PB continued. "Those Black Devils became the first Snow Devils."

"You followed in your grandfather's footsteps?" Janet turned her attention to Lieutenant Andrews.

"My father's footsteps, as well," John Andrews the third, stated. "I guess you could say that I was born to be a devil."

"I guess so," Janet agreed.

"You are about to become the twenty-third member of the Snow Devils. That means only twenty two other people before you knew our secret squad name," PB told her.

"My mother knows it," Johansen spoke out meekly.

"Both my parents know, too," St. Jean admitted.

"My wife, mother and brother, as well." Andrews put up his hand.

"I'm not sure, but I may have mentioned it to that pretty barmaid, the other night, when she brought us our second round," Billy Mankowski shrugged, as Lieutenant Andrews cuffed the back of his head. Everyone laughed.

"Well, it seems that you might be the last person on the planet to have heard of the Snow Devils," Janet's fiancé laughed and shook his head.

"Wait a second," Janet noted. "Did you say I'm about to become a member of the team? I thought I was in already."

"No, no, no!" the team responded, again in unison.

"You've already passed some of the requirements," PB told her.

"You've proven yourself to be a capable warrior on the battlefield," the Lieutenant stated and then added, "so bravery is definitely not the issue."

"You ate St. Jean's cooking and went back for seconds," Johansen ducked under a swat from the team cook before he continued. "So that proves you are certainly have the stomach to be one of us."

"And out of all of us fine specimens, you chose the runt of the litter to get hitched to," again Bobby slapped his best friend on the back. "Well, now that I think about it, I don't exactly know what that proves."

"It proves that she's just crazy enough to be one of us," PB interjected with a smirk.

"It proves that she has a pretty good head on her shoulders," Mankowski corrected his team mate.

"That only leaves one more thing for you to do, to prove you belong on the team," Andrews explained to her, as the whole team rolled up their sleeves, revealing identical team tattoos on each left shoulder.

She had seen the tattoo on PB's shoulder many times before. A black devil with a dagger in its mouth, holding a red spear and shield in his hands, stood above the words Ric-a-Dam-Doo inked in red, gold and royal blue.

"I'll be ready in five minutes," Janet told the group, as she got up from the table.

"It's almost two in the morning," PB reminded her.

"I know a twenty-four hour shop on Lancaster," she replied. "It's only a thirty minute walk from here."

Janet threw on a heavier t-shirt and some jeans. She joined the group outside in less than four minutes.

"What do you guys think about a red and gold and blue butterfly for my tattoo or maybe an angry hummingbird with a knife in its beak?" Janet joked, as she locked the flat door. When she turned toward the street all five men were staring at her.

"A little black devil it is, then," she laughed. Janet could not imagine a better wedding present.

"Lead the way, Recruit," Lieutenant Andrews instructed Janet. As she started down the sidewalk, the soldiers followed, marching behind in single file. From the rear, the team leader began to sing the team's marching song, "The Ric-A-Dam-Doo, pray what is that?"

"'Twas made at home by Princess Pat," the rest of the soldiers joined in.

By the time they turned onto Lancaster, Janet added her voice to the mix. While she was in love with one of them, she really did love the whole team. These were her new brothers.

CHAPTER 27

Slashing and Tripping

The present
Green Valley, Arizona

PB shouted at the shadowy female figure on the laptop monitor that he already knew to be Maria Morales. "I'm not going to give you one plug nickel until I talk to my wife."

Reese glanced over at Roger Novak. The FBI agent was standing only a few feet away on the other side of the Reese's dining table. Novak nodded his approval at the proof of life demand.

A half hour earlier, the Supervisory Special Agent had shown up at the Reese home carrying a laptop. He explained to the obviously distraught husband that the kidnappers had contacted him and would call back at 2:00 pm expecting to speak with Reese. Novak promised to help in any way that he could. When Reese had asked the agent about his bandaged hand, Roger described an embarrassing slip and fall. The kidnappers made contact precisely at 2:00 pm.

The computer screen filled with white light and suddenly Janet appeared. She was bound to a white chair in a completely white room. She was wearing her biking gear and had a gag in her mouth. There was a bright purple welt covering most of her left cheek. Tears had made tracks down both sides of her face.

"Janet, can you hear me?" PB called out immediately. Instantly she reacted to his voice, nodding emphatically.

"Let her talk," PB pleaded.

Behind Janet, a muscular man appeared on the screen. Completely covered in red from head to toe, the man looked gigantic as he towered over Janet. PB recognized both Nemesio Suarez and his horned mask from earlier video footage. After removing the gag from her mouth, the red devil turned to the camera and gently caressed the top of Janet's head for a few seconds. Janet cringed at his touch.

"Please don't hurt her," PB begged, as Novak stepped behind him. The video feed was two way. The microphone and camera were active on the laptop. The agent put a reassuring hand on the groveling man's shoulder, but inwardly he smiled. He couldn't wait to watch the tied up woman suffer. Maria had promised him some alone time with Mrs. Reese. His other hand, with the two middle fingers tightly taped together, ached like a son of a bitch. The earlier backhand slap across her face had only provided a small dose of satisfaction. The pain and humiliation of being bested by the tiny woman demanded much more. The FBI agent had never killed anyone in all his years as an agent, but felt like he could make an exception for the woman with the annoyingly piercing eyes.

"I told them about the hidden money, Donavon," Janet spoke, her voice sounding odd at first, still dry from the cotton gag. "Please do what they say and everything will be alright."

"Oh, God," her husband sobbed. "This can't be happening."

"Please, bring them the money, Donavon," she said. The big man rested his hands on her shoulders, prompting her to add, "You can trust Agent Novak, he will help you." The screen began to blur.

"I'll do whatever they want, I promise," PB shouted, hoping his wife could still hear him, when the screen transitioned back to the shadowed figure.

"I know you will, Mr. Reese." Even Maria's mechanized voice reeked with satisfaction. The man in front of Agent Novak looked terrified and helpless. Maria, once again, marveled at the fear that her brother evoked in people. Just his presence in the room had caused the Reese woman to spill her guts about the money she and her husband had hidden away, in stashes. And then, all Nemo had done was touch the woman's head and her husband, the former soldier, crumbled. Hector had been wrong to send Nemo away. Now that she was running this end of the business, her brother was back to stay.

Maria looked at her watch. Three minutes had gone by.

"You have twenty-three hours and fifty-seven minutes to round up five million dollars or you'll never see your wife again. Once I know you have the money, I will give you the delivery instructions."

"I understand," he replied between stifled sobs. PB noted that Maria's English was pretty good, but not as smooth as Hector's. There was a rehearsed feel to her delivery.

"Don't try anything stupid, or my large friend will have some real fun with your wife," she warned.

The screen flashed back to Janet. The man's big hands were now all over her chest. Janet wore a mask of indifference as she stared straight ahead.

"I won't," PB answered, sounding completely defeated, "I promise!"

The video feed went black. PB turned toward Novak. His face was filled with anguish, tears spilling from his eyes. The FBI agent actually felt some pity for the broken man.

"How will this work?" PB asked.

"All we can do at this point is to try and meet her demands," Novak answered as he walked back around the table. "Can you get the money?"

"Five million dollars," PB's demeanor brightened slightly as he answered the question. "No problem, we have a lot more than that stashed and buried all over the surrounding area."

That was partly true. PB and Janet did have enough money stashed away, but not buried in the desert. It was at several banks and investment firms in the form of bonds, stock trading accounts and good old fashioned savings plans. The *buried all over the surrounding area* part was strictly for Novak's benefit, in case PB needed to lure him away alone.

Novak was momentarily stunned at this admission. His greed kicked in at the mention of more money. Luckily, he was turned away from Reese at the time. He recovered his composure quickly.

"That's great for Janet's sake." He turned and smiled. "We can't let anything bad happen to her."

"No we can't," PB agreed, the totally defeated look returning. Then he sobbed softly, "I couldn't live without her."

Roger nodded. Reese's biography said he had been a hot shot hockey player, but that he'd only played one year in the big leagues. It was no wonder the pathetic pussy in front of him hadn't made it in the NHL. Roger had gone to several games over the years and those guys were tough and crazy -- slamming each other into the boards, not to mention all the slashing and tripping. That reminded him to make an effort to take in a few more Los Angeles King's games before his self-imposed exile to beaches and bikinis.

"I had better get moving," PB wiped his eyes with his sleeve. "I have a lot of running around and digging to do."

"Can I help?" Novak offered, as innocently as he could muster.

"Doesn't one of us need to be near the computer?" PB probed. "There won't be internet or cell phone coverage where some of it is buried."

"We won't hear from them again until 2:00 pm tomorrow," the SSA answered and then watched a remarkable transformation take place in front of him.

"Are you sure?" PB's back and shoulders straightened.

"I'm absolutely positive," the FBI agent confirmed, "I've worked on eight previous cases with this group."

"That's all I needed to know." PB walked over and got into the agent's personal space. He was no longer the soft sappy beaten man of only a moment ago. Instantly, there was steel in the former hockey player's eyes. The metamorphosis was astounding.

"You are going to tell me exactly where my wife is," Reese informed the Supervisory Special Agent.

"What are you talking about?" Novak asked as his good hand inched toward his shoulder holster. Faster than he could blink, there was a vice-like grip on the front of his neck. His hand stopped moving. In fact, he froze completely. Reese's other hand slid inside Novak's jacket and pulled out the Browning pistol that, earlier in the day, had been pointed at his spouse. He let go of the larger man's neck and stepped back and pointed the gun at the agent's left hand.

"Tripped and fell? My ass..." Reese asked and answered before continuing. "You didn't think I'd recognize my wife's handiwork?"

"But..." Roger began shaking his head.

"Save it Novak," PB cut off the FBI man. "Now slowly remove your backup piece."

Novak stared down the barrel of his own gun as he removed the small Beretta nine millimeter from his ankle holster. He handed it over grip first.

Janet never called PB, Donavon. It was the code they had, to do the opposite of what she told him. "Do whatever they say" was obvious, and "everything will be alright" meant that they were planning to kill both of them even if he cooperated completely. "Trust Agent Novak" confirmed what he already suspected. The ex-Special Forces soldier emptied the clips and ammunition from both guns and tossed them onto the easy chair that Janet had been tied up in earlier that day.

Novak looked at Reese quizzically. He was ten or eleven years younger and three inches taller than the man in front of him.

"This will go much easier for you if you just tell me where she is," Reese calmly looked the bigger man in the eyes, secretly hoping for a little resistance.

Novak clenched his right hand and swung it hard. His target dipped slightly to the side. The fist slid harmlessly past Reese's head. The ex-soldier's right knee came up crashing into Novak's solar plexus. The Supervisory Special Agent found himself doubled over and gasping for air. Then the two middle fingers of his good hand exploded with pain.

"That's for my wife!" These were the last words Novak heard before his world faded into a swirling black void.

An hour later, PB waved some smelling salts under the FBI man's nose. Novak's eyes fluttered open. As they came into focus all he could see was blue. Blinking a few times he realized that he was staring up at the sky. He was lying flat on his back. He turned his head to each side. There was nothing but hot desert hardpan and a variety of cacti as far as he could see in either direction. He tried to move, but his hands and feet were spread eagle and securely bound. Now both his hands throbbed with pain. Tugging them only made it worse.

"What's going on?" Novak asked out loud, not sure if anyone was around. PB's face appeared over his from behind, startling him.

"Like I said before, Roger, you are going to tell me exactly where my wife is." He smiled down at Novak. "Your life depends on it." PB stepped into full view. In his hands he held five frozen pork chops. Reese tossed four of them a few yards in each direction around the bound man.

"What are you doing?" Novak asked, eyeing the last chop in his assailant's hand.

PB stepped in between his legs and bent down. He grabbed the waistband of Roger's trousers and yanked upward. He then stuffed the ice cold chop into the crotch of Novak's expensive pants. Reese looked towards the sun. "There are a couple of hours of sunlight left," he estimated. "These chops will start thawing out pretty quickly. Shortly after that, the coyotes and bobcats will smell this meat and come looking for it." He tapped the front of Roger's pants for effect. "Did you happen to hear about the mountain lion that's been spotted in the area recently?"

The FBI man's eyes widened as he thought about where that fifth pork chop was located.

"I expect that one or more of these predators will zero in on this area within five or six hours. Two or three hours after that, they will get brave enough to come after pork chop number five."

"Okay, you win," Novak conceded. "Let me up and I'll tell you where she is."

"I'll let you up when my wife is here with me, safe and sound."

"No," Novak protested and struggled against his bindings. "What if you don't make it back in time?"

"You better hope that I do, G-man!"

Roger Novak's mind raced with images of hungry cougars, bobcats and coyotes all making unwelcome appearances. His allegiance shifted as he contemplated his best chance for survival. It was his turn to feel totally defeated, only he wasn't acting. Novak's freezing crotch was a further reminder that he needed Reese to return safely. Time was now of the essence.

"They have cameras monitoring the roads," he warned Reese. "They'll know you're coming."

"Let me worry about that."

"The ranch is more than two and a half hours away."

"Not for me!" PB unfolded a very detailed map of Northern Mexico. He put his finger tip in the center of it and began sliding it around. "Tell me when I'm getting warmer."

A few minutes later Novak heard an unexpected sound. An airplane engine started up not far behind his head. The engine began to race, as it powered up, readying for takeoff. He heard the sound of the tires crunching on hardpan when the plane started to move. Craning his head to the left he was able to see the small colorful plane as it left the ground.

Just how far out in the desert did he bring me? Novak wondered to himself. Once airborne, the aircraft immediately swung southward. Suddenly, Roger felt very alone and helpless. If Reese didn't return, he doubted that anyone would ever find him. He pulled against his restraints, they didn't budge. He yelled as loud as he could, hoping, against reason, that he'd be heard.

"H-e-l-p!"

Then he quieted himself, deciding not to unnecessarily alert the surrounding wildlife to his presence.

CHAPTER 28

Improvise and Adlib

A few hours earlier
The Morales Ranch, Mexico

Janet spoke into the studio camera. "I told them about the hidden money, Donavon." The kidnappers had an impressive, even elaborate, video-making setup. Behind her was a large green screen that would allow them to add whatever background the boss wanted, for the videos they produced. Lining the walls of the large studio were racks of wardrobe, props and set pieces. The ex-Interpol agent recognized the seedy stripper bar runway, from the girls' first video, leaning idly on its side. Someone in this group was certainly tech savvy. Janet suspected that it was the woman in the ranch house, operating the cameras remotely, who had set all this up.

Maria Morales was directing the show, of that there was no doubt. The dark-haired beauty was beyond the cameras, sitting at a bank of monitors. Everyone jumped when she barked out a command. She had forced Janet and Nemo to rehearse the simple scene several times.

"Please do what they say and everything will be alright," Janet added. She'd been coached on what she could and couldn't say.

"Oh God, this can't be happening." Janet could hear PB's voice, but she couldn't see the monitor from her vantage point.

"Please, bring them the money, Donavon," Janet improvised.

The moment the captive woman went off script Maria nodded to her brother. Nemo stepped onto the stage directly behind his hostage. He put his big hands on her small shoulders as a gentle reminder to say only what she was supposed to.

"You can trust Agent Novak, he will help you through this," Janet stated flatly as the recording light on the video camera in front of her faded off. The hands on her shoulders began to creep forward.

"I'll do whatever they want, I promise!" She heard her husband shout desperately. Janet knew that the opposite was true. He would come for her. She knew in her heart that her resourceful husband would find her. These people had no idea what was coming their way.

"I know you will, Mr. Reese." Maria's voice was smug. She had bought the hidden money story that Janet had woven for her.

The giant fingers on her shoulders drifted downward until they were brushing the top of Janet's breasts.

"You have twenty-three hours and fifty-seven minutes to round up five million dollars or you'll never see your wife again." Maria had adlibbed one of her lines, as well. In the moment, it had felt more dramatic. The sheet in front of her read - You have twenty four hours to round up five million dollars. Maria felt good about the change and continued reading her lines, "Once I know you have the money, I will give you the delivery instructions."

"I understand." Janet heard her husband's voice. Her hands had been bound to the chair rails to prevent her from sending hand signals, so she was helpless to ward off the pawing that her chest was undergoing as the video light came back on.

"Don't try anything stupid, or my friend here will have some real fun with your wife." Maria looked up from the monitor and sneered at Janet.

"I won't," her husband sobbed and then added, "I promise!" Janet knew the promise was meant for her and not Maria. The video light went out again. Nemo bent down and licked her neck.

"Nemo," Maria yelled at her brother in Spanish, "put her back in the cell!"

"We'll continue this later," Nemo whispered into Janet's ear. Then he straightened up and walked off. "Juan Carlos can do it."

The tension in Janet's muscles eased a little with every step further away that the big man took. A sigh of relief escaped her lips as he walked out the studio door.

"Our husbands are so weak without us," Maria laughed at what she believed to be an inside joke between the two women. Maria could not get past or forgive Hector for not revenging her honor. She'd obtained poison to get rid of him. It would look like a heart attack. Supposedly swift and painless, he deserved that much, at least. She walked over to Janet and lifted her chin. "Tomorrow, both of our problems will cease to exist," she laughed again and followed the same path out that her brother had taken a minute earlier.

"Juan Carlos, put the Gringa away," Janet heard her say from the other side of the wall. Janet rubbed her chin against her blouse. If anything, Maria's touch felt even more vile than her brother's. From the sounds of it, Hector Morales was also the target of Maria's wrath.

Juan Carlos entered the studio. Janet hoped he would not be abusive, too. She noticed as he came toward her, that he had a pistol tucked into his belt. Before she could formulate a plan, Raul stepped through the door behind him. She would have to wait for PB to arrive. She knew that he would find her.

Under the watchful eye of Raul, Juan Carlos removed Janet's restraints and marched her back to the cement block cube that was her temporary home. The door closed and locked, she was alone once again except for the hidden cameras, of course. She had glimpsed the four views of her cell on the bank of monitors before they had switched over to the studio camera feeds. She knew they were watching her. Janet walked back and forth, loosening up her cramped and tense muscles. She began at her fingers and worked her way down to her toes, alternately flexing and relaxing each muscle in preparation for what was to come. This was a ritual she'd begun as a dancer, and then repeated before Tai Kwon Do matches, and whenever she had time before any strenuous activity. The petite fifty-four-year-old vowed to be as ready as possible for whatever lay ahead.

.   .   .

The tiny red, gold and royal blue plane circled once over Reese's private storage compound. Looking down he could see the dirty FBI agent staked on a high spot below. PB had picked that particular spot to place the agent because you couldn't see the eight foot high wire mesh fence that surrounded the compound from that vantage point.

At the north end of the compound, behind the spread-eagled agent, a large sturdy barn was all that remained of the ranch yard that had once occupied the property. The original barn door had been removed and a wide hanger-type had been added. Besides the plane, the modified barn was also home to a pair of Polaris RZR all-terrain vehicles and a Monaco Class A motorhome. In one corner, there was a large fully-stocked weapon safe with several practice targets leaning against it. In the opposite corner stood some specialized martial arts fitness equipment, not found in the local gyms. The retired couple trained faithfully here every week. Located at the end of a long dirt road, the closest neighboring property to the secure compound was over two miles away. That property, like this one, had been abandoned years earlier and had also been purchased, at auction, by the Reeses.

PB pointed the ultralight aircraft south and opened up the throttle. The couple had chosen this small plane for its outstanding STOL, short takeoff and landing capabilities. This type of aircraft, outfitted with large low pressure tires, was a popular choice for bush pilots who often needed to take off and land on a dime. The manufacturer claimed that you could take off within sixty feet and land in under two hundred and forty feet. PB had halved both those numbers in practice runs.

This particular Carbon Cub SS had been custom built for Janet and PB at the Cubcrafter factory in Yakima, Washington. Powered by a one hundred eighty horse Lycoming engine, it was soon cruising at 135 knots just under the plane's ten thousand foot ceiling.

While in the air, PB radioed in and filed a flight plan to a private airstrip at Magdalena that he had flown into several times before. He then phoned his pal, Ronaldo, who operated and maintained the small airport and explained his intentions. Magdalena was located about forty miles south of the Mexican border. However, he would not be landing there. The Morales ranch was located approximately sixty miles further west, along highway thirty-seven, between Puerto Penasco and Caborca. Both cities were located within the province of Sonora. Radar would track the small plane in both US and Mexican airspace.

As PB neared Magdalena he radioed his intention to land. At the same time he paid close attention for information that other planes may be flying in the area. Things were pretty quiet at the small strip, as he had expected. The red, gold and royal blue ultralight made its approach toward the single runway. Radar lost track of the plane when it got below 150 feet.

Flying at an altitude of seventy-five feet PB announced his arrival and successful landing over the radio to anyone who might be listening. Only Ronaldo noticed, as the plane flew on past the end of the runway and banked to the west. PB gradually added power to the throttle as he rose to a hundred forty feet.

Half an hour later, PB had slowed his cruising speed down to eighty knots, as he watched for the final landmark provided by Novak. There they were, sticking out like The FBI agent's broken fingers, faded red twin barn silos three miles east of his target. He banked north and flew a wide berth around the kidnappers' location. In the pasture, behind the Morales barn, there was a watering dugout lined with Mesquite trees on either side. The trees provided some shade for the livestock on hot summer days. They would soon hide the Ric-a-Dam-Doo-colored plane.

Half a mile out, PB killed the engine and started his silent, gliding, descent out of the quickly-setting western sun. The tricky part of the flight started now. Even the best maps and GPS systems did not account for old farm equipment, rock piles, livestock or any number of obstacles that could be waiting for the little plane in the landing area PB had chosen. Google Earth had provided a snap shot of the pasture to PB's smart phone. However, things could have changed since the satellite image had been taken. With the engine shut off, there would be no flyby. The risk of being seen would be too great.

PB would have to hope for the best and trust that he could find some space to land the agile plane safely. PB was purposely flying light, as well. The clothes on his back, a small first aid kit, his trusty Para Ordnance, Janet's Walther, a knife and a few extra clips for each gun was all he'd brought in the plane. The lighter the load, the quicker they could be airborne if a hasty escape was needed.

Retreating wasn't what he had in mind, but he definitely wanted the airplane to be in flying condition after the landing, just in case.

When the landing site came into view, PB breathed a sigh of relief. A hundred yards of empty ground, picked clean by horses and cattle, lay between the pasture fence and the trees he'd hide the plane behind. He could see nothing but a few cow pies in his landing path. Even the livestock cooperated, congregating at the far end of the pasture. PB checked his airspeed. It was fifty knots and slowing. He gently touched down at the stall speed of forty knots and the plane rolled quietly behind cover.

"This ends today," he said to himself, as he vaulted over the pasture fence. He'd gone less than thirty steps when he dropped and flattened himself to the ground. A figure emerged from the barn.

Raul Torres left the barn and headed for the house. He had just brought pork and rice tamales out to Juan Carlos and the captive woman. Maria had gone back to the mansion for the night. Raul quickened his pace. He didn't like leaving Rosa alone with Nemo.

Behind him he hadn't noticed the small dust cloud that was just visible above the barn or the dark body lying prostate a mere thirty feet to his left.

Inside the house, Rosa might have glanced at the bank of security monitors when a shadow crossed past one of them, had not Nemo been pestering her as he did whenever Raul was out of sight. He was still dressed in the creepy, tight red leathers from the video performance earlier that day. At the sound of the front door opening, Nemo flipped Rosa's small pony tail and walked away. She rolled her eyes. It was like being back in high school.

CHAPTER 29

Where is the Cougar?

The present
The Morales Ranch, Mexico

When he wasn't eating everything in the house or teasing Rosa, Nemo liked to watch the Reese woman. He'd moved an easy chair in from the living room and placed it in front of the monitors dedicated to the holding cell.

She paced back and forth like a caged cat. Nemo was mesmerized by the easy athletic way she moved. She was much more interesting than most of the junk on regular television. Rosa had commented earlier that the older woman prowled like a cougar. Maria and Raul had both laughed, but he didn't get the joke. He had a good laugh though, when Juan Carlos told them about how she'd broken the foolish FBI man's fingers. For a woman in her fifties, she was pretty feisty and she still had a very trim body.

He put together another plate of tamales and grabbed a Coke from the fridge, took them back to the computer room, and settled in front of the monitors. Nemo's eyes slid from the first monitor to the second, then the third and finally the fourth. He jumped up. The food in his lap went flying. The woman was gone.

"She's gone!" he yelled loud enough to wake the dead.

Rosa and Raul rushed to the monitors. The cell was empty. The top monitor revealed a black rectangular hole where the door had been swung wide open. Rosa pushed Nemo out of the way so she could rewind the video feed. Raul, simultaneously, tried to raise Juan Carlos on the intercom. His partner didn't answer.

Rosa had barely turned the rewind knob, on the playback machine, when the Reese woman ran back through the dark opening, in reverse, and the door slammed shut.

"This just happened a few seconds ago," Rosa told them. "Maria will have our heads if we don't get her back."

"There," Nemo pointed at one of the other security monitors. A figure sprinted across the barnyard towards the gravel road that led back to the highway. Although the sun had set, there was still enough light to identify the figure as the Reese woman. It was also clear that she had Juan Carlos' big gun.

"I'll get her!" Nemo shouted, as he moved towards the door.

"No!" Rosa ordered. She couldn't trust that Nemo would return the woman in the same condition as she left. It would be healthier for all concerned, especially those that didn't happen to be Maria's sibling, if Mrs. Morales never learned about this event. "Raul will bring her back."

Raul reached behind his back and pulled a shiny Smith and Wesson 1911 forty-five from his waist band, clicked off the safety, smirked at the big man, and then sprinted out the door. Nemo didn't carry a gun. He stood there pouting like a big kid. Rosa shook her head and pulled a cell phone from the desk drawer.

"You go out to the barn and check on Juan Carlos." She activated the screen on the smart phone. "Find out how this happened."

Nemo didn't like taking orders from anyone besides Hector or his sister. He replied sarcastically, "Anything for you, Doll Face."

"Take this with you," Rosa instructed, ignoring his comment. "It is hooked into the security grid."

He grabbed it and his leather balaclava from the top of the monitor bank and went out the way Raul had, still sulking.

Less than a minute after hugging her husband, Janet ran out of the barn. She was the bait in PB's divide and conquer plan. She had her trusty Walther tucked into the back of her bike pants along with two spare magazines. She brandished the much heavier Colt Bisley revolver that her husband had liberated from Juan Carlos, waving it around so that it would be noticed.

PB watched her departure carefully from inside the barn. They both were aware that the road was monitored and her escape would be quickly discovered. One of the four guards, which Janet knew about, had already been incapacitated. If more than one of the remaining captors gave chase, PB would have to follow. If only one did, it would be PB's job to take care of those that remained.

Thirty seconds after Janet had raced down the gravel road, a small engine roared to life near the house. Seconds later, a man on a four wheel ATV tore off after her. The bright lights from the machine bounced down the road. Less than a half a minute following that, the silhouette of another man appeared at the side of the house. This one walked towards the barn. PB backed away from the dark doorway. Slipping into one of the empty horse stalls, he tucked back against the wall, well hidden in the shadows. Familiar barn odors reminded him of farm life on the prairies. He hadn't seen any horses in the pasture, but he could smell their distinct equine musk around him.

The Para Ordnance rested, locked and loaded, against his thigh. In his other hand, he held a length of freshly-braided rope that he'd taken from the old cowboy. While he waited, Reese took the opportunity to stretch his muscles. Similar to Janet's routine, it had been a habit he'd picked up as a hockey player many years earlier. It helped him relax and get ready for action.

Seconds passed slowly. The deathly silence of the barn was broken by the sound of six shots echoing from a distance. Good girl, he thought. Janet was following the plan perfectly. Now her pursuer would assume she was once again weaponless. PB turned his attention back to the barn entry. The other man should arrive at any second.

As Nemo made his way to the barn, the screen on his phone brightened. He looked down at it. Rosa had activated the new thermal cameras on the property and forwarded the video feed to his phone.

There were two heat signatures in the empty barn. One was motionless, but the other was making small movements near the outside wall. Nemo rerouted towards that side of the building. As he got closer, his own image appeared on the screen. When the two images were directly across from each other, Nemo set the phone on the ground. He had no pockets in the padded leather suit. He pulled on the mask. Six shots rang out about a quarter of a mile away down the road. He hoped that Raul hadn't killed the woman. He had big plans for her. The big man backed up a couple of steps, dropped his shoulders and charged at the barn wall like an NFL linebacker.

A noise from outside the barn caught PB's attention too late. The wall he leaned against exploded inward. He was sent sprawling out of the stall and into the central area of the barn by what felt like a ton of bricks crashing into his back. His gun clattered loudly on the concrete, after it flew from his hand. PB rolled away from the dark figure also sprawled on the barn floor.

A vice-like hand clamped onto his ankle and yanked him back. Thick arms circled his mid-section from behind. They squeezed tighter and tighter. Air began to spill from PB's lungs. He beat on the giant's forearms, to no avail. He reached behind his head. PB's fingers clawed against firm leather.

PB had not felt strength like this in another human being before. The arms continued to squeeze tighter and tighter. His lungs were almost empty. He'd black out if the situation did not change soon.

One of his flailing feet managed to find purchase on a stall divider. He pulled hard until he could reach it with his hand. Using his new-found leverage, PB slammed the huge body into the divider once, twice, three times. The arms held firm.

"What is he doing?" Rosa had said to herself seconds earlier, as she watched the infra-red blobs on the monitor. There isn't a door there, she thought. Suddenly, the large blob converged with the smaller one. She gasped, realizing the beast had gone right through the wall. She made the sign of the cross with her left hand as she whispered, "He really is the devil."

With her right hand she flipped a switch. The barn's interior lights came on. Inside the barn, there was the barely audible whirring of server motors as a camera swung from its usual view of the entrance over towards the working area of the barn. This camera didn't have zoom capabilities, but Rosa could clearly see Nemo and the other man on her monitor.

"Surprise," Nemo taunted in Spanish, continuing to squeeze. As his eyes adjusted to the light, he caught the profile of his squirming captive and laughed. "I recognize you from the video! You're the pathetic husband of my new girlfriend."

A vision of Janet invaded PB's darkening mind. He would not abandon her to this madman. Using all his remaining strength, PB twisted and arched, flipping the huge body, back-first, onto the stall rail. They hung suspended for a couple seconds, then started to tip backwards into the stall. Finally, the vice-like arms released. PB flung himself forward. Air rushed back into his lungs.

PB's hand dove to the sheath on his hip. It was empty!

"Looking for this?" Nemo held up the Special Ops knife, laughing. "Weapons are for wimps."

The giant slowly rose, separated from his quarry by the stall rail. He tossed the knife over his shoulder. As he came around the railing, Suarez looked even larger than PB imagined he would. The physical contrast between the two was startling. At five foot nine and a hundred sixty-five pounds, PB had the slight but well-tuned physique similar to his boyhood idol, Bruce Lee. The man across from him was close to a foot taller and a foot wider. At three hundred ten pounds, Nemo wasn't as trim as he had been ten years earlier, but he hadn't lost any of his muscle mass. The big man in front of PB reminded him of Lou Ferrigno, when he'd portrayed the Hulk on television, only blood red instead of green.

"You must be the big bully I've heard about," PB replied, using the Spanish he and Janet had learned since moving to the southern Arizona. "The one that likes to prey on and kill helpless little girls."

"I'm going to enjoy killing you, little man," Nemo replied, flexing his considerable muscles.

PB slowly moved to his left and then to his right, making a show of assessing the leather-clad giant from head to toe. The man's muscles were too big. They were great for intimidation. Suarez was amazingly strong, no doubt about that. PB had already discovered that while wrestling with the muscle-bound giant. Big muscles were heavy and required great amounts of energy. If he had the time, PB would simply keep his distance and wear the man out. But he had other pressing business. Remembering the out of control rage he'd witnessed in the video, PB shook his head, then laughed and taunted Muscles with the truth.

"I'm afraid, my big friend, that this is not going to end well for you."

Nemo blinked. The little man's behavior stunned him for a second. No one ever laughed at him. And certainly, no one spoke to him in this manner once a fight had begun. His temper flared and he lunged at Reese, eager to finish crushing the life out him. The other man jumped back just out of his reach. Nemo relaxed a bit; that was more like it. The little man was scared, just like everyone else, even if he didn't appear to be.

"I'm going to have a lot of fun with your wife," Nemo taunted back, as he pulled off the leather balaclava and set it on a nearby railing. He licked his thick pudgy lips and sneered. "If she isn't already dead, I'm going to make her bury you. Then we'll dance on your grave before I tear the clothes off her sweet little body and..."

"You are never going to touch her or any another woman again," Reese interrupted him.

Nemo lunged. The quick little man, again, hopped out of his reach. Nemo was an Iron Mike Tyson or Smokin' Joe Frazier style of fighter. A brute that came straight at you, as if demanding that you show him what you've got, certain that he could dish out worse punishment than he'd receive. More often than not, Nemo's first or second punch knocked his opponent senseless. Here in the real world, there was no referee to stop the fight. When you fought Nemo, you either ended up in the hospital or in the ground. The hospital wasn't going to be an option today! He was already tired of this crap. It was time to inflict some pain!

"You're even uglier without the mask, Suarez," PB taunted him.

Nemo seethed inside, but managed to control himself. The barn walls were getting closer. He would either grab Reese this time or have him trapped in the corner. Then the hurting would begin. Nemo leaned forward and charged.

PB expected the attack. He faked another jump backwards but leapt sideways this time and ducked under an out-reached arm. The big man had carelessly committed all his weight and momentum straight ahead and couldn't correct himself in time. PB slammed his knee hard into the huge left thigh as it went by. Big muscle, big hurt!

A charlie horse couldn't adequately describe how the big guy's leg must have felt after PB's knee struck the target perfectly, just above the knee. That had to feel more like a charlie clydesdale! PB flashed back to one he had received in grade school that had rendered him unable to walk for an entire recess. The big man turned around awkwardly, all his weight now resting on his right leg. PB shifted back and forth, dancing on his toes. The big man would be unable to kick for at least a few minutes. PB now had four striking weapons against two and he intended to take advantage.

"A real man would never strike a defenseless woman," PB said, then spat on the floor in disdain.

He darted forward to just within striking distance of the big angry fists. PB had already sprung back out of reach when they struck outward. He slid to the big man's right and faked a kick. As the man took the bait and brought his hands down to block it, PB danced to his left and landed three quick jabs to the unprotected midsection, the last striking a kidney which had less muscle protecting the area. There was a loud groan and, quite predictably, a huge fist came swinging around. PB let his momentum carry him further left. He spun around and delivered a roundhouse kick. There was a loud cracking noise as his size nine and a half hiking boot collided with the huge hand. The impact had been so jarring, PB wasn't sure for a second whose bones had broken.

He stepped down on his foot. It was bruised but not broken. The leather-gloved hand a few meters away looked worse for wear, hanging at an odd angle. Now, it was four striking weapons to one.

To Rosa, who continued to view the fight on the monitor, the small man's movements were balletic, especially, when compared to Nemo's brutish actions. It was as though she was watching an old video game production of *Beauty and the Beast*. She found herself enjoying this part of the show as the ugly, bothersome Beast got his ass kicked. So enthralled with the action, Rosa didn't even bother to look up when the front door opened. She'd heard the quad pull up to the house and correctly assumed that Raul had returned with Mrs. Reese.

He marched right up to his wife.

"You're going to have to go down to the barn and help that big idiot," Rosa said over her shoulder.

"Let's just watch a bit longer," Janet spoke.

The female voice behind Rosa caused her to stiffen immediately. She turned to see the Reese woman standing behind Raul with a gun in either hand, pointed at each of them.

"I think it is almost over, anyway," Janet continued, and as if on cue, her husband delivered the *coup de grâce*.

PB danced right and left and up and back. It was hard for the injured man to keep up to these quick movements. Once PB got into the rhythm and position he was looking for, things happened fast. A flying scissor kick to the chin rocked the big man back. PB then spun low, sweeping the good leg out from under the teetering giant. Seeing stars, and already off balance, a little over three hundred pounds of muscle and bone smashed through a stall railing and landed hard on the concrete. There was a loud gasp-like grunt as this time the breath was taken from the big man. He'd never get it back.

Nemesio Suarez never saw the descending elbow that crushed his windpipe.

The moment his elbow struck home, PB did not waste another moment on the convulsing man. He did not take killing anyone lightly. The ex-Special Forces soldier was very aware that Nemo's face would join the many others that often haunted his dreams and thoughts. He would contemplate tonight's actions many times. But right now, Janet was his only concern. PB retrieved his knife and semi-automatic and headed quickly out of the barn, sprinting towards the house. His adrenalin levels were still high as his senses probed the darkness around him for signs of danger.

CHAPTER 30

Pilates and Tae Bo

The present

The Morales Ranch, Mexico

PB found Janet, and her two captives, waiting for him in the house. After witnessing the spectacle in the barn, Raul and Rosa were very cooperative. They could not have imagined that any one individual could survive a fight with Nemo, let alone dispatch him as easily as the very average-sized man in front of them had. PB took Raul down to the barn and locked him in the holding cell with the now conscious Juan Carlos.

When he got back to the house, Rosa was showing Janet the computers. Rosa had kept video archives of every kidnap victim, including the murder of Tabitha Winger. There was more than enough irrefutable proof to put all of the kidnappers, including Hector, Maria and Supervisory Special Agent Novak, away for life.

They spent the rest of the night putting together evidence and making calls to Interpol and the FBI. Janet had Rosa make hard copies of everything. They sent several hundred hours of video and audio to Sarah at Interpol and Novak's boss at the FBI.

Worried that Hector and Maria would inevitably get tipped off and flee, it was decided that the local Mexican authorities be kept out of the loop as long as possible. It would take several hours to put together a joint Interpol/FBI/Federales task force. Maria Morales and possibly Hector, as well, were due back in about three hours to give Mr. Reese the ransom delivery instructions. PB also forwarded the coordinates and gate code to the property where Novak could be found, to the FBI.

Then he took Rosa down to the barn and put her into the cubical with the other two. Once satisfied that they were not going anywhere, he turned his attention to the large body in the stalls. He decided to leave Nemo where he was and began a search for a blanket or tarp to cover the dead man. All he could see were a couple of horse blankets. They would barely cover half the large man. A few minutes later he found a narrow set of stairs leading up to the loft. He ventured up them.

.   .   .

Maria woke up early. She was excited. Today order would be restored to her world. Everyone would be reminded that you didn't mess with the Morales family. She was running the show now. The whole kidnapping business had been her brainchild anyway. Hector wanted to walk away from this cash cow. For what? So he could play with his little steel business? It was laughable. At this point, she didn't care anymore.

She'd been dissatisfied with Hector for a while. His lack of action after she'd been kidnapped, from her own home, had been the last straw. For more than a year she'd thought about running away, possibly with Leo, her masseuse, and had even been hiding money away. Lately, though, it occurred to her that she needn't go anywhere. Hector was the problem and with Nemo's help, that problem would soon disappear.

The kids loved their father, but men and father figures were replaceable. Besides, she'd grown up without a father and had turned out just fine.

Maria went about the morning doing all the usual things, getting the kids to school, buying a new pair of shoes and heading to the club for a special massage. But today felt different. Today, truly, would be the first day of the rest of her life. Maria felt more alive than she had for years. Hector, the fool, had warned her about revenge. But revenge felt great, wonderful even. She would watch that wretched couple squirm and die this very day. They should never have messed with Maria Morales! Novak understood. He had begged for some alone time with the Reese bitch. Maria had granted the request for two reasons. First and foremost, to further punish the Reeses and, secondly, to get more leverage on the FBI man, which may come in handy sometime in the future. It occurred to Maria that she was pretty darn good at this. Los Diablos Rojos would be feared, once again, now that she was running things.

After her massage Maria showered and put on the blood red leather outfit she'd purchased that morning. Diabla Roja got into her car. The stereo was playing loud American music. Maria hated Mexican music, which was all that the local stations played. Thank God for satellite radio. Cheryl Crow was singing. What a perfect song for today, Maria smiled as she passed a handful of pesos to the valet. "A change will do you good. Yes, I think a change will do you good." Maria sang along, as she sped off towards the ranch. It was time to get this show on the road.

Maria didn't bother switching cars or stopping at the lookout, so she made good time getting out to the ranch. After all, this wasn't a typical kidnapping. Neither the police, nor the

FBI, other than Novak, would be involved with this ransom. Soon she'd have the five million dollars that her foolish husband had let slip through his fingers. She pulled up to the front door and went into the house. She spotted, what she assumed was Rosa sitting at her computers. She stood in the computer room doorway.

"Rosa, we should have some footage of Nemo roughing up the Reese Bitch. Tell him that he can do anything he wants to her, but he can't kill her. I promised that pleasure to Novak."

Maria had decided, while driving to the ranch, that the bitch's husband might need some extra incentive to bring the ransom money in person. "Have the boys remove her clothes and then send in Nemo."

There was no response to the demands made by Maria.

"Did you hear me, Rosa?" Maria asked firmly. "Now that I'm running the operation, things are going to change around here." When she still got no response she demanded, "Look at me when I talk to you!"

"Rosa doesn't have to listen to you anymore."

That voice! The bitch's voice coming from the computer station startled Maria. Maria glanced at the cell monitors. Rosa, Raul and Juan Carlos sat and stood in the cell where the Reese woman should have been.

"What is going on here?" Maria cried, as Janet Reese stood and turned to face her.

"You are going to spend the rest of your life in prison," Janet told her, waving the Walther PPK at Mrs. Morales, for emphasis. "That's what."

This shouldn't be happening. Maria's mind raced with questions. Why hadn't Novak contacted her if there was a problem? Where was Nemo? How much did they know? Maybe Hector had been right. Then she remembered that they had several of the region's judges on the payroll, along with the Mayor and Chief of Police. She couldn't contain a sly smile.

"I don't think so," she replied smugly.

"Oh, I should have been more specific, "Janet continued, "I meant to say the rest of your life in an American Prison."

"You will never get me across the border."

"You and your crew kidnapped Americans, assaulted Americans, raped Americans and killed an American. For that you will be tried in America."

"I don't care, I'm Mexican. You will never get the extradition through our courts."

"It is already arranged."

"That is not possible," Maria asserted.

"I found a powerful ally," Janet explained. "You might remember Tabitha Winger, the girl your brother murdered."

A look of recognition crossed Maria's face.

"I see that you do. Well, as it turns out, her mother is now Congresswoman Winger. She has been working with lawmakers on both sides of our border to combat cross-border kidnappings."

"When Mrs. Winger learned that we had found her daughter's murderers," Janet paused for a second, then continued the narrative, "the Congresswoman used her considerable influence to push extradition through immediately."

"Agents picked up your husband and children half an hour ago," Janet informed her. "Your home and bank accounts have been seized," she continued, noticing that Maria reacted more noticeably when she mentioned the bank accounts than her family. Still feeling a little stung by the way Maria had casually ordered her rape and murder just minutes before, Janet decided to drive the verbal knife a little deeper and give it a little twist with a small lie. "Including the cash you have stashed at the country club."

Maria gasped, her knees buckled slightly; no one knew about the money in her extra locker. She'd cleverly been returning half of the items she purchased around town for cash refunds. That was her money! Her safety net! This could not be happening!

"You will pay dearly for this," Maria promised, her face masked in hatred. "My brother will hunt you down and tear you apart." She suddenly wondered where Nemo was. She hadn't seen him on any of the monitors.

"I hate to be the bearer of more bad news, Maria, but your brother..." she was about to continue when Maria's purse flew at her head. Janet ducked just in time. When she looked up Maria was gone. Janet flew out of the room and through the kitchen after the woman. At the doorway to the entry, a swinging broom crashed into her gun hand and the door frame. The pistol hit the floor and bounced all the way back into the computer room. The broom's head snapped off, turning the handle into a sharp spear. The splintered point stabbed at Janet. She leapt back, barely in time.

Maria appeared in the door brandishing the wooden weapon. There was fire and blood in her eyes. Janet kept one eye on her as she searched for the gun with her foot. She couldn't find it. Maria stepped forward.

"I don't know how you managed to do all this," Maria told the other woman, "but you will not mess with my life ever again, Bitch."

Janet dodged a menacing jab. She needed to avoid getting trapped against a wall, so the retired agent feigned to her right, drawing another joust from the younger woman, and stepped left into the open.

Maria screamed in frustration when she missed the target. She swung the sturdy broom handle angrily at the woman who was ruining her life.

Janet tried to slide further left but her foot got caught on a kitchen chair leg. She ducked, but the handle slammed into her shoulder, sending her tumbling over the chair. By the time she got turned face up, Janet felt, more than saw, the pointy end plunging down. She was able to twist out of the way just in time, eliciting yet another scream of frustration. With both feet, she kicked the chair into Maria's shins. Maria went down, too.

Both scrambled to their feet. Janet had a slight head start. The makeshift spear hung between them, with the point on the floor. Janet jumped onto it, snapping it out of Maria's hand.

"Puta!" Maria yelled, stepping back, but not backing down. She was not afraid of the smaller, older woman -- in fact, far from it. All the Pilates, spin classes, weight lifting and Tae Bo classes she'd taken over the years were about to pay off. She was raised in the streets. She could still fight. Diabla Roja circled her prey. Little did Maria know, she was facing a devil, as well; a Snow Devil.

"Shall we take this outside?" Janet lowered her shoulder and charged the younger woman. Standing in the entry hall, Maria couldn't dodge left or right. There was more power and speed than she expected from the smaller woman and she was driven back hard. They crashed right through the original wooden entry door, weakened by the sun of many hot summer seasons, and tumbled outside.

.   .   .

PB realized he felt little or no guilt over the evil man's death. Reese hoped that this was due to the type of man Suarez had been and not because he no longer held human life as sacred as he once had. Maybe it was a little of both. He honestly wasn't certain.

As he neared the top of the narrow stairs, PB could see that the loft had been converted into living quarters. He could tell instantly that the old cowboy made this his home. Two walls of straw bales, stacked four high, separated about six hundred square feet of space from the rest of the large barn loft. Off to the left, in the corner, stood a three piece bath, partially hidden by eight more bales. He could see an old claw-foot bathtub, with a single brass faucet attached to it. There would be a choice of either luke-warm or luke-warm water.

Beside the tub was a three foot by three foot by three foot wooden box. On it rested a metal basin, an alabaster pitcher, a large bar of soap, a straight razor and a tooth brush in a metal glass. From where he stood, at the top of the stairs, PB could just see the nose of an almond toilet bowl beyond the box.

On the other side of the short bale wall was a standard-sized bed covered with a bright, mostly red and yellow patchwork quilt. The bed was made and the corners looked tight. The old man obviously had discipline in his life. In the center of the space sat a well-worn brown leather sofa. Across from it, on another wooden box was a thirty-two inch flat screen Samsung TV with a satellite receiver in front of it. A power cord and coax cable ran across the floor to the outside wall and disappeared through a small hole in the floor.

The kitchen, of sorts, had no running water. There was an old two door fridge, white with chrome handles. Next to it were three ramrod straight two-by-twelve planks, eight feet in length, resting on a pair of saw horses. On this home-made counter were a George Foreman grill, a toaster oven, a slow cooker/crock pot, a small microwave and another metal basin. On a single plank below rested a few plates, bowls, cups and a utensil holder.

PB could hear, and smell, a hearty beef stew bubbling inside the crock pot. He walked over and turned the unit off. Lifting the lid only reminded him that he hadn't eaten in a while. He had to admire the way the old bachelor had put this living space together. The place was clutter free and nearly spotless. He wondered if the man was simply an employee caught up in this mess. The courts would have to figure these things out.

PB decided that he'd better keep moving, so he headed over to the bed. The quilt would just about cover the body below. As he got closer he noticed several blue ribbons hanging on the wall behind the bed. They were for bull riding and bronco busting. Tacked next to them hung a picture of the old cowboy standing behind a table, displaying woven and braided goods.

Though he couldn't know it at the time, when the joint task force later searched the loft thoroughly, they would find hundreds of other photos. Pictures of drugged or sleeping young girls in various stages of undress. There would be no leniency for Juan Carlos, a willing participant in the kidnapping ring.

Reese pulled the light quilt off the hard mattress and went back down into the barn. He covered the body with it and a horse blanket. He took no pride in having bested such a large man. We all have strengths and weaknesses. Nemo had been big and strong, PB quick and skilled. Speed and talent took the day this time, but the ex-Special Forces soldier knew that no one won every battle. If he kept getting into these situations, sooner or later, he'd be under the blanket. As much and hard as PB continued to train, he knew that his thirty-year-old self would kick his fifty-seven-year old ass every time. PB bowed his head, for a few moments, thinking of lost friends and acquaintances, then left the barn.

An unexpected sight startled the tired Canadian. There, by the house, was Maria's Mercedes. He hadn't heard the vehicle approach. Sore foot be damned, he triple-timed it across the yard. As he approached, there were shadows dancing in the morning light, beyond the far side of the house. He could soon hear the sounds of a struggle. The black Para Ordnance slid smoothly from waistband to hand. A forty-five caliber bullet sat ready in the chamber as a thumb kicked the safety off. He poked his nose around the corner. Janet spotted his arrival immediately. She'd been expecting him. Her subtle, almost imperceptible, nod told him to stand down. Maria's back was to him.

Maria's designer leather outfit didn't look quite so smart, now that it was dirty and torn from more than a few trips to the dirt. Maria's breath had become ragged; her shoulders heaved. The last ten minutes had replaced the fire in her eyes with a dull determination. Maria lifted her heavy arms into the classic boxing pose, stepped forward and jabbed at her opponent.

Janet hated the woman but had to admire the fight in her. She wasn't quitting despite the whooping Janet had already administered. The older woman bobbed and weaved, easily avoiding Maria's fists. The fight reminded Janet of a dance routine. It was all very rhythmic and predictable. Jab, jab, jab followed by a knee strike, side kick or punch. Sometimes there were four jabs, occasionally, as many as six, followed by a kick or punch. This time it was four jabs and a knee strike. Janet slid to her left, delivered a jab of her own into an unprotected ribcage, and kicked the back of Maria's other knee.

A sharp pain flashed from her side and leg as Maria fell to the gravel, once more. Small stones bit into her once-manicured hands and blood dripped from previously silky-smooth knees and shins. Welts and aches covered her pampered body. Why wasn't this working? Maria's training partner at the club, Manuel, had convinced her that she was a natural fighter. Tae Bo was supposed to keep her in shape, plus teach her deadly fighting skills.

However, no amount of Tae Bo could have prepared her for Janet, who'd trained almost daily for the last twenty years with the Snow Devils and, of course, her husband. Maria struggled to her feet and turned around. She noticed a man standing in the shadows. He was far too small to be her brother. The shadowed man was shorter than either Raul or Juan Carlos, too, unfortunately. Maybe Hector had arrived to save her.

"I think she's had enough," the figure stated in English as it moved into the light.

Maria's aching jaw dropped when she recognized the bitch's husband.

"Awe," Janet kicked some dirt in mock disappointment, "but I was just getting warmed up."

"I can see that," PB walked up to Janet, his gun trained on Maria. "Save some of that energy for me." He put his other arm around her shoulders and pulled her tight.

"I don't understand," Maria said, trying to put the pieces together. "But how did your husband get here without *my* instructions?" she questioned, as she struggled to her feet.

Janet shook her head. "When you dance with my devil, you end up getting burned!" She stretched up and kissed her hero on the cheek and then whispered, "Ric-a-Dam-Doo, Sweetheart." In this case, the Special Forces catchall phrase meant I love you, thank you, and job well done, all at the same time.

"Ric-a-Dam-Doo," he replied, as a small smile crossed his lips. PB's eyes and gun barrel never wavered from Maria.

Five minutes later, Maria was in the holding cell with her compatriots. She dropped to the floor in the corner and wept tears of self-pity. No one went over to comfort her.

A short while later, the team of Federales, Interpol and FBI agents arrived at the ranch. PB and Janet turned over the prisoners and the evidence. The new task force was to take all the credit for the arrests. Congresswoman Winger arrived on site to personally thank the Reeses. She promised to keep their names out of any and all proceedings. Janet and PB walked

WAYNE A D KERR

away satisfied that, this time, the job had been done properly. Los Diablos Rojos would never hurt another innocent soul.

Janet slept in the tandem seat behind PB, as he piloted the plane homeward. It gave him time to think about all the men he had killed. Most, like Nemesio Suarez, had been vile, psychopathic human beings. However, they were all husbands, brothers, fathers or sons. Someone had loved them. Well, most of them. Nemesio Suarez was his tenth kill! He had reached double digits, a fact that didn't please him at all.

Some people got tattoos or carved notches on their weapons to memorialize these events. PB's gun remained unblemished, but another notch did scar his soul.

CHAPTER 31

Josephine's Saddle

One week later
Mount Wrightson, Arizona

Janet took a deep breath of the pine-scented air. She looked down at Green Valley, a little more than three thousand feet below where she was currently standing. She and PB would miss this place and close friends they had made over the past few years. They'd finished packing that morning. Their furniture and most belongings were already in storage. With their cover blown, a new home was a necessity. That afternoon they were heading north to find one, but not before one last hike to say goodbye to the area.

Sweat trickled down her back. Janet and PB had taken the much more challenging route to the saddle. Vault Mine Trail was steeper and more difficult than either Super Trail or Old Baldy Trail, both of which were favored by most of the hikers in the area. Vault Mine Trail was a great workout and worth the extra effort. As a reward for their efforts, Janet brought out a couple of homemade granola bars and some apple slices to eat as they shared the fantastic view. There was still some ice in the water bottles that PB pulled out of his pack. They always carried lots of water with them on hikes.

"How is your foot doing?" she asked her husband. The swelling had gone down on his bruised foot the day before. He had assured her that morning that he was fit for duty when she'd suggested a hike.

"It's doing just fine," PB told her. "Do you want to continue up?" he asked, as he raised his eyes towards the peak of Mount Wrightson. It would take another two hours of climbing to reach that summit.

"I was thinking of a slightly different form of exercise before we leave," she teased him.

PB leaned over and kissed his wife passionately, then jumped up from the log they were sharing, grabbed his backpack and double-timed it towards Old Baldy Trail.

"Last one down is a rotten egg," he called over his shoulder.

Janet laughed out loud as she stood, gazing down at the beautiful valley for a few more seconds before heading after her husband. She knew he'd be waiting for her just around the bend. Wherever or whatever was ahead, she knew she could handle it with PB at her side.

The End

ABOUT THE AUTHOR

Wayne A D Kerr was born and raised in Biggar (New York is big, but this is Biggar), Saskatchewan. Twenty years ago, along with his wife and daughter, he moved to the United States. When not reading or writing adventure novels, he is probably hiking, biking or playing tennis.